THE SEEKER

One Man's Struggle with Faith and Marriage

A Christian Novel

by

Terry Dodd

Xulon
PRESS

Other Books Authored by Terry Dodd

Uncommon Influence. A gripping business/science fiction novel of the power of advertising, and of those who would use it in a devious attempt to influence the minds of others. The only novel ever published set in the uniquely personal advertising medium known as promotional products.

"Just when you think you've got the story figured out, a new twist develops . . . like a hall of mirrors."
—Bobby Bowden, Head Football Coach, Florida State University

250 pages, 6" x 9" paperback. Out of print, but with limited availability through amazon.com and barnesandnoble.com.

Ultimate Encounter. Fast-paced Christian science fiction novel and stand-alone sequel to *Uncommon Influence.* The book's theme evolves from the UFO enigma and a quest for reciprocal communication with UFO occupants. Whether benign curiosity or sinister presence, God remains universal for there cannot be competing Creators.

"Add one part Robert Ludlum, a measure of Gene Roddenberry, and a pinch of Mickey Spillane, then bring it all to a boil through the sure-handed pen of a veteran Christian author . . . "
—David Hubbell, M.D., Emory University School of Medicine

270 pages, 6" x 9" paperback, available through pleasantword.com

The Foursome. A compelling and compassionate Christian novel set against the background of a golf match among four strangers. The players are felled by lightning, yet the match miraculously continues. With eternal life on the line one man's faith is matched against doubt, ignorance and pride.

"I could not help but be convicted by the parallels between my human struggles in golf and my very personal relationship with the Lord."

— **Chris Cupit, Rivermont Golf Club Manager**

350 pages, 5 ½" x 8 ½" paperback, available through selahpublishing.com

Life's Toughest Lessons. A true-story window into two lives in difficulty. After decades of the author's having wandered in spiritual darkness he and his wife finally become equally yoked in their Christian faith, thus prepared to deal with cancer's imminent assault on her body. Close to death, Judy asks Terry to look back after she has passed to see how God has used her to further His Kingdom. In her characteristically unselfish nature she also prays that he will find a new wife.

"A true Christian's walk with God brings Terry from a mountaintop marriage through the valley of death; emerging to new love and a second chance at happiness. I found inspiration and hope for my own journey through grief."

–**Gloria Overvold, English Teacher and Stephen Minister, Retired**

309 pages, 6" x 9" paperback, available through xulonpress.com

PREFACE

As this book's subtitle suggests, *The Seeker's* story focuses on one man's struggle with not only the underpinnings of marriage, but with Christian faith itself. Yet the story is much more than that in the sense that these two elements are critical gifts from God to man. As Eugene Peterson so eloquently states in his introduction of *The Message* paraphrase of the Bible, "If we don't have a sense of the primacy of God, we will never get it right, get life right, get *our* lives right."

In writing this book I acknowledge my undying love and gratitude to both my late wife Judy and our 45 years of marriage, and to my recently married wife, Helga. From them I have learned the critical one-sentence lesson/secret of a successful marriage: **Developing a servant's heart and intentionally growing in one's love for his or her spouse.**

Interestingly, my own three-year active participation in Stephen Ministry overlapped my life with each of these two godly women, though they never met nor had I met Helga until sometime after Judy passed. My Stephen Ministry training and service has also provided me with a special appreciation for the institution of marriage as God has ordained it.

With respect to marriage as one of the two themes of this book, I have attempted to apply a major part of the story through a particular book of the Bible–*Song of Songs*. This Biblical book is rarely referenced in either sermons or non-fiction books, and perhaps never before in a fictional setting. It is my purpose to present *The Seeker* as a convincing witness that men and women were created physically, emotionally, and spiritually to live in love.

Christians read the Scriptural book of *Song of Songs* (sometimes entitled *Song of Solomon*) on several different levels. These have been described by *The Message* of the original Greek and Hebrew languages as 1) the intimacy of marital love between man and woman, 2) God's deep love for His people, 3) Christ's Bridegroom love for His church, and 4) the Christian's love for his or her Lord. Within level number one I have chosen to go with a modernist story interpretation which includes Solomon, the Shulamite maiden, and her shepherd-lover, rather than the more traditional interpretation of one man (Solomon) and the Shulamite woman.

For this perspective I reference much material (with express permission) from Tommy Nelson's non-fiction *A Study of Love, Sex, Marriage and Romance*. Consider Nelson's comment: "Romantic relationships affect everyone. Do we think that God has given us desire and passion without any instruction? Has He given us romance and tossed it out like a grenade? Did God say 'play around with it and you'll figure it out?" No, He has given us an entire book (The Holy Bible) which deals with all of this and more."

Lastly, on these themes of faith and marriage, a full appreciation of how God intended marriage to be for those who love and whom God loves, is simply not possible without faith in Him.

Halfway through writing the first draft of this novel my wife and best friend, Helga, and I viewed for the first time the classic film *Somewhere In Time*. We were both captivated by what has been called the most romantic love story ever filmed. I was so taken by both the story and its music that I immediately went to SIT's web site and joined my first fan society since my parents signed me up for the Lone Ranger Safety Club when I was six years old. And since timing is sometimes more important than time itself I was led by this film to introduce what I consider a most unusual and endearing closing story element (although I will obviously have to leave this to readers to judge).

Importantly, I also want to thank the following: my friend, fellow-author, sometime golf partner, Bible teacher and spiritual mentor, Wayne Clark; my faithful proofreader, Pat Anderson; two courageous friends, Valorie Deel and Bradley Dykstra, each of whom provided me with short but valuable feedback from their reading of an early draft of the manuscript; the senior pastor of my church, Steve Wood, who troubled himself to not only read the (nearly) finished manuscript on short notice, but provided me with the book's back cover endorsement.

In addition, I thank my children and their spouses for their ongoing love and support—Wendi and Kevin and their children, Abigail and Karsten; Jason and Wheng; Martin and Betty and their children, Mitchell and Eric; plus Helga's daughter and her spouse, Tracie and David and their children, Tyler and Aaron. And finally, I again thank my wife Helga, not only for her critical proofreading, but also for much IT help and the loving encouragement that a committed marriage produces between husband and wife.

Terry Dodd

TABLE OF CONTENTS

CHAPTER 1

ENDING A BEGINNING

"Sign here and the contract is sealed," the attorney said with a rueful note to his voice. Peter Wysong and his soon-to-be ex-wife were sharing the same divorce attorney, but she was not present.

"I will," Pete said, nodding his head as he took pen in hand. To that he added, "I hope this is the last time I ever say those two words." Thus had his divorce from a marriage of seven difficult years officially ended. He was now 34 years old and had just yielded custody of his six-year old son. He and his wife had been separated for a full year and still he had absolutely no clue as to how they had failed so miserably in their marriage. It was ironic, he thought, that although he now equated his failed marriage with a significant failure in life, why had he not made more of an effort to avoid that defeat? He still believed the blame was largely hers. So what could *he* have done about that? It was the 18th of December and he would have plenty of time alone over the coming weeks to think about the how and why of his unhappiness.

"You know, Pete," the attorney volunteered, "if you ever do say those two words again in a matrimonial sense you would be wise to first say it to your Maker."

"Oh? Is that my gift from the man whose Christmas I just financed? You know, I share the same view I once overheard a friend of mine say to someone about Christian faith: 'I don't care what *you* think. Just don't try to ram it down *my* throat.'"

"I'm sorry, said the attorney. "Let me try putting it more palatably. You're discouraged, you're wrung out, and at this moment you also claim to have no direction for the rest of your life. But whether or not you realize it, you have been greatly blessed in life. Take it from me and a lot of other guys who have found themselves at the bottom of life's barrel at one time or another. There *is* a way up and out of your funk."

"And exactly what would that road look like?"

"The cross of Christ."

"I figured that's what you were going to say. And that would solve all my problems? Gosh, I didn't realize it would be so easy. Look, we tried that route. We were married in a church. But that didn't keep our marriage together. Dannie was never anything but a nag; first it was about money, then about her parents, then about my business travel, and finally, about how to raise our son. You know something? I think I'm better off with Manianity than Christianity."

"Manianity?" the attorney said.

Wysong sighed. "It's just what you might think," he said. "Belief in man rather than in Christ."

It was the attorney's turn to sigh. "The only problem with that solution," he said "is that man can't save himself. I don't mean to aggravate you at a time when you're particularly vulnerable, my friend, but allow me to make a point about what you just said."

"You mean you wouldn't mind aggravating me at a *better* time?" Wysong said, while managing a smile. "Okay, barrister. Take your best shot."

"You said you were married in a church, implying that that alone should have made all the difference. My point has to do with numbers." At that latter statement the attorney let out a little grunt accompanied by a comment interrupting his train of thought. "Actually, quoting numbers is one of the complaints my wife has about me, although she does so with both grace and humor." With that he continued his point. "Anyway, these are worth pondering: 80% of couples who live together before marriage end up divorced.

60% of couples married by a justice of the peace divorce. And sadly, 40% of couples married in a church ultimately resort to divorce."

"Are you resting your case?" said Wysong. "I think you just made mine."

"I haven't finished," said the attorney. "When the fog of numbers fully lifts we see something very different. Only one out of 1,000 married couples who study their Bible *and* pray together . . . end up divorcing. In other words, neither a couple's living arrangement nor wedding ceremony offers odds of a successful marriage when compared to a couple's studying the Bible and praying together. And I'm pretty sure I know why. Faith and trust in God come before family."

"Maybe so," Wysong responded, ready with his counter-attack, "but that 'until death do us part' thing requires a little too much faith. I mean, a 20 or 30-something spouse will be a much different person ten years later, let alone after 40 or so years of marriage."

"But that's my point," the attorney said. "We live by faith and not by sight. In any event, while God is good, not one of *us* is. Merry Christmas, Pete. And thanks for the business."

"You're welcome," Wysong said facetiously as he stuck out his hand. "Always glad to help the underprivileged."

The attorney took Wysong's hand and shook it genuinely, saying, "I wish you God's continued blessing, but until people begin to understand what marriage is truly all about, divorce attorneys like me will never seriously suffer for lack of work."

CHAPTER 2

REFLECTION

O ver the following week Wysong reflected upon the attorney's closing words. More than any other comment, one in particular bothered him. That was the statement that he–Pete—had been blessed in life. *Which had been the greater blessing,* he thought, *the marriage or the divorce?* He flashed a wry smile at the thought, but then focused his thinking on a different perspective. He couldn't really define it, but something had begun inching its way into the back of his mind even as he had been outing his marriage.

In real time he was standing in his home bathroom, staring into the mirror. He pointed at himself as his thoughts formed. *You spent a year living with a woman* before *you married her and then spent a full year separated from her* while *married to her. What is it you don't get about marriage? More than that, what is it you don't get about life?* Then came his summary thought. *Is it possible that the biggest troublemaker in my life is watching me from this mirror every morning?*

After having spent the loneliest week of his life moping around his North Atlanta area condo while his ex-wife had taken their son, Billy, to visit her parents in southern California, Wysong was ready to return to work with renewed energy. With a new enthusiasm he suddenly began filling up the next six weeks of his day planner with territory account appointments. That would take him up to late January and the year's biggest trade show, in Las Vegas.

A month and a half later it was show time. He departed by plane a day–actually, a night—early for the nearly week-long show at which he would work most of the booths of the seven promotional products industry lines he independently represented in traveling his seven-state territory between Memphis and Miami. After the flight and a long shuttle ride he checked into the headquarters casino hotel. As he was leaving the front desk he heard someone call his name. "Pete! What's your hurry, buddy?"

As he turned towards the voice he saw his long-time friend and Texas distributor, Sam Sampson. "Sammy!" he said. "You're a sight for these cheap-fare red eyes."

They shook hands warmly. "Same here, man. Sorry to hear about your divorce."

"Thanks, but it was a long time coming. I'm glad to be out of it. What's up? You don't usually come to the show a day early like we rep-tiles."

"I have a special meeting early tomorrow morning. Hey! Why don't you join me? I'll buy your breakfast."

Wysong shook his head. "Naw," he said, trying to beg off. "They don't want reps at distributor meetings. Heck, I'm even thinking of bugging out of a *rep* breakfast in the morning, let alone going to one of yours. Maybe next year."

"Phooey," Sampson said. "You sound like a man trying to disengage from life. All the more reason you need to be up and about something productive. And this isn't a distributor meeting. It's for everyone. There'll probably be 50 or so of us for a continental breakfast and a speaker."

"What's it all about?" Pete said. "'Industry Complaints R Us?'"

"Cynic!" Sampson said. "Actually, we meet to thank the Lord for having blessed our lives. And we have a special marriage testimony from someone who recently lost his wife. I think you could benefit from coming."

"Oh, no!" Wysong said as he slapped his chest in mock distress. "First, my divorce attorney, and now one of my best friends. Hey, I've been blessed enough through losing a nagging wife!"

"Come on, you wienie," Sampson said. "Divorce is traumatic for anyone, regardless of who is to blame. It's time you started to let yourself recover. I'll knock on your door at 7:00 A.M."

Pete rolled his eyes but said, "Okay, but I'm only along for food and yuks."

CHAPTER 3

TESTIMONIAL

At the early morning meeting Wysong was surprised to see a number of people he knew, including several fellow reps and a few distributor customers. He even saw some supplier personnel whose faces were familiar, if not their names. He shook hands with those he knew. Some seemed surprised to see him, a few tried to hug him. The would-be huggers' efforts were met with surprising body rigidity. Pete's friend, Sam, was the facilitator and after offering an opening prayer of thanks he introduced the speaker.

"Good morning, gentlemen," the speaker began. "My name is Crawford Morland. I answer to 'Craw,' and I'm delighted to be here with you. Mine is a simple message this morning, but I want to preface it with something I heard on the radio as I was getting dressed to come over here. It went like this: 'When you were born, you were crying and every one around you was smiling. Live your life so that when you die, you're the one who is smiling, and everyone around you is crying.' Someone should say 'Amen.'" Many laughed and several did.

Morland looked out over his well-dressed business audience and nodded in Sam's direction. "There is a four-word phrase in a verse from the book of Ephesians that reads, 'Husbands, love your wives.' If you would indulge me, may I see a show of hands of those in the room who are either married now or *have* been married."

Pete reluctantly raised his hand as he looked around to note the very few who did not. He wondered how many fit into his own category. "Good," said the speaker, "I like maturity in an audience." The group laughed again and Morland smiled broadly as he began his talk in earnest. "Gentlemen, we see bitterness, insults, and animosity presented in the media as the norm. How much more desirable it would be to see some focus on true love–to see stories about a husband unashamedly cherishing his wife." He paused for a moment to allow that idea to settle in amongst his audience.

"A friend of mine recently said of his late wife, 'I have lost my princess.' That's the way I felt about my wife of 25 years whom I lost six months ago. My question for you is this: How can you married men love your wife in a more princely way? And for those of you who have lost a wife—either to death or divorce—and may find yourselves marrying again some day, this especially applies to you. Why? Because you will then have a fresh opportunity. By a show of hands, how many of you who have been through a divorce think you could do a better job with a do-over?" About one-third of those who raised their hands the first time raised them again.

Wysong felt as if he had been struck squarely between the eyes. He didn't want to raise his hand and wouldn't have if Sam had not been in the room. As he did so, however, the speaker looked quietly from one raised hand to another before asking three rhetorical questions. Wysong felt as if the questions were being asked of him: "Where were *you* in your failed marriage?" he said. Secondly, "Did you think it was a game?" And thirdly he asked, "Did you think it was simply something to be tried for a while before you moved on? Please pardon my bluntness," he added. "I am not speaking to you out of judgment, but out of conviction." Without being charged Wysong nevertheless felt guilty, but would have been unwilling to admit it to anyone.

Morland then acknowledged the earlier show of hands, saying, "Thank you for your honesty. I know that wasn't easy for any of you. But take heart. God causes or allows all things, thus you can be certain He hasn't forgotten you." The speaker took a drink of water and continued. "I have three 'L' suggestions for you men with regard to your wives, present or future. 1) Listen - Enjoy those tender times when she knows you will hear what is on her heart and mind. 2) Love - Treat her always as the person you value more than anyone else in the world. 3) Lead - Guide the way into prayer and intimate fellowship with the Lord."

Wysong felt caught in an emotional whirlpool. *Why is everyone attacking me?* He told himself that he was turned off by the message, but he also knew his heart had been seared. Guilt was on the one side and trauma on the other. On the spot he reaffirmed for himself that his life was rotten. He spent the balance of the hour in total distraction from the speaker's remaining words, searching inside himself for answers. It did him no good, however, for he found no stream of either understanding or solution, only emptiness.

Almost as soon as the speaker had begun–it seemed to Wysong—he heard him say, "And that's how my wife was lost to me, the princess of my life. Although I know that she is much better off now than before, I nevertheless struggle with my loss. The good news, however, is that I am determined to process this experience as a lesson, for I am yet blessed through our Lord and Savior, Jesus Christ. Before I close, allow me to share with you this short, anonymous poem:

"Honor your wife and in love with her dwell,

Yield to the Savior and all will be well;

Peace He will give to both husband and wife,

Blessing their marriage with joy throughout life.

"Before I pray us out," he continued, "I want to thank you for your time and interest and ask you to remember this: The child of God may face tribulation, distress, even persecution. At times, life may be hard and suffering may be acute, but the problems of this life do not abrogate the eternal promises of God for the life to come."

As they walked out the door together, Sam said, "Pete, you seemed preoccupied. I apologize if you think I shanghaied you."

Wysong shook his head. "No," he said. "Right now I think I *want* to be ticked off with life. At the same time I really don't want

23

to suffer the consequences of such an attitude. I don't know why I can't seem to dump this spade I'm carrying around."

Sampson looked puzzled.

Wysong noted his friends's expression and said, "You know! For the hole I'm digging for myself."

"Oh, of course," Sampson remarked facetiously. "What was I thinking? Well, it's probably true that we don't know what we've been missing until it arrives. But from what I hear you saying you might be awakening to something. I recommend you start talking to someone."

"Talking?"

"Yeah. They're called 'counselors.'"

"It's too late for that. I'm no longer married. Remember?"

"That's the point, doofus."

CHAPTER 4

ADVERTISEMENT

Wysong was back home from what he referred to as the 'smoke and mirrors' show, anxious to hit the road in calling on accounts. He noted that there was nothing much to catch his attention from either e-mails or postal mail from the week before, except for something from a local church. He had seen the church's name many times before, but what netted his mind was the flyer's header: "Post-Mortem of A Marriage." He turned the flyer over to this lead-in message: "Come as you are from the golf course, tennis court or yard work at 6:00 P.M. for our Saturday Sabbath service. Instead of watching Elvis reruns, hear about the true King." *What has a church service to do with divorce counseling?* he thought.

The explanation followed. A line of copy read: "After the service hear from someone who has dealt with a divorce probably not unlike your own sad experience." At first reading, Pete was offended at the writer's sense of humor, but then he laughed. *Sad experience? That's me. Maybe what I need is a fresh perspective.* He put the event on his calendar for when he returned from the coming week on the road.

At the Saturday evening's service he was instantly reminded of his discomfort over the few times he had attended church with his ex-wife. He was certain that was mostly due to her nagging, although he had always felt uncomfortable with the message of man's depravity . This message, ironically, was focused around the same verse the speaker in Las Vegas had quoted: "Husbands, love your wives." His thought: *There must be a lot of this going around.* All that thought really said to him, however, is that divorce was not only becoming more common, but perhaps inevitable.

The pastor began speaking about how marriage thrives in a climate of love and respect. It was at that early point that Pete unplugged, justifying himself by the logic of circumstance. *Hey, it takes two to make a marriage. I certainly couldn't make her love and respect me.* He could hardly wait until dismissal. At that time the congregation was reminded of the service follow-up for those interested.

It was announced that several Stephen Ministers were going to be talking to a breakout group immediately following refreshments in the gathering area, and all were invited to sit in. That's what he had come for, but he had no illusions about it being of much benefit to him. He imagined his interest was more a matter of distraction, although a single related idea had been softly playing in the back of his mind.

There were about ten or so people in attendance and one of the two leaders opened the session by sharing her own experience with divorce, followed by her testimonial of a successful second marriage. Wysong didn't see a connection for himself since he didn't have a girl friend. In closing, the speaker painted a graphic perspective of her personal pain associated with the trauma of divorce. Against his inclination, Wysong found himself straining forward as the speaker's words suddenly began to speak to his own self-denial of grief—not only over his failed marriage, but to the ill-conceived loss of regular contact with his young son.

"Ladies and gentlemen," said the speaker, "please hear me on this next point. When we speak of the reality of grief associated with divorce–regardless of the reasons behind it—we are talking about pain. The pain that we describe is not that of a football player's broken bones or the pulled muscles of a golfer too late in his season, but of a pain that penetrates the spirit of a person and plunges to the deepest recesses of the person's being. It is a pain that grips the soul like a carpenter's steel vice pincers a piece of wood. And with that relentless pain comes an excruciating sense of loss, almost as of mourning."

The speaker had everyone's attention, as if she had been piling one brick of understanding on top of another. She continued, saying, "Good judgment comes from experience. And a lot of the pain of divorce comes from bad judgment *decisions*." At that, most of those in the room probably wanted to look away, but where would they look when the object of the speaker's comment was within themselves?

To that brick she added yet another. "We use the term *grief* to describe pain that assaults the deepest level of our being. I quote R. C. Sproul's metaphor about broken hearts not breaking like a glass that falls on the floor, or like bones that are shattered in an accident, but rather this: 'The broken heart really describes a weeping soul, a soul that is cloaked in the darkest night.'"

In closing, she brought into play the profound grief Jesus experienced when He noticed the women weeping for Him even as he struggled to move forward towards Golgotha. His wounds from the terrible flogging and the load of His own cross were taking their physical toll. "Yet," the speaker said, "in Luke's narrative we hear Jesus' words as He spoke to those bystanders, 'Daughters of Jerusalem, do not weep for me, but weep for yourselves and for your children.'"

The speaker then made her offer. "Any of you who would be interested in having a Stephen Minister with whom to share confidentially on a regular basis, please see either me or my associate before you leave tonight." At that, she turned and introduced her male associate, who had not said a word to that point. He smiled and raised a hand in greeting to the group.

Wysong's initial reaction was quick to form. *How lame would someone have to be to need a stranger at a time like this?* But as he gathered up his papers to leave he hesitated. *Yeah. Seriously lame* was his affirming thought. But then another thought crowded that one out. *You know what, Wysong? That's you! Lame. And sad.* He went forward.

One woman was talking to the female speaker while another man was speaking to the male associate. Wysong drifted off to one side of the room so as not to overhear their conversation, supposedly busying himself in looking at various notices pinned to the cork bulletin board. When the man departed he went up to the speaker's associate and stuck out his hand saying, "Pete Wysong." With skepticism in his voice he added, " Tell me again exactly what a Stephen Minister is all about."

The man shook his hand firmly and said, "Well, Mr. Wysong, it's good to meet you. My name is Will Shoemaker. Thank you for that question. I could give you a lot of ministry definitions, but the quick and easy one is that Stephen Ministers are trained for their listening ministry. Whoever is assigned to a care receiver is likely more interested in hearing about what's going on with that person than anyone else in their family or circle of friends."

That was not quite what Pete had expected to hear but still he said, "I might be interested."

"Do you belong to this church?" Shoemaker asked, merely as a point of information.

"No," Wysong responded with a trace of self-pity. "Does that make a difference?"

"Not at all. I would be happy to answer any questions you have. Beyond that–should you be interested—here's a brochure along with a name and phone number. It belongs to the lady you just heard speak. Is there anything you would like to share with me regarding your interest?"

Wysong, a salesman himself, was nevertheless a cautious recipient of anyone's "pitch." "Naw," he said as he took the card. "I'm good for now, but I appreciate your time. I'll read your brochure."

"You're welcome. May God continue to bless you." With that, they shook hands and Wysong left.

As he walked to his car he wondered at Shoemaker's parting statement. People kept saying that to him and it irritated him. He didn't understand how the phrase "continued blessing" could apply to people suffering negative life experiences. He would think about making the phone call.

CHAPTER 5

THE REFERRAL

Early Monday morning Wysong Consulting hit the road to Birmingham, Alabama. The plan was to call on distributor accounts from late morning that same day until late morning on Friday, at which point he would head home. At mid-week he called on one particular account and his partner wife, with both of whom he had done a fair amount of business during each of the previous five years he had worked as a multi-line rep. As he finished his call–and knowing by their own admission that they were strong in their Christian faith–he asked a question. "What do you know about Stephen Ministry?" The business owner was immediately enthusiastic and said he had heard much from others—both in and out of his church—to recommend the ministry.

Early on Friday morning he decided to ask the same question of his single largest account in the city, which happened to be last on his week's call-schedule. Wysong knew him not to be a man of any particular faith, but following his product presentation he decided to ask the question anyway

"Stephen Ministry?" the customer said, his body language indicating more annoyance than interest. "What is that? A church?"

"No, it's a ministry within a church. They call it a 'listening ministry.' As I understand it, it's for people dealing with recent loss, divorce, family illness, that sort of thing. Have you had any experience with them?"

"Well, Pete," the distributorship owner began, "I'm not a regular at church and I've never heard the name. But if you're looking for some sort of counseling concerning your divorce, I think I should find a good support group outside of a church-administered program."

"Why do you say that?"

"Because there are as many divorces by people who go to church as those who don't. Besides, your horse is already out of the barn, isn't it?"

Wysong was a little taken aback, but he tried to roll with the punch. "Hey, I'm not dead yet."

"No, of course not," Wysong's customer said, "but your divorce is final, isn't it? Look, you're still a young man. Go on line. Find yourself someone and make the most of life. Frankly, I think organized religion is a crock. With or without it, life and death are the same."

"What do you mean?" Wysong said, hoping for meaningful clarification.

The distributor laughed and said, "Hey, you live and then you die."

"You think that's all there is?" Wysong responded in all seriousness. "What about life after death?"

The distributor looked at Wysong as if he were a child asking for an increase in his allowance. "Look," he said, "you can believe anything you want. The human condition is what we make of it. I think that's in the Bible. You know, eat, drink and be merry, for tomorrow we die. Well, I have an appointment. Thanks for coming by, Pete."

Wysong left his customer's office with far less resolve about what to do with his situation than before he had entered. True, he was still young–not yet half way through his 30s–but he had been up and down so many different trees that he now found himself prone to answer whistles coming from nearly any direction that seemed authoritative, if not authentic.

He had witnessed divorce firsthand long before his own marriage. His parents had not only divorced before he was ten years old, but the husband of his mother's second marriage hid his pornographic addiction from both of them until his associated infidelities finally caught up with him. Yet another marriage ending in divorce. Thus had Wysong taken to college with him parts of the only two models of male-to-female relationships he had known.

Only standard exhortations at his mother's side had instilled in him a clear difference between right and wrong, but then conscience existed in everyone for that purpose. What he lacked was an owner's manual. He had no sense of how to treat a woman as an equal, much less any notion of sacrificial love. And among the things he had not come close to grasping was the most important one of all: a personal relationship with his Creator. He knew *of* God, but he did not *know* Him. It was not surprising that he knew little of how to earn another's trust and nothing of *placing* trust in another, much less in God.

CHAPTER 6

LAUNCH

For the next 12 months Wysong doubled up on his new life as a single. He began driving to his territory on Sunday afternoons so that he could make his first account call early on Monday mornings. As the months went by his account sales grew and he added two additional and significant lines as well. And although his time-in-territory increased he managed to be home most weeks in time for a Friday night date with *someone*, the result of his link-up with a dating service. By the end of the year he had dated more than twenty-five different women at least once. On occasion he even took advantage of his out-of-state travels by linking up on line with his dating service. More than one fellow rep had asked if he was having a good time, to which he would honestly answer, "Certainly!"

But he was not happy. In fact, about the only joy in his life seemed to come at son Billy's ball games, which he frequently visited. His ex sometimes attended, but more often found it convenient to be absent, allowing Pete the privilege of game duty. Being present for an hour-and-half's ball game, shouting encouragement, and making dinner of a hot dog and french fries with his son was good duty for Wysong-the-father.

During a particularly slow time at an Atlanta trade show he shared some of his life's frustrations with a fellow rep. "Ken," he said, "you seem to have it altogether. Your wife and some of your family work with you in the business. You represent some solid lines, and you seem really happy. I wish I could say the same for myself. What I seem to have in life–aside from my boy–is a decent business, the revenues from which mostly go to fund superficial dates. Who knows how long any of this will last?"

"I appreciate the compliment," his friend said, adding, "but I don't worry about either the business or life itself, and I doubt if either my wife or God would approve of extramarital dating. Here's my story, short and sweet: I have been blessed by the Lord in so many ways it's all I can do to praise Him for whatever comes along, even if that blessing sometimes takes the form of a beating."

"What does that mean?" Wysong said. "You can't tell me you're actually thankful whenever you get knocked down. I mean everyone occasionally loses a good line, has a transmission go out, or gets sick."

"No, I'm not thankful for problems themselves," his friend said, "but I trust that if the Lord doesn't keep me out of the furnace, He'll at least meet me there."

"You know," Wysong said, shaking his head, "I have no idea what you're talking about. I've heard that same kind of statement from more than one of those phoney TV evangelists as they connive to suck money out of homebodies with little life and fewer resources."

"Um, sorry," Pete's friend said, "I didn't mean to upset you, but I understand where you're coming from. At one time I felt the same way. But shortly after I met my wife-to-be I got over it. I was amazed at how she handled adversity, turning to her faith in God and trusting that He was still in control. As a matter of fact she led me to the Lord. From that point on I began–if at first, slowly–to learn that life simply isn't about me. And since coming to accept Jesus Christ as my Lord and Savior I have had a relationship that blessed God and saved me. That's my longer testimonial. Pete, would you join us at church this Sunday?"

Wysong had just been given more than he bargained for. "Honestly," he said, "I wouldn't. I don't know where I am right now, but I think I'll eventually find my own way. Thanks, anyway."

Another full year passed. Wysong hadn't changed anything in his life except for a few of the smaller lines he represented. One evening, as he was sitting at home with his computer trying to write a fresh bio for himself for yet another dating service, he had a flash of inspiration. He had analyzed his past two years' dating experiences and realized that he hadn't found more than two or three women he had wanted to date for a second time, and none at all for a third. Worse, he couldn't figure out the reason. All had been reasonably attractive and many had interesting backgrounds, yet none had really appealed to him. It is true that on several occasions he had been tempted to pursue things merely for the potential sex a relationship might represent, but something always seemed to prevent his taking action.

So what's my problem? Is it really them? Or do I need a radical change? Like what? Consider the people I know with happy marriages, like Ken and his wife. H'mm. It seems to me that most of the men I know and admire have what they refer to as "a Christian life and a Christian wife." Maybe what I need is a Christian woman, whatever that means. Within another hour Wysong had written and submitted a creatively reworked profile to a Christian matchmaking service, something he had never before considered. In completing his profile form he portrayed himself as a Christian interested in dating Christian women only.

A week later he began reviewing matches which had been submitted for his consideration. One profile in particular caught his attention and he inquired of her with his own profile. Much to both his surprise and delight, she responded in kind. In fairly short order they had exchanged photos and added a minimal amount of information about themselves. For his part he had labored in constructing even the bare-bones Christian comments section of his profile.

He was taken by the fact that the respondent to his profile had been married once before and had a six year old child–a girl only two years younger than his son Billy. She was forthcoming with respect to her strong Christian faith, leading Wysong to sparingly state what he had made up as his own. In the "special interest" category, however, he took notice of her check-off of "old movies." At least on that point Wysong could truthfully echo a similar interest.

After only two weeks of wide-ranging yet general e-mail chatter on both sides, he nevertheless managed to set their first date. Hoping that he had sold himself as someone who met her standards, he was anxiously awaiting her arrival for dinner at a pre-arranged restaurant location.

Marlene Neuman was approaching the restaurant where she was to meet her first date through a dating service of *any* kind. As she passed the front door to a side area parking slot she thought she recognized what might be her date standing near the entrance. He was wearing a leather jacket and tie, which is what he had said to watch for.

As Wysong stood outside the restaurant in the early evening June sunshine, he was tempted to wave at the woman he, too, thought might be his date as she had slowly driven by, apparently looking for a parking space. He resisted the impulse. As she parked her car out of his sight Marlene Neuman hesitated before getting out of her car, but then reluctantly reaffirmed her commitment to "try this one time."

As she approached through the parking lot Wysong tried to hide his casual glances in her direction. He had agreed to meet her at this, her choice of a familiar salad buffet restaurant. He figured that she likely considered this to be a safe-harbor. As she got closer to the entrance he caught her eye and subtly pointed in her direction, saying, "I'll bet you're Marlene. I'm Pete."

They had not talked by phone, only communicated via e-mail. "Hi, Pete," she said. "My name is pronounced Mar-lena, German pronunciation. The second syllable carries a long 'a' sound for the 'e'."

"Mar-lane-eh," Wysong phonetically pronounced the name. "That's beautiful," he said. "Like the old time German movie star, Marlene Dietrich."

"That's it exactly," she said, impressed at his association.

Once inside and seated with their salad selection, Pete started the conversation rolling. "Tell me more about yourself and your family, Marlene."

Now that she had met him in person she was happy to share her story. She had actually followed his initial e-mail lead in not telling him much in the way of personal information. That cautious approach seemed to be appropriate for starters. But now was the time to be more open to this interesting guy.

"My faith in the Lord has preserved me," she said in an unassuming manner, "after having lost my husband to the war in Iraq. I'm an administrative assistant to the president of a large German-owned company. I've been there for about eight years. I just got my promotion to this position last year, and I love it."

"Do you speak German?" Wysong asked, taken by her striking looks, warm confidence, and upbeat attitude.

"Yes," she said. "My parents were missionaries and we lived in Bremerhaven–near the North Sea in Germany–for eight years, until I was twelve. I grew up in the church, but didn't really come to walk with the Lord until my college years. My family had moved back to the States just before I entered university. I think a lot of young people fall away from God during that period of their lives, perhaps because of their sudden freedom. But I sought Him anew and He drew closer to me. I met my future husband at school and within two years of graduation we were married."

"How long has it been since you lost your husband?" Wysong said, already feeling a little uncomfortable with her several references to God, but taken by both her personality and appearance.

"Three years," she said. "Since then my life has been the church. Well, that isn't quite true. After God, comes Amanda—my lovely little girl—then my job, and finally my church and its activities." She took the last bite of her salad and said, "Not to change the subject, but I noticed on your resume that you like old movies also. What's your favorite?"

Based on her profile information Wysong had anticipated that question. He had thought about it in advance and his instinct was to respond with something humorous, such as "any movie with a football theme or Bruce Willis in the lead, or both," but he resisted the impulse. Instead, he again was truthful in replying, "*Singing In The Rain.*"

Her jaw dropped perceptibly, her eyes brightening. She leaned forward and said, "Really! That's one of my favorites also. What do you like most about it?"

Wysong had never thought about why he liked the film, but *Singing In The Rain* was the only film he had ever watched more than twice. "Oh, I don't know," he said. "But as I think about it, three things come to mind: the singing of course, but also the dancing and the humor. Sometimes the title tune just crowds into my head for no reason and I begin singing a couple of its lines, often when I'm in the shower. What a threesome they were in that film," he said in all sincerity. "Three headliners, and each one a wonderful singer-dancer: Gene Kelly, Debbie Reynolds, and funny man Donald O'Connor."

Marlene was nodding her head. "For sure," she said. "Great film. I can see you really know it. As I said, it's easily in my top five. But then, about ten years ago I learned for the first time of an incredible romance movie made about 30 years earlier. Others had often mentioned it to me because they knew of my film interests. I rented it once and immediately bought a copy. Since then I've probably watched it two dozen times."

Wysong was taken by her enthusiasm and asked follow up questions. "Really? What's the title and what's it about?"

"*Somewhere In Time*," she said. "It's a love story about a man who sacrifices his life in the present to find happiness in the past. It's become a cult classic. I'm even a member of its fan society."

Wysong found that a bit eccentric since he had never joined any sort of fan club, even in his adolescence, but the way in which she spoke of things—her gentle yet confident attitude—and her physical attractiveness all greatly appealed to him. "And what do you like most about that film?" he said.

"Touché," she said, smiling at his handing her own line back to her. "The whole story. It's so wonderfully romantic. And the music. Talk about *Singing In The Rain* getting into your head, the theme music to SIT is absolutely haunting. And the lead line by Jane Seymour during her first meeting with Christopher Reeve in the beach scene—'Is it you?'—kills me every time I watch the movie. Actually, I just like everything about it; from the story line and dialogue to the period costumes." She took a deep breath. "Sorry," she said. "I didn't mean to go on like that. Enough about me. Tell me about yourself, Pete . . . and how you came to know the Lord."

Wysong swallowed twice before putting down his fork and saying, "Okay, but first let's load up on soup and whatever." As they walked through the secondary buffet line he thought, *Wouldn't you know it? She keeps coming back to the religion thing. What do I tell her beyond the generalities I shared with her on line? What were those words I used in the profile, the ones I borrowed from a creed I printed out from an on line church bulletin?*

Back at their booth he twice pointed at his billowed cheeks when she said he could talk whenever he felt like coming up for air. When he could no longer beg off he said, "Well, who am I? You already know that I'm two years older than you. And I've told you about being raised in a divorced home and not being able to count on either my mother or my father. I managed college in spite of that, with a little scholarship and a lot of part-time work. English was my major and I've been working at being an independent multi-line representative for only my second job since graduation."

"You're a traveling salesman. Right?" she said.

"You could say that, but you'd be wrong," he said as he forced a laugh at his own line while forking another bite of salad. "I don't actually sell anything. I promote my suppliers' products to distributors who sell custom imprinted products from my lines to their clients. I really like what I do, even though it involves a lot of travel."

Wysong was hoping she might have some follow-up questions for him, but she had none. He sensed she was waiting for him to get to the second part of her earlier two-part question. No one spoke for an awkward moment or two, so he broke the silence with a diversionary tactic. "I confess that I made the mistake of marrying a woman who wasn't ready for marriage. Well, I guess I wasn't either." Sighing, he added, " Out of that came Billy." He stopped for a moment and smiled. "Yeah," he said, nodding his head over the memory of a recent discussion with his son. "He's so funny."

"Funny how?" Marlene said, adding to her encouragement of him with a genuine smile.

"Well," Wysong said, "he has to make a decision about whether to play baseball or soccer next year, since the seasons overlap. He likes both and he said he had figured out the answer. He wants me to tell the coaches that he's going to play both sports, but in alternate weeks!"

"That *is* funny!" she said, laughing. "My Amanda thinks she would like to both play softball and take dancing. I want to support and encourage her in whatever healthy interests she would like to pursue." She nodded her head in affirmation and then there was a short but awkward moment as she struggled to find a segue for something that was on her mind. She apparently could not think of a good transition so she simply said, "But your marriage didn't work out."

"Not at all," he said. "Five years later came the divorce. Frankly, we never really got along." Wysong didn't want to continue with that line of thought so he tried to wrap it up. "What else can I tell you?"

"I'm sorry for you and for your divorce," Marlene said. "I believe strongly in commitment to both spouse and marriage. I put great stock in humans being primarily created to be spiritual people and to do great and wonderful things in these short physical lives. My cause is to live my life for Jesus." She hesitated before continuing. "Pete, I have to ask you something personal. Since a marriage takes two to make it work. Where do you think you went wrong?"

At that moment—had she known Wysong better—she might have been able to translate his facial expression and body language. It was almost comical in that it reflected a combination of self-righteousness—in blaming his ex for most of their problems—and his desperation at finding himself increasingly open to the lie he had created in order to meet this woman to whom he already felt drawn. He suddenly had no idea how he might survive his luncheon date. But he also knew he had to answer for her a question he had never really tried answering for himself. He answered the immediate question the only way he knew how. "I'm sorry to say that I simply don't have a clue."

Marlene had a look of surprise on her face. "You mean it's been almost two years since the divorce and you're still clueless about the reason for it? I'll bet some counseling would help you pin that down." She immediately regretted saying what she had and added, "Sorry, that's none of my business. Okay. Where do you go to church? And how did the Lord reveal Himself to you? I think I actually asked you that in an e-mail, but you didn't answer."

"I didn't?" he said. "Well, I'm in between churches right now." He looked around as if searching for something—anything with which to redirect her attention. With nothing coming to his rescue he decided to plunge forward. "I went to church a few times with my ex, but we didn't care for the pastor. And for another thing, I thought the congregation was full of hypocrites. Do-gooders on the surface, but I knew a few of them pretty well."

"Hypocrites?" she said, raising her eyebrows in mock surprise. "Really? You mean, more so than in everyday life?"

He didn't pick up on her tone, but he nevertheless fidgeted with his fork, saying, "Well, let's say I hadn't expected that. After my divorce though, I did try one other church." Then, thinking he might get some traction by adding to his statement, he said, "As a matter of fact, I even went to a Stephen Ministry orientation, but nothing came of that. The thing is, I'm on the road every other week. It's pretty hard to find the time to get involved."

Nearly ten awkward seconds passed with no one speaking. Pete was desperately hoping his response had been adequate and that she would nod, maybe even smile. But no. The ball was still in his court. He attempted to change the subject. "Do you like sports, Marlene? I think your profile said you did."

"Peter," she said, raising her right hand a few inches from the table top as if it were a stop sign, "about the personal profile you provided to the matchmaker service . . . it," she hesitated before continuing . . . "well, it said you were walking with the Lord. Now, only God knows the nature of that relationship between you and Him, but you haven't yet shared anything with me in that regard. Let me ask a different question. What's the most important thing in your life?"

Wow, he thought, *maybe I just dodged a bullet.* "That's easy," he said. "My job! I'm committed to it. Well, of course I love Billy." He didn't know what her point might be so he tried again to steer things back to her. "How about you?" he said. "You're working as an administrative assistant aren't you? Born and raised in Germany, didn't you say?" This woman was very different than any he had ever met. *She seems genuinely interested in who I am, with no need for superficial conversation.* He pondered that thought with a concluding one. *That may be both good news and bad news.*

"I understand that your job is very important to you," Marlene said. "Mine is to me, too. And your son is very important to you, of course. I know I would do anything to protect and care for Amanda. But there is one thing that comes before either of them. The Bible talks about comparisons between loving God and loving other people and things–literally any one and any thing–*less* than Him. I trust in the Lord in all matters, including the terrible emotional pain of having lost my husband, even though I still don't understand. What about *your* faith, Pete? Where does God fit in?"

Pete's jaw sagged. The motion itself was likely imperceptible to Marlene, but it carried significant meaning. *What did she just say?* No one had ever asked him such a thing. He recovered enough to pose a defensive question in response to hers. "First, let me ask you about something you just said. Where do your parents fit into the loop of things that are important to you?"

"I love my parents," she said, "even when they disappoint me. They're family, just like my daughter. But when I left my mother and father I cleaved unto my husband. And although I lost him, I never lost the Lord."

"I don't know much about those things," he said. "Can you elaborate?"

Wearing a disappointed expression, she said, "Many have had the sad experience–as have you–of being forsaken by a father or mother. And I understand that people suffer broken homes, differences in belief, addiction to drugs or alcohol. And for that matter," she added, "even psychological isolation, but we can't allow ourselves to be emotionally crippled by such losses."

"I have to respectfully disagree," Wysong said, knowing that he might well be digging a hole for himself. He simply did not know how to let go of the spade's handle.

Marlene gracefully took up the challenge. "Yes," she said, "but even as we carry some of that pain into adulthood and other relationships, God never changes. He is both our primary and our ultimate resource. Scripture is very specific in that respect when it says, '*Though my father and my mother forsake me, my Lord will receive me.*'"

"I've never heard that," he said, confused about where she was taking the conversation.

"Pete, I've learned that God can take that forsaken place in our life, fill that void, and heal those hurts, with the bottom line being that His love is sufficient for all of our needs."

If Wysong had been surprised by Marlene's earlier answer, now he was in awe of her explanation of it, although he didn't understand it. He had tried to be honest with her. *Where can I go from here?* he asked himself. "Intellectually," he said, " I think I understand what you're saying, but emotionally that's another story. You sound as if you have had personal experience in this regard."

"Well," she began reluctantly, "my father and mother didn't get along well. As I said, I love my father. I loved my mother, too. She passed away a year ago. But she didn't love me. She even tried to abort me. Not once, but twice. I didn't learn about that until I was an adult. For a while I questioned God, but when I got to thinking about it and went to the Bible for comfort and answers, I found both and I have since forgiven her."

Pete was intrigued by this woman who seemed to be so well grounded in life. "Do you always go to the Bible for answers?" he said.

"Much of the time. To whom else would I turn with big questions, but to the Creator?"

Wysong was trying to assimilate what she was saying about having dealt with difficulty. "And your point is that you managed to wait until you got through things before you regained your happiness?"

"No. No. Not at all," she said, reaching over to momentarily cover his hand. "What I mean is that we *do* get through everything, *because* there is a God in heaven. But we don't have to wait until things are fixed to have joy. I have always had the peace of Christ in my life, in spite of difficulties."

Wysong shook his head, saying "That doesn't sound reasonable to me."

"You're right," Marlene said. "It does pass understanding, but that is what God tells us. It's in the Bible. Colossians 3:15."

Pete had a thousand questions, but he could only think of one. "Okay," he said. "I guess I can understand about your job, your parents, and even having lost your husband, but do you really mean God is more important to you than your daughter?"

"Yes. I would give my life for Amanda. The thing is that we all die, but the Word of the Lord will never change, never perish. And because of Jesus—who sacrificed Himself on the cross for us—believers will share everlasting life with Him. But you know that, don't you?"

"To be honest, I don't."

"Pete," she said, looking him squarely in the eyes, " You don't have a personal relationship with the Lord, do you?" He could read sadness in her eyes as she continued. "Now that's your business and I am certainly not judging you, but why did you say you did, and in those very words?"

Peter Wysong was–at that moment–experiencing the single most embarrassing and painful moment of his life. Worse, he was wounded by the truth of what she was saying. He very much liked this woman. He found her to be not only engaging, honest, and attractive, but oddly–at least for him to admit–*spiritually* attractive, even though he didn't really know what that meant. What could he say in response? There was only one thing he could think of to say.

"You're absolutely right, Marlene. Frankly, I don't even know what 'walking with the Lord' means. As to why I lied, I can only say that every single one of the women I have dated before lacked what you have, although I have no clue as to what that is."

"I appreciate your being candid about your dishonesty, " she said, "but it also hurts."

"I hope my confession didn't come too late," Wysong responded, but with a sinking feeling.

"I think you're confused," she said. "I clearly stated on my profile that I am not interested in meeting a man who is not in possession of belief in Jesus Christ as Lord and Savior. I don't want to hurt your feelings but I perceive that while you have pro*fessed* some degree of faith, you clearly po*ssess* none. Now that is one thing. You have the right to go your own way. Most people do. But it is quite another matter to have lied about that."

Wysong paused before replying. *Surely she won't dump me for that if I'm contrite enough.* He dropped his head into his hands for another moment before looking up at her and saying, "I am guilty as charged. I apologize for having misled you but let me add something I consider as important as the admission itself. I like you very much and hope you can forgive me enough for a second date." In closing his appeal he felt that a light touch might help, so he said, "What do you say, Marlene–German pronunciation?"

Without hesitating, yet with an obvious sense of resignation in her voice, she said, "I say 'no,' but I don't say it in anger, merely in disappointment. There are no degrees of honesty, Pete. Timing has purpose, however, and this has no chance of working out. I am truly sorry. Thank you very much for lunch." With that, she got up and left. Pete remained at the table, holding his napkin in one hand and resting his chin in the other. As the waiter approached he said, "Will your lady friend be back, sir, or would you like your check?"

CHAPTER 7

RETREAT

Wysong went back to his apartment and threw himself at his business for the next two weeks. He also returned to his once regular Saturday morning routine of playing racquetball. Work followed by vigorous exercise always helped him to clear his head. Whenever Marlene and their personal encounter flooded up into his consciousness, he did his best to will it into subjection. But it wouldn't stay buried.

One day, he wheeled both the baggage of that experience and all of his various sample cases into the offices of Herb Hammond, a long-time distributor friend in a small community just East of Tampa. No sooner had he finished a shortened version of his usual presentation than he proceeded to unload his hidden agenda. "Man, I am miserable," he said. "And I don't really know why. I've dated dozens of women over the past two years and I never once felt like I do at this moment. And to make matters worse, my last date dumped me before we could get to dessert. Why? Because I'm not 'walking with the Lord,' as she put it." In concluding the woeful story for his friend he managed a final self-righteous expression by saying, "What kind of Christian perspective is that?"

Hammond leaned back in his office swivel chair and assessed what he had just heard from the rep he had come to know, like and respect. Both he and Pete had discovered early on a common enthusiasm for life that was totally outside their mutual alma mater, Florida

State University. "Peter, my boy," he began, "I suspect you're not telling me the whole story. But let's dig into it a little further and maybe I can shed a little light on your dilemma. In return, however, I expect you to cover our pizza dinner at Babe's. You have a problem with that?"

Wysong wanted to answer with something snappy such as, "It's a deal, so long as you focus on selling one or more of my lines exclusively for the next month," but he didn't. He was wrung out over the issue and settled for a simple, "You're on."

"Okay," Hammond said as he now leaned forward at his desk. "Get out your pen and paper and take some notes, pal. I've known you long enough to read you like a book. First of all, whether you know it or not you're already in "like" with this woman who dumped you. The fact that she is so different than all the other women you've dated is probably a big part of it. As for the matter of her perception that you aren't a man of Christian faith, she's right, isn't she? I mean, that's obvious if for no other reason than you haven't denied her statement."

"For crying out loud," Wysong objected, "why should that make a difference? I don't have a problem with *her* faith. Why should she have a problem with mine?"

"Oh. I'm sorry, Pete." Hammond said as he expressed mock facial pain, "What *is* your faith?"

"Okay," Wysong said, nodding his head, "let's call it like it is, *lack* of faith. But what's the big deal?"

"Well, I'm guessing she has already told you. Probably something equivalent to not being equally yoked with respect to spirituality. Now, is there anything you're *not* telling me?"

Wysong slumped down in his chair, resignation flooding his countenance. "Uh, yeah. There is. I lied to her."

Hammond sat upright and feigned mock outrage. "Now if that doesn't tear it," he said. "A little lie. Women these days! Imagine her wanting a prospective suitor to level with her from the get-go. What's your generation coming to?"

"Hey," Wysong said as he, too, sat upright in response to his friend's light-hearted yet accurate response, "we belong to the same generation!" Then he added, "I know. I know. I screwed up big time. But for the moment let's deal with the facts. Where do I go from here?"

"You can't get there from here, my man." Hammond said. Then he pressed a forefinger to his lips, leaned back in his chair and turned his head slightly in looking away, apparently in deep thought. After a full 30 seconds of silence Wysong had all but reached the end of his resolve to keep his lip zipped until his confidant spoke. Sensing that, Herb leaned forward and said, "Okay, tell me how things ended. I mean, aside from your having left the restaurant with your tail between your legs. Did she throw you a bone of any kind?"

At that Wysong began animatedly pointing at Hammond. "Bingo!" he said. "Until you just mentioned it, I had forgotten something. She made a point of saying she wasn't actually angry with me. In fact I think we got along great . . . that is, until the religion thing. True, she turned me down when I asked her for a second date. But all she really said was that she was "disappointed."

"And what are you trying to make of that?"

"What I now make of it, Inspector Clouseau," Wysong said, "is that if I can gain an understanding of the direction from which she's coming, I might still get that second chance."

At that, Hammond burst out laughing and said, "Yeah. Right. That is, if she doesn't marry and have four kids in the meantime." Hammond once again settled back into his chair. Then, in a serious tone he said, "You should hear yourself. Do you honestly believe that if you can fake sincerity, you can still win the day? Forget it. Now here's what your 'Aunt Landers' would tell you: If you want to get serious with this woman who has you so bothered, you'll have to first get serious with yourself."

For the second time during their conversation something his bold friend said had spoken to Wysong. A vague idea that had been beating around the door of his mind suddenly began pushing its way through. He couldn't wait to get back to Atlanta to check it out. "Herbie-boy," he said with a broad grin, "a plan is incubating in this mush brain of mine, and I have you to thank for it. Let's go get that pizza and I'll tell you all about it."

CHAPTER 8

MENTOR

B arely home from the week's road trip, Wysong picked up the phone and called the church he had recently visited. The receptionist answered and Wysong said, "Yes, ma'am. Could you give me the name of the person who led the break-out group some months ago on Saturday evening? It was about your Stephen Ministry program. I need some help."

He was given the name of the church's Stephen Ministry leader and he called and made an appointment to see her. He showed up at her office the next day and she listened to what he had to say, making it very clear that she had no interest in judging him. In response to that he surprised himself in sharing something he had not intended. "I'm not only lonely," he said, "but suddenly I feel like I'm invisible."

Recovering from his temporary lapse into self-analysis, Wysong proceeded to give her a short version of his divorce, the rebuff for his lack of faith by someone in whom he had become interested, and his visit to the Stephen Ministry information break-out. He didn't mention either having lied to his date or his ulterior motive in merely gaining a better understanding of her faith. The idea which had come to him was much longer on the "understanding" aspect than on "faith" itself.

"Mr. Wysong," she said, "it sounds to me like you could benefit from sharing with someone who would truly care. I'll be happy to assign a Stephen Minister to you."

Within three days Wysong received a phone call from the same man he had met at the end of the break-out session. The initial appointment was set for 4:00 P.M. the following Friday. The leader acted as the go-between and both the timing and the place were suggested by Wysong. He didn't want to meet at his own apartment because of the usual disarray with which he seemed to struggle in combining his home with a business office, and a laundry room with a kitchen sink, all of which seemed to remain full of items in need of attention.

The minister called the next day to confirm the appointment. "Wilson Shoemaker here, Pete. Remember me? We spoke at the church about a year ago."

"Of course. I've been expecting your call, Mr. Shoemaker."

"Call me Will. I'm looking forward to getting to know you. From what I understand, our program has been explained to you. We can certainly meet at my home. I normally meet care receivers at either their home or at a convenient restaurant, or even in the narthex of our church, but if that's your preference, it's a plus for me. I'm retired from my former industry and I'm home quite a bit. In fact, if you're usually in town by four o' clock on Fridays, that should work quite well."

They met for the first time exactly as planned. After they had each shared something of their lives, with the dominant time naturally being given over to Wysong, the Stephen Minister said, "Let me understand problem number one. You feel your lack of a true understanding of Christianity is what is preventing you from further dating a young lady you've met once and been given the heave-ho? That doesn't sound quite complete to me. Are you leaving anything out of the equation?"

"Mea culpa," Wysong said. "I lied to her on my dating service profile and again in our first e-mails. I didn't think it was a problem. Don't most people in this country claim to be a Christian if you ask them?"

"I don't know. Do they? In any event, that doesn't make it right."

"I've thought a lot about this," Wysong said, "and I don't understand why it should be such a big deal to her, either about my faith or the lack of it."

"My friend, you have put your finger on exactly what God warned the Israelites about, and why His words on the subject apply to us today. Those who don't follow His ways are by definition, pagan. God's point was that intermixing and intermarrying between believers and pagans would cause the Israelites to be led astray. And that is precisely what happened. Your would-be lady friend understands this. That–along with your lying to her–are the reasons she dropped you before she had a chance to become attached to your charming self."

"Well," Wysong said defensively, "I still don't get it."

"You will, in time," Shoemaker said. "I at least applaud you for your honesty with *me*, but tell me some more about yourself."

Wysong realized he had taken a couple of hits in the last moment or two, but he was none the less eager to tackle the project. He would make allowances for Shoemaker's bias. Even though he was quite a bit older than himself, he seemed to know what he was talking about. Having read the material he had been sent concerning Stephen Ministry, however, he felt he first needed to qualify something. "Okay, you're being straight forward with me, so let me do the same with you. My situation might be a little different from what I understand your ministry's usual care giver-to-care receiver relationship is like."

Shoemaker smiled. "And how different might your needs be?"

"I want more than your ears in this deal. I want your knowledge. I want to know what you know about the Bible and the Christian faith. I mean, intellectually I want to understand what's behind such verses as '*Though my father and my mother forsake me, my Lord will receive me.*'"

Shoemaker was amused. He said, "You're doing research so that you can impress—and possibly win—this young woman at some point in the future. Is that correct?"

"Well, her or someone like her," he answered truthfully. "You put it pretty bluntly, but it's a fair statement."

Shoemaker nodded and said, "I see. I've read the brief statement you provided relative to your background. Tell me about your marriage and the relationship you had with your ex-wife."

"I don't know what that has to do with anything," he said with a sigh, "but I'll give you the Cliff's Notes version." Wysong wasn't really interested in being analyzed but Shoemaker was obviously looking for something, so he felt he had better play along. *How can I sum this up?* he thought. He began as best he could. "As I see it, marriage is . . . well, to be straightforward . . . except for the sex . . . two people in a paper relationship committed to dealing with ongoing crises. Actually," he said as he sighed again, "I read that somewhere, but the fact is it's close to my own experience. That's how it was with my parents and that's how it was with my ex-wife and me."

"That's all of it?" Shoemaker said.

"Yeah. Well, not quite, to be honest. As I look back on things, I think I really saw my marriage as an acquisition. I mean I liked what came with the deal. You know — regular date, house- keeper, cook, sex partner. In a nutshell, my philosophy was–I guess still is—that it's better to wear out than rust out." He knew he had a stupid grin on his face, but he didn't care, although he wasn't sure why he had thrown in that gratuitous one-liner. Simply because he had read that, too? Or maybe to lighten the conversation? He was wondering what kind of reaction that was going to bring from Minister Shoemaker.

Will didn't so much as blink as he said, "Tell me, who was protecting your wife during your marriage?"

"Protecting her?" he said with a puzzled expression. "From whom?"

"From yourself." Shoemaker could barely believe the sum of what he had just heard. He didn't doubt that some couples acted in such a fashion when they were first married, perhaps even after they had been married for a year, or even many, but he had never before heard anyone actually *claim* such an attitude.

"I don't know what you mean," Wysong said. "I didn't have to protect her from myself. She was my wife. It wasn't long into our marriage before I realized that she had the same attitude about me as I had about her."

"What an amazing coincidence," Shoemaker said, being unsuccessful in not wanting to give in to his bias. "I wonder where she could have gotten the idea? Please excuse my being so forthright, but with that attitude you're lucky to have escaped losing no more than a wife, custody of your child, a house and an alimony payment. I mean, you could have met with a serious accident. My point is that you seem to be missing most of what it takes to make a successful marriage."

Wysong was surprised at Shoemaker's comments. After all, weren't churched folks mostly side steppers and tip-toers, even if they professed—or in Marlene's church jargon, 'possessed'—faith, along with a dogmatic approach to their religion? *Well, I still need to make the most of this,* he thought. "Okay, professor," he said, "could we include your short course on these 'lessons about marriage' into my crash course on Christian faith?"

Shoemaker said, "Would you excuse me for a moment? I'll be right back. Help yourself to Mrs. Shoemaker's home-made chocolate chip cookies. May I bring you a root beer or some ice cold peach tea?"

"Oh. Thank you very much," he said, wondering what the early break was all about. "I don't mind if I do help myself to a cookie. And a bottle of water would be fine."

Shoemaker went out into the kitchen and said to his wife, "I don't know what I'm getting myself into here. This guy wants to work me for his own selfish ends. I don't know whether to kick him out of the house or thank the Lord for sending him to me."

"Are you asking me for my opinion, Will, or are you using me for a sounding board? I'm okay either way, honey."

"You know it's the former. You may have even heard something of what he said."

"No, I didn't, as a matter of fact. I was cooking, not listening. In any event, Will, you aren't the message, you are only the messenger. It's up to you to decide if you might be the instrument by which this young man is to gain the very things that could save his life, not to mention his soul. And remember, too, that you're not only a Stephen Minister, but a Sunday School teacher as well. Could you not provide him with teaching as well as caring?"

Shoemaker didn't need to ponder his wife's wisdom. With a wry grin and a subtle head nod he said, "Thank you, sweetheart. You are right on, as usual. But this assignment is going to take a lot of prayer. I don't know exactly how it's going to work, but 'Lord, here am I.'"

As he came back into the room he handed a bottle of water to Wysong and said, "Okay, my friend, let's do this. I'll see you again next week. Same time, same place, unless I hear differently from you before then. May I briefly pray us out?"

"Uh," Wysong said, surprised, "if that's a part of the program I guess it's okay. But I'm not a praying man, understand."

"I understand very well," Shoemaker said, "and I take no offense." He bowed his head, paused a moment, and said, "Thank you, Almighty and Gracious God. May You guide the two of us as we take on Pete's challenge in making this an opportunity for both of us. In His holy name. Amen."

CHAPTER NINE

SECOND MEETING

W ysong showed up at the Shoemaker home on time for his second meeting. As the two engaged in small talk for a few minutes about their past week, Wysong reached out to figuratively scratch a bothersome itch, saying, "I have a personal question. I notice that you and a lot of other Christians wear a cross. I have always thought that a little boastful. Don't take offense, but I have never figured out the thinking behind the wearing. I know it represents a belief in Christianity, but why the need to advertise the fact?"

"I'm not offended at all," Shoemaker said. "In fact, I'm impressed that you would bring it up. In my own case I wear this particular chain-necklace cross because my wife gave it to me as a birthday gift. But the underlying reason is as you say, an advertisement. "This," Shoemaker said as he tenderly lifted up with his thumb and forefinger the inch and three-quarters by one inch 18-carat gold cross of nails overlain with the Star of David, "is a symbol that proclaims to the world—whether on a person or on a building—that the blood-stained wooden cross of Calvary is our only hope of forgiveness and salvation. In other words, I wear it prayerfully to let people know of my personal faith." He was going to let it go at that, but then added, "I have been working for God for more than 30 years, but I am not saved because I am working for Him; I am working for Him because I am saved."

"That was well said," came Wysong's reply, although not grasping much of what he had heard. "You sound like a straight arrow."

"The truth is," Shoemaker said, "God took this 'crooked stick' of a person and straightened him out, giving me a new nature altogether."

"Well, I just heard 'the rest of the story' didn't I?"

"Yes, you did." They had taken seats at the coffee table and Shoemaker added, "That's a good start for the day. Now I have a few questions for you, but first I want to clarify something."

"Shoot, Mentor," Wysong said, trying to keep things light, yet he knew he was also being marginally disrespectful of the man who was 25 or so years his senior.

Shoemaker gave him a little smile and said, "My friends call me Will. Remember?"

Wysong nodded and said, "Sorry," but he was feeling only marginally chastened.

"That's quite all right. You made an excellent observation a few moments ago concerning the nature of Stephen Ministry. Now, if I am to also share with you from a teacher's perspective, then it is important for you to know one thing about our relationship. Any time you feel your level of having invited me to share with you is being exceeded, you need to speak out. As much as I would like to think otherwise, I know I can neither 'educate' nor 'argue' anyone into the Kingdom of God."

"Don't worry, Will. I'm only seeking intellectual apprehension, not faith."

"Fair enough." Shoemaker said, flinching internally before asking his first question. "During the time of your seven year marriage, who was your best friend?"

"I don't know. I suppose my college buddy, Wally. We've done a lot of stuff together over the years. Still would be if he hadn't moved back to Tallahassee a couple of years ago."

"That's an interesting answer. I'm not a marriage counselor, but I know a few things about successful marriage. I've been happily married for 41 of my 61 years. The most important person in the world to me is my wife. I have a lot of friends, but none a better friend than her. Some people refer to such a relationship as 'soul mate.' I'm certain you've heard the phrase."

"Well, that isn't how it was for me," said Wysong. His expression was not one of guilt, only truth. "My ex and I had other roles with each other," he added.

"Really? I assume she *was* a friend, however, even if not *the* friend. You've already mentioned the sexual role, but were any of your other mutual roles that of partner?"

Wysong wrinkled his brow and said, "I don't know. I hadn't really thought about that. I was certainly her banker. I loved her, if that's what you mean. Well, at least I did in the beginning, until she began nagging me about everything. But tell me, why should a husband and wife have to be friends as long as they each get what they want out of the marriage?"

Shoemaker sighed, but this time he managed to avoid also shaking his head. "There is a very simple reason for that," he said. "The friendship factor is what drives the other roles in marriage. Did you and your ex ever seek marriage counseling?"

"Actually, yes. When we first started talking about divorce I agreed to see a counselor, and we did. All that accomplished was seeing our arguments moved from our home to his office. Look, I know I made a bunch of mistakes during our marriage, but I'll wager that a jury would agree that I was right a lot more often than she was."

"You think you can be right and married at the same time?"

What is this, he thought, *a pop quiz on the first day of school?* "Look," he said, "if you're right, you're right, married or not. Wimps wilt. Besides, even the Bible says that men are head of the house."

"Really?"

"I don't know chapter and verse, but I know it's in there somewhere."

"You are absolutely correct about that," Shoemaker said, nodding in agreement. "In the apostle Paul's letter to the Ephesians he *does* exhort wives to submit to their husbands, just as the church submits to Christ in all things. But do you also know that Paul devotes twice as many words to telling husbands to *love* their wives as to telling wives to *submit* to their husbands?"

Wysong met the statement with a shrug.

"I see you are dismissing the point, but why?" Shoemaker said. "Do you know what Paul meant by loving one's wife?"

"I have a pretty good idea," Pete said, grinning.

"Maybe you don't," Shoemaker countered. "I beg your indulgence for letting me share with you three things with regard to loving one's wife, and . . ." he hesitated for effect " . . . none of them include *making* love. Consider these few words."

Wysong frowned at whatever might be coming up as his teacher/minister took out a white 5" x 7" card and boldly wrote on it. Pete could easily read the card from across the coffee table where he was sitting. It read: "1) Sacrifice. 2) Well-being. 3) Care." Shoemaker turned the card around and said, "What do these three things mean to you?"

"I'm not sure," he said with more than a trace of sarcasm. "Tell me."

Shoemaker ignored both the tone and the body language. "In order for a wife not to fear submitting to a man who treats her with tender, self-sacrificing care, this is how a husband is to love her."

Wysong said, "Now you're going to have to translate that for me."

"Certainly." Shoemaker pointed to the card on which he had written the three headings and said, "This is how a man is to love his wife: 1) Be willing to *sacrifice* everything for her. 2) Make her *well-being* of primary importance, and 3) *Care* for her as you would care for your own body. This is what Paul's verses about love and submission are all about."

"Well, that's quite enlightening," said Wysong, trying to hide his boredom. "That would indeed make a man to be admired, but I doubt this actually works for many married couples."

"Why do you say that?"

"It's idealistic, that's all."

"For the sake of argument," Shoemaker said, "can you admit that such practices would be holy living? That is, don't you think marriage is a holy union?"

"Holy? I don't really know what that word means."

"Okay, let's look at that. The chief characteristic of holiness is being set apart to a sacred use. That also properly describes matrimony. Look, Pete," Shoemaker said as he turned both of his palms upward, "let me wrap things up for today by making the point that those same verses we've been talking about in the book of Ephesians simply tell us this: As husbands we are to love our wives just as Christ loved the church and gave Himself up for her. That was done by Jesus to make her–the church–holy, cleansing her by the washing with water through the Word."

"Whoa, whoa, whoa," said Wysong, putting up a hand. "I don't have a clue as to what you're talking about."

"All right, let's back up. Try to think about this as you're driving your territory next week. Just as Christ wanted to present His bride, the Church, to Himself as radiant, without stain or wrinkle or any other blemish–that is, holy and blameless—husbands, too, ought to love their wives as their own bodies."

Wysong had a look of surprise on his face. "That's in the Bible?" he said.

"Yup. Almost verbatim. Look it up in Ephesians, chapter five. Do you have a Bible?"

"Uh. Actually, no."

"Take this one. It's yours. See you next week. And Godspeed, brother."

CHAPTER 10

LIBRARY CARD

W ysong left for Nashville, Tennessee early Monday morning. He could drive there in fewer than five hours and then discount the time by an hour as he passed into the Central Time zone. He would easily be able to keep his day's first distributor appointment at 1:30. He also knew of a city library only a few blocks from his motel. He immediately proceeded there after checking in well before 12 Noon.

At the information desk he asked for the self-help section. The librarian responded with, "You'll have to wait your turn, sir. All the computer stations seem to be occupied at the moment."

"No," he said, shaking his head, "I mean hard copies. You know, books." She gave him a look of minor irritation as she pointed him to the area in question. He valued a library as much for its ambience as for being able to flip the pages of a book. With books spread about a work table he was captain of his research vessel. A few moments later, however, he felt he was hardly master of anything.

He was thinking about Shoemaker's words from Friday afternoon. *What had he said about saying 'no' to self-help? That made no sense. Wait a minute. On the way out the door I remember him giving me something that I stuffed into a pants pocket. Was I wearing these same . . .* he reached into his right back pocket and pulled out a single rumpled page. It was a short article torn from some publication called *Our Daily Bread*.

He glanced at the title: "Is Your Life Out of Control?" He flattened out the paper and leaned forward at his table as he began reading the text. He was stunned. Here, in print, was a sub-head of the very question he had been pondering. "Is self-help the answer?" The article went on to explain: "Consider how others have fared in this regard. The ancient Israelites were always getting into trouble for trusting human strength rather than God's." He consumed the balance of the article, including the closing sentence about what people do when they find themselves in difficult circumstances and seem to be powerless. Then he read it a second time, but with no better understanding of its meaning: "Not only is the Lord our strength and our shield, but by trusting in God we are helped." *Helped? Helped how?*

Wysong put down the paper and sat back, deep into thought: *Who is the author of such a counter-intuitive perspective?* He turned the paper over. On the back side were listed chapter and verse references from several different books of the Bible. He wadded up the paper and shot it in a low arc towards a nearby wastebasket. "Nothing but net," he said aloud, and then added, "Phooey on that notion. I'm the one who got myself into this funk. I can get myself out. 'Trust is a must' is a bust." A man seated at the next table looked up and frowned. Wysong stood up and left without having availed himself of any of the material for which he had come.

CHAPTER 11

THIRD MEETING

"Hey, Pete. Come in," Shoemaker said in greeting. "How was your week?"

"Business was fine, but I didn't think much of the article you planted on me decrying self-help. What was your point?"

"Have a seat my friend," Shoemaker said, ignoring Wysong's opening. "Care for some iced tea or a soda?" He directed him to a couch across the coffee table from where Shoemaker would sit. "I thought you might find the article relevant to your search for intellectual understanding of trust. What is there about trusting in the Lord that bothers you?"

"Okay, for the sake of argument suppose I said I believe in the existence of God, but that I don't trust him. What then?" Wysong folded his arms against whatever might be coming next.

"Well, since you put it that way let me apply a little logic. If one believes *in* God, why wouldn't he *believe* God?"

"That's a hypothetical question to my hypothetical position. Logic would say abandon the point."

"Okay," Shoemaker said, as he smiled at his new friend's determination to cling to what he wanted. "How about an analogy? People run from God in fear, just as squirrels run from us whenever we appear on their scene in refilling a feeder. They don't know we provide for them. People run from God in fear without knowing that He loves them and richly provides them with everything for their enjoyment. For example, can you make the connection between God's love for us and marriage?"

Wysong tried to analyze what Shoemaker had just said. *Is he trying to trick me?* He took the bait anyway. "No," he said. "I don't see that."

"Okay, here's a hypothetical question: What is more meaningful in life than to discover we are loved by someone? My point is that just as knowing God's love for us is such that He never takes His eyes off of us, a man and woman should likewise have as their goal of marriage putting each other before themselves."

Wysong once again presented his hand-up-palm-outward trademark signal. "For any two people to really be convicted about that wouldn't there have to be something in it for each individual? What would that be, aside from a 50% share in sex?" Before Shoemaker could respond, Wysong threw a second grenade into the bunker. "The hard reality is that in my marriage I stood for nothing when it came to religion. I guess that's where I still live. Why should I move?"

Shoemaker was surprised in feeling energized rather than frustrated by Wysong's comments. "I hear what you're saying," he said, "and I appreciate your being so candid. But as to your question, let me address the contributions of spirituality to a marriage."

Wysong realized that he wasn't going to be able to steam roll Shoemaker merely with outspoken opinions, so he simply shrugged.

Shoemaker took the shrug as assent and proceeded. "A recent article on the subject focused on what the author called an IQ test for one's soul. The guy is a theoretical physicist and he deals with what he calls 'spirituality quotients.' In other words he was interested in causing his readers to stop and take stock of how spirituality actually expresses itself in day-to-day life. I think it is especially relevant to married couples. First, consider the synergy in marriage, one plus one is equal to more than two. Are you with me so far?"

Wysong absorbed the comment for a moment before responding. "Okay. To your way of thinking marriage is the potential for each to support the other as well as themselves."

"Precisely!" Shoemaker looked around the room as if there might be others present. Grinning, he said, "Someone say 'Amen.'

Now," he continued, "the author had a series of 20 multiple choice questions. The higher the score one honestly registers, the greater it indicates he is led with respect to spirituality. Of course, that is, relative to the average population."

Wysong slowly shook his head and said, "I'm trying to bear with you, but what exactly are the supposed benefits to magically grow out of this 'spirituality?'"

"That's the incredible part,"Shoemaker said enthusiastically. "His premise is that higher scores appear to indicate things like those individuals healing faster from illness and surgery, recovering more easily from alcohol and substance abuse, coping better with stress, trauma, and emotional loss, being less likely to suffer from depression, and . . ."

Wysong interrupted. "Yet another example of an 'expert' underpinning his argument with the results of his own survey."

"It wasn't a 'survey,' Pete," said Shoemaker, ignoring Wysong's by now-familiar sarcastic tone. "And the author mentioned another critical item in this connection, which is that the more spiritual one is, the more likely one is to feel happy and optimistic. Give me the courtesy of thinking this next point through. Think of situations from the perspective of a married couple who tenderly and with self-sacrificing love care for one another. Can't you imagine the upside of that?"

"Maybe there's a reason why I don't get it," Wysong said, again shaking his head, but this time also tightening his lips. "I've never personally seen that model. Besides, marriages come and go all the time, and at an increasingly greater rate year after year. I think it's human nature."

"But it wasn't so in the beginning."

"What do you mean 'in the beginning?'"

At that, Shoemaker stood up, stretched, and smiled yet again. "Great question," he said, "Thank you for the segue into next week's meeting. Same time? Same place?"

Wysong was a little startled at the abruptness, but he nodded in the affirmative.

"Good," Shoemaker said. "At that time I'm not only going to explain how it was 'in the beginning,' but I'm going to introduce you to a song. In fact, a Song of Songs."

CHAPTER 12

DOUBLE WHAMMY

The next week Wysong took a call from the CEO of his largest line, one he had represented for ten years and had grown in sales dramatically every year from the first. A decade ago the sales manager for the company had first contacted him by phone and then had flown down from Kansas City to interview him before negotiating a contract for their line of custom advertising playing cards. Now, the CEO was speaking. "Pete, you know I've brought my son into the business. You met him at our last big sales meeting up here."

"Of course," Wysong said as he instantly wondered about the call. It was rare to talk to the company owner other than at sales meetings. "He's been doing a great job for a young man just learning the business."

"Thanks," the CEO said. "He's actually dryer behind the ears than you think, but the point is it's time for me to cut back. I'm giving him general sales responsibility. Naturally, he has his own ideas about things. I don't necessarily agree with them, but he wants to go forward with in-house sales reps rather than with independents."

Wysong's heart skipped a beat before accelerating. "I'm not going to be happy about this, am I, Ian?"

The CEO said, "Here's the thing. I don't want to make you mad and cause you to bad mouth us to your distributors. I'm going to pay you full commissions for the next quarter, then half commission for the following quarter, and half of that percentage for the third quarter. And you won't be representing us for any of that time. Fair enough?"

What can I say? He's killing me here! But then again the reality is I've never heard of a supplier paying off a dropped rep this generously. "You're my biggest revenue line," he said. "I can't deny this is going to hurt. But I appreciate your fairness." His thoughts went much deeper. *What an understatement about the hurt. The line accounts for nearly one-third of my revenues!*

On Friday he returned from his road trip, his reaction to the loss of his largest line still acute, only to open a letter from his struggling American-made cap line. The owner got right to the point: "Pete, I'm sorry to say that business is so poor–what with the foreign competition–that I have to terminate your representation. This is effective immediately. In accordance with our contract I will pay you for thirty days. Keep your samples but we would like you to return any remaining catalogs."

Great! Within the space of one week I have effectively lost more than 40% of my monthly revenue through no fault of my own. He picked up his cell phone and punched in the number of the one person in his life he knew who would honestly care about his circumstance. "Will," he said, "my boat is taking on water. I need someone to count cadence for me while I bail."

Shoemaker could tell from both Wysong's false bravado and tone of voice that he probably wasn't exaggerating. "What's the problem, Pete?" he said.

"Nothing much," he said. "Two of my supplier accounts have just dropped anchor through the floor of my boat. Before the end of the year almost half of my revenues will have followed, with no reduction in my cost of doing business. What's the thought for the day, minister?"

"My gosh, I'm sorry to hear that," said Shoemaker. "If you don't mind a little humor, my friend, I'm thinking of what my best friend told me when my first business went under. He said, 'Perspective, my friend. Perspective. No matter how successful you become, how confident or well known, when you die the size of your funeral will still pretty much depend upon the weather.'"

A surprised Wysong offered a subdued laugh and said, "That's all you have for me?"

"No. Of course not. You're due to come over here yet this afternoon and I'm anxious to hear the whole story."

CHAPTER 13

UNRAVELING

Wysong rolled his SUV into Shoemaker's driveway and parked. He was met at the door with a hearty hand shake and a clap on the back along with three brief yet genuine words of greeting: "Come. Sit. Talk."

"You see," Wysong began within seconds of taking a seat in Shoemaker's modest North Atlanta metro home, " I own this huge ball of twine, and the loose end seems to have snagged itself on something that won't stop running in the opposite direction. In other words, both it and I are unraveling." With that he proceeded to fill his host in on the week's events. When he had finished he shook his head and said, "Man, I'm not only down, I could be headed out."

"I can sympathize with you, Pete, but there is a much better direction to take. You laughed at that funeral-and-weather perspective I mentioned earlier on the telephone, but it actually has a great deal of merit. Let me give you a personal example. During times of my own setbacks–that is, after I began walking with the Lord—I have always tried to remind myself that I am nevertheless living victoriously."

"That sounds like some kind of Polyanna."

"Not really. God never promised His children that they would go through life buying low and selling high. What He did promise us is that in the world we would have pressures, affliction and difficulty. Now this is an important part of what you're trying to intellectually understand about faith. In walking with the Lord we are given a supernatural grace to walk through our tribulation with a peace and rest that passes all understanding."

"That sort of statement has passed my understanding more than once," Wysong said with a slight head shake."Are you certain you don't know a young woman by the name of Neuman?"

"Okay," Shoemaker said, knowing full well to whom his student/ care receiver was alluding. "I know this isn't an easy concept to grasp the first time around. Or the second, for that matter. Let me put this another way. Pretend for a moment–for the purposes of an exercise–that you *have* active faith in God. Can you give me that?"

"What do I have to lose?"

"Good. Now given that you have active faith you would then have confident patience that you would overcome, just as Jesus did, which is exactly what He tells us. Thus, with that confidence you would have certain hope in both this life and the next. Am I making any sense?"

"Hell no! Hope in *what?*" Wysong didn't grasp *any* of what Shoemaker was saying.

The teacher/minister thought for a moment. "See how this works for you," he said. "Understand that Christian faith is tied to the return of Jesus Christ–the Son of God—and the inexorable events woven into the fabric of that return. With that in mind, let me give you a question to think about during this coming week. This is it: What is our purpose in life?"

Wysong only hesitated a moment before saying, "I hope I can come up with something better than 'Live well and prosper.'" He snickered at his own answer before adding, "I obviously don't have a clue. Maybe that's part of why I'm here, talking to you."

"And that's why we're doing a little cultivating. We'll be planting, fertilizing and growing for a while yet before the harvest."

Wysong smiled and said, "Yeah? Well, I hope I don't rot on the vine before we bring in a crop." He glanced at his watch and said, "Look, I'm going to be late for an appointment." As he got up to leave, however, he stopped in mid-step and said, "Hey. Didn't you forget something? What about that cryptic 'song' business you threw at me last week?"

Shoemaker nodded and said, "Oh, that. It's the start of a simple little book from the Bible that addresses love, sex, marriage and romance."

Wysong lifted his chin and said,"Now that beats hearing about the Farm."

"What doesn't?" Shoemaker said. "See you next week. Call me if you feel the need. I'm always available. At least up until 10:00 P.M."

CHAPTER 14

PONDERING PURPOSE

Wysong left Shoemaker's home with a question he had never seriously considered. *Do I have a purpose in life?* During his territory drive-time to Tampa-Clearwater on Sunday afternoon he questioned, he speculated, and he pondered, but for all of that he came up with nothing on which he could hang his hat. *For crying out loud*, he thought, *what* do *I believe?*

As if in rehearsal for sharing with his teacher/mentor/minister at the end of the week–owing him nothing whatever in that regard, but having no one else who would care–he continued trying to nail down an answer to Shoemaker's nagging question. But the more he thought about it the more he seemed to generate questions rather than answers.

Why should I bother to seek goodness? his thinking began. *Why should anyone? Isn't man's basic goodness of heart good enough; well, aside from the perennial existence of war, crime, prejudice and poverty? On the other hand, knowing how complex is both the universe and man, how could it be that we actually exist without a purposeful Creator? What do we owe God, much less our fellow man? Or is it the other way around? Okay, God is one thing, but Jesus is a god of a different color. And what do I do with the notion of evolution, the affirmation of which is prevalent everywhere around us? Nuts! I don't know what I believe.* Before he could reach his driving destination that day he consigned everything to a single thought, having no idea that he had just prayed: *If you're there, God, please show me.*

"Focus, Doofus," he said aloud as he mentally slapped himself. He was pulling up in front of a distributor's office and so added another aloud line: "It's show time, boy!"

An hour and a half later, upon concluding his presentation and seeing that the last salesperson had departed the show room, Wysong said to the owner, "Randy, I'd like to ask you a personal question."

Surprised, but interested in being asked for his opinion on something, Wysong's customer said, "Sure. What do you have?"

"Only this. Do you believe there are clear and absolute standards for what is right and wrong?"

Taken aback, the distributor paused for a moment before scratching his head and raising and then lowering his eyebrows. "Is that all? Let me see. I don't get this question a lot, you know. Okay. I say yes."

Now it was Wysong's turn to be surprised. "Thank you," he said, "but your answer prompts a second question. What is your guide for determining those standards?"

"That one I can answer without having to scratch this balding head. I preach it to my salespeople: practical experience and common sense."

Wysong didn't understand and debated with himself whether he should point out the obvious contradiction in the two answers. On the one hand the man said he believed in absolute standards (true for everybody) and on the other, experiential guides (true for me). He could reasonably guess what Shoemaker might say in response to what he had just heard: *"In other words, you have admiration for God but dismiss the only entity that claims to speak for Him?"* That wasn't too far from where Wysong had been living for a very long time.

Then, without further encouragement, Wysong's customer amended his comments by saying, "I believe in myself. I believe that what I do and how well I do it defines who I am. In other words, you gotta' go get 'em. But you know that, don't you, Pete? After all, you're a go-getter. Right?"

"Right," he said. "Thanks." As Wysong headed out the door and towards his car he thought, *That was a lot of help. I guess from now on I'll leave that question in the bag.*

As he headed home at week's end he was still thinking about the distributor's answers to his questions. Wasn't he saying that the cause for which we are living and dying is us? If that is the case, then how could Shoemaker charge him with failure in his half of his marriage, when all he was guilty of was doing what he thought best? And by extension, wouldn't that also apply to his faith . . . or the lack of it? He was confused.

CHAPTER 15

THE SONG BEGINS

As Wysong showed up on time at Shoemaker's doorstep, the inside door was open, implying that someone was expected. One ring of the doorbell immediately brought the host. "Pete! Good to see you, my friend. Come in."

Before he could even take a seat Wysong said, "I've been trying to work out a plan to challenge some of the stuff you've been sharing with me, but the fact is I've been running around in circles. I simply can't figure things out."

"Sit down and relax," Shoemaker said. "Care for your usual drink?" Shoemaker nodded towards the bottle of water sitting on the coffee table in front of his guest.

"Thank you. Yes," Wysong said as he took a seat. He had a look of distraction on his face as he added, "I suppose you're hot to get started with the mysterious 'song' book lessons."

Shoemaker nodded. "I am, but if you want to talk about other things, by all means do."

"Oh," he said, shrugging, "I don't have anything specific. Things may come up."

"Then hang on," Shoemaker said, rubbing his hands together in anticipation. "I can tell you that before we finish this study some weeks down the road, you may look back at this as quite a ride. Now, paraphrasing my favorite author and pastor on the subject of love, sex, marriage, and romance, Tommy Nelson asks this question: Has

God given us desires, drives, and needs and failed to give us any guidance through what can be treacherous ground?"

Before Wysong could attempt answering Shoemaker's rhetorical question the minister/teacher said, "I think not. On the contrary, He has actually given us a reference–obscure as it may be—for these very things." Opening and then holding up his Bible to where he had placed his bookmark, he said, "This is the little 'Song' book of the Bible I have been referring to, one of the five poetic books of the Old Testament."

"Poetic?" Wysong said, not expecting poems as a reference. "As opposed to what?"

"As opposed to the historic and prophetic books of the Bible."

"What about the Gospels?"

"You'll recall that those are in the *New* Testament."

"So," Wysong responded with mock sarcasm, "the first pop quiz of this course was a trick one. Are you saying there's a book in the Bible that's an actual love story?"

Shoemaker nodded his head and said, "That's an interesting question. I might simply say 'Yes,' but from the perspective of God's love for us being the inspiration behind *all* of the books of the Bible, they are *all* 'love' stories. But Song of Songs is different in that it is a *romantic* love story. Not only that, it deals with what many of us–judging from the figures on marriage and divorce–either do not understand or have not properly learned."

Wysong saw an opportunity to inject a little humor into the conversation and jumped in with, "Then what we have here is the biblical version of 'the Birds and the Bees?'"

"Actually, that observation isn't too far off," Shoemaker said. "In fact, there are seven different and distinct subject areas that make up the book. I want to try to cover them with you over the next few months."

"I feel like I'm back in seventh grade," Wysong said. "Why don't we fast forward through some of this?"

Recognizing his charge's warning signals of boredom, Shoemaker shifted gears. "This might be a little advanced for seventh grade when you consider the subtitles: attraction, dating, courtship, intimacy, conflict, romance, and commitment. Any questions before we begin?"

"Yes, as a matter of fact," he said, still not content to move on without a little more substantive input. "Who is your usual audience for this stuff? Adolescents? I've been out of puberty for several years."

Shoemaker had anticipated such a comment and said, "I know what you're thinking, Pete, because I've been here before. The fact is that neither you nor I ever mature past being able to learn. God *can* help anyone who is teachable. And *may* God help those who aren't."

With that, Shoemaker gained a little traction with Wysong who said, "Come to think of it, I guess I did invite myself to this party." Nevertheless, he figuratively folded his arms.

Shoemaker nodded and said, "By way of introduction, our Song of Songs–or, as some refer to it, Song of Solomon–has, as one of its key verses something you'll probably find titillating. It reads like this: 'I am my lover's and my lover is mine; he browses among the lilies.'"

"That's Scripture?" Wysong said in challenge.

"Yup. You need to know that the book itself has been much debated in terms of its meaning but it has been widely used—and I believe, rightly so–by believing couples to greatly enhance the likelihood of a successful marriage."

"That's a bold statement," Wysong said, "but, even though the horse is already out of the barn for me, I still might be able to learn something." The new student leaned back into the recliner and took a gulp from his water bottle.

Shoemaker continued on his light starting note. "Thank you, Mr. Wysong. And I agree that you aren't dead yet. Even though you're freed from one failed marriage, it's entirely possible–in fact, highly likely — you might find another romance somewhere down the road. As we go along try to look both backwards and forward."

"I'm tuned in," Wysong said as he made a quick motion with the two forefingers of his right hand from his eyes towards Shoemaker's.

"Then listen up as well," Shoemaker said, humoring him. "At the beginning of a romance there are two questions each person should ask. They are these: 'What kind of person am I attracted to and what kind of person is attracted to me?' Seems simple enough, I know. But the reason for this is that many people continue to date the *same* kind of person, and thus continue to experience the same problems in dating relationships."

"That's interesting," Wysong interjected. "Because that's what led me to try a very different dating approach from what wasn't working. Of course, I didn't really get out of the gate with Marlene, but that's another story."

"But you *were* attracted to her?"

"Absolutely."

"Do you know why?"

"Not really."

"Consider that who a person is attracted to shows a great deal about the character and personality of him or her. That's the basic point that guru Nelson makes in his study of this subject, that who we are attracted to–and therefore date–is ultimately going to be–or should be—the person we marry."

"Now *that* is a big leap," Wysong said, "even though it would seem to be logical. Explain it to me, professor."

"I'll do better than that," he said. "I'll illustrate it through the girl of the Song of Songs. She is a Shulamite maiden living in Solomon's court and is expressing her thoughts of her absent shepherd lover and herself to Solomon's court ladies. She states that to her his name is like 'purified oil.' By that she means a man's name is a man's character. Now think back to some of your own relationships, Pete. What do you think God would say about your own character?"

"I don't care for that question," Wysong said, making no attempt to mask his pride.

"Is that because it hurts?" Shoemaker prodded.

"Yes," Wysong said, allowing a little defiance to surface along with pride.

"Okay, here's a different way to approach the question. What do you think is meant by the verse, 'It is better to be lonely and single than lonely and in a marriage?'"

"I can only guess. In a marriage there is supposed to be someone besides yourself to think about?"

Shoemaker gave him a thumbs up. "Bravo. That's a good way to put it, but you can drop the 'supposed' part. And harking back to the single life, someone has wisely said for a woman's benefit, 'If he will not obey God as a single, he will break your heart as a married man.' To a woman what do you think that would mean?"

"I don't care for that question either," he said.

"Okay," Shoemaker said, proceeding in spite of Wysong's attitude, "if God has told us in His Word that sexual intercourse as a single is against his will, and if a guy persists in disobedience in this respect, how will he then obey God in his marital life in honoring his wife?"

"I knew I wouldn't like your answer. In spite of the morality of what you're saying this is still an uphill climb for men."

"For some, yes. After all, today's print, electronic, and film media preach that immorality means freedom, perversion is natural, and commitment is outdated."

Wysong stretched what he knew was the teacher's meaning. "Are you saying that God doesn't think sex is important?"

"Hardly, but Scripture contains guidelines for its use, as well as warnings about its misuse. But sex is *always* mentioned in the context of a loving relationship between a husband and wife."

Wysong put up the sign for a time-out. "Wait a minute, coach. First of all, you say there is great variance in interpretation of the Song's meaning. So, are you saying this book is a literal story about married love, or is it some kind of allegory, or even something else? I'm wondering how much stock should be put into the book."

"That's a good question. Personally, I–and many others—think it is an historical story with two layers of meaning. On one level, we learn about love, marriage, and sex; and on the other level we see God's overwhelming love for His people. In any event, it's important to remember that we are loved by God, and therefore we are obligated to commit ourselves to seeing life, sex and marriage from His point of view."

"*His* point of view," Wysong said, emphasizing the first word. What about an individual's point of view? I think I'm getting a headache. What, exactly, is the lesson here?"

"How about this from Proverbs: 'What is desirable in a man is his kindness.'"

Putting his hand to his forehead, Wysong said, "I think my headache stems from confusion. What I'm wondering is where we are going with all of this. I also see by my watch that my evening's date is coming up. Can we continue next week?"

"Of course," Shoemaker said, "but in the meantime I have a short reading assignment for you. It might help you with your question. And this time I won't slip it into your pocket." With that he handed a printed and folded piece of paper to Wysong.

CHAPTER 16

CHARLOTTE'S WEB

On Monday morning Wysong was headed to Charlotte, North Carolina. He was still puzzling over one of Shoemaker's comments, the one about the 'art' of attraction. He had never heard of one person's attraction to another referred to as 'art.' It was all too deep for him.

He had decided that given the opportunity he would ask another of his distributor friends to render an opinion on things. As he got closer to Charlotte he bounced around on the radio dial from one local station to another until he heard someone say, "Life is like a game of cards." *What's this?* His follow-up thought was facetious: *I lose my line of playing cards and right away I hear some joker on the radio taunting me.*

The speaker was affiliated with a Christian ministry group out of Michigan called RBC. The speaker was trying to illustrate his point and said, "We have to work with what we're dealt. Consider that a new, unshuffled deck presents the cards in a predictable order. Once the deck had been shuffled an adequate number of times, however, there is no reason to react with disbelief or surprise to whatever card turns up. You can call it science, or art, or whatever you want, but the result is indisputable."

The statement made sense to Wysong. He could easily have made the same assessment. What surprised him was the particular analogy about to come. The point was that information *not* rooted in a consistent view of life becomes like a shuffled deck of cards. The speaker's qualifying explanation was, "In that situation we no longer have a coherent conception of ourselves, our universe, and our relation to one another and our world. As a result, with our information-immune system inoperable, we don't know how to filter things." Wysong nearly freaked out at the next comment. "Take King Solomon, for example," the speaker began on a further illustrative note.

Wysong repeated the words aloud. "King Solomon?"

The speaker continued. "In the midst of unparalleled wealth Solomon degenerated from the incredibly prolific and profound author of most of the book of Proverbs to flagrantly ignoring the counsel of the God who had given him power and wisdom. Now, unlike Solomon, everything Jesus said and did reflected a consistent view of reality."

Wysong listened to the commentator's supporting statements, but remained rooted in the unlikely moment's connection to what Shoemaker had been sharing with him. Then, as the speaker began closing his comments, Wysong refocused. "In the ultimate sense," the radio voice said, "Jesus is like our unshuffled deck of cards. All order, design, and purpose begin and end in Him."

Wysong shook his head in confusion. Or was it merely obstinate thinking? He didn't know which. Was it his lot to always question everyone and everything?

The next day he again asked one of his customer-friends a question following his product presentation. "Jeff, I want to pose a philosophical question for you, although some might prefer to call it theological."

"What do you know," the customer wise-cracked, "a rep straying off-message."

"All right, cut me a little slack here," Wysong replied. "Do you think it's possible to turn our backs on the moral order of a Creator and seek unending information rather than truth?"

The answer he received was, "Huh?"

With a laugh Wysong waved him off and said, "Forget it. I'm really talking to myself." As he walked to his car, he could only smile as he shook his head in thought. *You should have seen that coming, Doofus. You either asked the wrong question of the wrong person, or his answer was your reward.*

CHAPTER 17

TRIBULATION OF SORTS

Within minutes of Wysong's showing up on Shoemaker's doorstep Will was led to say, "What's wrong, Pete? You look like you've just lost two more of your lines."

"No, " he said, shaking his head, "although I haven't replaced either of them. The problem is that there is really no way to effectively lobby for new ones. At least not in a broadcast form. All I can do is wait for prospective lines to come to me, based on my reputation."

"Then take heart, my friend. Based on what I personally know of your work ethic, time will surely bring you a line or two."

"The truth is," Wysong said, "I know you're right. It's happened before. My real problem is impatience. But that isn't what's on my mind. I want to talk to you about a much bigger problem."

"Oh?" Shoemaker said with a look of surprise. "Tell me about it."

Wysong made a slow gesture with upturned hands before dropping them to his sides in frustration. "It's my ex," he said. "She's moving to California."

"I see," Shoemaker said, "and she's taking Billy with her."

"Yup."

"Let's talk about that. We'll shelve the planned lesson until next week."

"Thanks," Wysong said as he reached for a drink from the cold bottle of water waiting for him on the coffee table. "I've checked

things out. The terms of our divorce actually address such a situation. If she moves, she still retains primary custody. I have the same
visitation rights as before, of course, providing I can manage it. Yeah,
right. At best I'll probably be able to see him only twice a year."

"Your attorney didn't cover that for you before you signed
off?"

Wysong sighed. "I didn't tell you about that. We shared the
same lawyer. It was a relatively amicable divorce and I didn't want
the additional expense of a second attorney. I never considered the
possibility of her moving from the Atlanta area. She's lived here
for more than fifteen years, but shortly after our divorce her parents
moved from Ohio to California to be near a sibling of Dannie's who
was in a stable marriage. Will," Wysong said, his lips quivering with
emotion, "I'm losing my son."

Shoemaker placed his hand on Wysong's shoulder and said, "I
hear what you're saying, and I'm terribly sorry. I know this is not
going to be easy for you. All I can offer is my friendship and my
prayers. . . and . . . one other thing. Something for which I think
you're now ready."

"What is that?"

"Just this," Shoemaker began. "It's time you began trusting
yourself and your circumstances with the Lord. I'm going to pray
for that right now." With that, he bowed his head, saying, "Almighty
God, my friend Pete has been laid low. Worse yet, he may not have
reached his lowest point. I ask for grace for him, Father, that he
might come to know you and thereby have *your* strength to rely
upon. Amen."

Wysong was taken by surprise at his mentor's praying for him,
but he wasn't offended. "Thank you for the prayer," he said. "I can
use all the help I can get."

"Pete," he said, "there is more to it than that. It's important for
you to know that you aren't alone. Although you perceive your recent
losses as great, the fact is that the greatest loss of yours and anyone's
was our relationship with God. But that was forever addressed on
the cross and that gift is available to anyone who seeks it."

"I suppose that should be comforting to me," he said, "but it
isn't." Surprised at his own statement he said, "H'mm. Maybe that's

what comes with *having* faith rather than merely knowing about it, huh?"

Shoemaker was quick to respond. "Boy, was that well said! Let me follow up. For a long time I, too, tried to stay dry under that leaking umbrella until I realized that merely knowing *about* God would never make the difference. And it didn't happen for me until I experienced brokenness."

"Brokenness?" Wysong said with emphasis. "I'm broken, man. Not only is my business sucking air, but I'm about to lose my son. What does God want from me?"

"What He wants is for you to understand what being broken means, about being broken by the knowledge of one's sin. And beyond that a knowledge of Jesus' costly grace and the Almighty's incredible mercy. Let me illustrate this for you. Recall that your definitive words to me when we first met were that you wanted to know what I know about having a relationship with God."

"Yes. What about it?"

"Do you have a coin with you?" Shoemaker asked.

Wysong's interest was flagging, but he dug into a front pants pocket and came up with a quarter and handed it to him.

"Thank you," Shoemaker said as he placed the coin in an upturned hand. "God's grace and mercy might not *seem* to be linked, but I have learned that they are. Take this two-sided coin, for example. Let one side stand for the grace we receive from God for all the things we have in life that we *don't* deserve. You know, the life and breath and good stuff we take for granted. Let the other side stand for the mercy we receive from God for not giving us what we *do* deserve. You know, the things we can figure God finds disappointing in us. Now watch this."

Wysong was doing precisely that, his curiosity back on board.

Shoemaker proceeded to flip the coin up into the air and catch it. "What is it?" he said.

"Mercy," Wysong said as his mentor removed his hand from the arm upon which he had slapped the coin.

"Grace or mercy," Shoemaker said, "it doesn't matter. We are blessed in either event." With that he handed the coin back to

Wysong, saying, "I never cease to wonder at how much those two gifts mean to me."

Wysong sighed and said with a twinkle in his eye, "You know, lately I've been wondering about something. Am I better off being physically mugged by a stranger or spiritually challenged by a friend?"

CHAPTER 18

BACK TO THE SONG

Wysong did not have a good business week in town. He did book the following week's appointments for eastern North Carolina, but in the meantime he had only managed to call on a very few accounts in the Atlanta area. The only 'plus' had been the previous weekend when he had been able to spend more time than usual with Billy. He took him for his first-ever round of miniature golf and then enjoyed light conversation with him as he cooked while Billy did his best to keep his mind on setting the table for his favorite dinner—spaghetti.

Afterward, he sat the eight-year old down for a serious talk. He began awkwardly but sincerely. "Son, you know daddy loves you very much. And so does mommy. Unfortunately, we can't all live together because mommy and daddy argue too much. I know that's hard for you to understand, but I will *always . . . always . . .* be your daddy." He had to turn his head and disguise his tearing eyes with a cough.

Billy didn't understand. He said, "That's okay, daddy. I'll come and see you."

This time Wysong reached for his handkerchief as he said, "I know you would, Billy, but you'll have to wait until I come to visit."

"But when?" the boy said as he began wiping tears from his own eyes.

Wysong could barely gather himself enough to continue, but after a moment he managed to say, "You and your mother will be moving to California in a few weeks, but I'll make you a promise. Even though California is a long way from Georgia, as soon as I can come out to your new home you and I will have adventures like we've never had. We're going to visit all kinds of places when I get there, from Disney to the ocean. And you can start dreaming about that anytime you want." He knew his words were totally inadequate, but he didn't know what else to say.

"But I don't want to go," Billy said through his tears. "I don't want to leave you. Why can't you and mommie do better?"

At day's end all Wysong could do was hug his son as he returned him to his mother. He was already grieving what he considered an unfair loss. What had his mentor said about brokenness and loss being the great leveler? He had been thinking about that, but still hadn't been able to grasp its meaning. How does a person place a theme of hope in the same sentence with "when the rains come?"

It was mid-afternoon on Friday, close to his time to visit the Cobbler, as he had begun referring to Shoemaker. He had even mentioned to someone during the past week that he would be "seeing the Cobbler" when asked what he would be doing when he got home from his road trip. He didn't bother to elaborate, but he chuckled to himself in noting that the person had glanced at his shoes.

Shortly after their greeting and an update, it was Wysong who set the tone for what would be the session's focus. "Okay, enough about me," he said. "It's time to get on with your 'dating song.'"

"It's the *art* of dating," Shoemaker corrected him. "And it's hardly *my* song. They are words inspired by the Designer of Life. But let's begin. As everyone knows, once a person is attracted to someone, the dating process begins. What would you say is the *best* kind of dating?"

"I don't know what that means . . . unless . . . maybe . . . getting to actually know one another?"

"Bingo!" Shoemaker said. "Whatever the couple does or wherever they go, the point is not only to get to know one another, but in the process build respect for one another. Do you agree with that?"

"No argument."

"Good. Dating is really nothing more than observation. It is through this process that one learns whether the next step is in order, which is courtship. We'll talk about that next time, but in the meantime consider that there are three things needed in a relationship. Those are time, cultivation, and restraint. Here's my question: How does one cultivate respect with their mate?"

"For some reason Wysong was paying closer attention than at anytime since they had begun meeting. "By honoring her?" he said. "By not trying to force her to make a decision she doesn't want to make?"

Shoemaker looked up from his notes, surprised. "Hey, are you looking at my papers? I'm impressed. Yes. You honor her by keeping your hands to yourself. One hand in another is one thing. What you have to guard against during dating are the face-to-face, mouth-to-mouth and body-to-body steps."

Wysong's resulting expression had the effect of his having raised his hand. "Okay," he said, "I understand about two of the three relationship items; spending time and cultivating interests. The 'restraint' thing you have mentioned before, but I have to say this is a lot more challenging in real life than it is in a Bible study. You aren't telling me the subject is actually addressed in the Bible, are you?"

Shoemaker took Wysong's question as a cue. "In a way that you would never imagine," he said. "When the Song's verses speak of the Shulamite woman missing her shepherd-lover and the fact that she is lovesick for him, she says, 'Let his left hand be under my head and his right hand embrace me.' She then qualifies her statement by saying to her companion maidens of the moment, 'I adjure you, that he will not arouse or awaken my love until it pleases me.'"

"Translate that for me," Wysong said. "I've now read all eight chapters of Song of Songs twice and I still don't understand what's going on."

"Okay. In this second chapter, King Solomon woos her as a new member of his court, but her thoughts are of her absent shepherd-lover. She tells the court ladies about both him and herself. She is saying there is a time for love and sex, and it should not be aroused outside of marriage. She contrasts this to what the score-keeping Solomon was trying to accomplish. In other words, as one Bible commentator so insightfully tells us, 'love is not a thing to be bought or forced or pretended, but a thing to come spontaneously, to be given freely and sincerely.' As a side note, if Israel had followed this simple rule, it would not have been unfaithful to Jehovah God."

Wysong nodded tentatively, saying, "Now let me get this straight. She's in love with her young shepherd who's elsewhere tending his flocks, while old Solomon is dealing with an unrequited desire."

"Poetically put, my boy! That's what I'm saying. Now think about comparing immorality to the law of diminishing returns. What does that say to you?"

"H'mm," Wysong pondered that for a moment before responding. "Let me hazard something," he said. "The further one's relationship develops–that is, the deeper one's physical relationship goes—the more is needed."

"That's it," Shoemaker said with obvious enthusiasm for his student/care receiver's apparent progress. "Without restraint, individuals often look back and regret what they have done."

Wysong had a regretful look on his face as he said, "I can't say as I've ever considered that until this very moment."

"Don't beat yourself up. What's done is done, yet lessons are for the learning. I want to throw you one more question before we wrap up for today. The point of it isn't intended for any purpose but communication. Give me your best one-word guess for the greatest need for women, and another one-word guess for men."

"You're right about the 'guessing' part," Wysong said. "Okay, how about this one for women: faithfulness. As for men, I've gotta go with sex."

"You were flying high earlier, Peter my man, but you just crashed. Faithfulness is what women *expect*. Tenderness is what they *want*. As for we men, respect actually comes in well ahead of sex."

"I know better than to challenge you on that, but I also need to think about it."

"Challenge me all you want. I'll only go to the Word for my answers." Shoemaker glanced at his watch. "Time's up, my seeker friend. This is *my* date night. My wife should be home from the senior center any minute. We're going our for dinner somewhere.

See you next week." With a wink he said, "Same place, same song . . . Wysong."

"Cute," Pete said with a broad smile. "Then we'll take up the 'courtship' thing. That's second base, isn't it? Last time out with my dream date I didn't get out of the batter's box, much less to either first or second base."

CHAPTER 19

REFLECTION AND COURTSHIP

Wysong took his concerns for Billy's upcoming exit from his week-to-week life with him on the road. Likewise, he reflected on the weekly lessons he was being exposed to by Shoemaker. He was having trouble taking to heart the connection between marriage and faith, but the witness observed of Shoemaker's own life certainly corroborated what he was hearing. He had met and liked his wife, had heard inspirational stories about the Cobbler's own life and successful marriage, and understood that he was a man who had a personal relationship with Christ. In addition, Wysong realized that his stated purpose of research was likewise being met. He wasn't seeking God, but merely hoping to gain an understanding of why and how others do. Now he was asking himself why? His answers were revealing. *Because I don't want to make the same mistakes I have in the past. All I want is hope for a better future.*

He had missed the previous week's regular session with Shoemaker because of a regional trade show that kept him out of town until late Friday evening. A week later he was ready to resume their regular get-together. It didn't take long for them to get down to the business at hand because of Wysong's interest in the courtship aspect of their study.

"How would you describe courtship?" Shoemaker began.

"Um, I guess I would call it an extension of dating."

"Yes, that's true, but it's also much more than that. My author-pastor friend of this wonderful study compares dating's relationship to courtship as 'kicking tires.' With respect to courtship he is referring to the beginning of sacrifice and commitment. Courtship is when two people know the other is special and want to know more about them. In other words, while dating is observation, courtship is depth."

"Depth is risky."

"Of course," Shoemaker said, "but do you know why?"

"Something can go wrong?"

"Okay, but which is better? For something unacceptable to be discovered before the fact of marriage, or after?"

Wysong nodded in agreement and said, "I'm reminded of the song, '*Little Things Mean A Lot.*'"

"Big *or* little," Shoemaker said with emphasis. "There are certain things that simply need to happen during courtship."

"On the other hand," Wysong said, still trying to justify his initial position with respect to Marlene, "don't you think that by sharing too much too fast the relationship can be escalated too quickly?"

"Only if that means putting your hands on your partner too soon. I'm referring to things like having the wisdom to evaluate the character of your partner, having consistency in your dating relationship, communicating, and having patience to let the relationship grow in God's time."

"Man, I'd have to take my notebook along on dates," Wysong said. At that, he saw the opportunity to throw in a real life experience and get Shoemaker's reaction. "But what if your partner won't forgive your past before you can get to courtship?"

"Did that happen to you, Pete?" Shoemaker asked sympathetically.

"You're doggoned right it did . . . if I do say so self-righteously."

"Good boy!" Shoemaker said as he chuckled and reached out to Wysong for a fist-tap. "Let me put this another way. Would your partner be more likely to forgive something in your past after marriage than before it? Even more importantly, how is it that we could not forgive someone when God has offered each of us forgiveness for all of *our* sins–past, present, and future–through the sacrifice of His only begotten son?"

"I see the point now. I wouldn't have before."

"Of course, where there is no confession there is no forgiveness. Not forgiving someone can be dangerous to your health. It's like swallowing poison and expecting the *other* guy to die."

"That's funny," Wysong said, "but it also makes perfect sense."

"I know," Shoemaker said, nodding his head and smiling. "That's why I borrowed the phrase. Something I think is even more profound is a question my pastor friend Nelson once asked a singles audience. It's one of the most revealing questions I have ever heard on the subject of dating. He said, "Do you find yourself kissing another person before you are willing to hold his or her heart?"

"Wow. That has to fly in the face of the way most men think."

"Don't be so quick to judge others by your own standards, Pete. I'll give you a personal example. Before I married June I was looking for a godly woman. When I found her I courted her in a godly fashion. And when I married her it was no surprise that we had a godly marriage."

"I'm envious," Wysong said. "Weddings don't end up that way very often."

"No, they don't," Shoemaker said, "but what I'm describing is not a wedding but a love relationship. A wedding ceremony does not create love between two people. The ceremony is planned *because* of an already existing love relationship."

"But," objected Wysong, "a relationship doesn't always have to involve love."

"You're right, just as a prayer to 'receive' Christ doesn't create the love relationship with God. Rather, a love relationship birthed in someone's heart creates the desire to invite Him to be Master of his or her life."

"I see the connection between the two but on the former matter, there comes a point during courtship when your lips and hands want to wander. Analyze *that* for me."

"It doesn't need analysis," Shoemaker said. "It merely requires restraint. When two people are feeling very close to one another and truly believe they are in love, they simply need to 'catch the foxes'."

"They need to *what*?"

"Don't you remember? That's from our Song. I'll read it for you. 'Catch the foxes for us. The little foxes that are ruining the vineyards, while our vineyards are in blossom.' This refers to resolving your problems as they come up. You said it yourself; it's the little things that tend to thwart us, more so than the bigger ones."

Wysong wasn't following and said, "How does that fit in?"

"Quite well, actually," Shoemaker said. "It's all about cultivating love without fertilizing lust. To put it another way, a couple must know that God's Word is very clear about sex before marriage. Violating that premise is one of the most common 'foxes' that can destroy a godly relationship."

Wysong shook his head and said, "Not many people hold to that position these days."

"That's the problem," Shoemaker said in response. "People today commonly treat sexuality outside of marriage as recreation. They prefer a 'new reality' to God's Word. What has happened is that truth has been replaced with evil. Yet, truth remains truth."

"But what if the woman takes the lead?"

"You can't hide behind that, Pete. It's the man's lead to either take or forfeit. When Adam chose to eat the apple Eve brought him from the forbidden tree of the knowledge of good and evil, he merely forfeited his lead, even though he blamed her.

Shoemaker glanced at his watch. Before he could comment on the time, however, his student, care receiver, and friend stood and said, "I know. It's your date night. I'm out of here."

CHAPTER 20

ON THE ROAD AGAIN

Wysong was en route to the Florida panhandle and the adjacent southeastern Alabama area. He would be seeing a number of accounts he especially enjoyed visiting. I-85 South from Atlanta is a relatively low-traffic route for an interstate highway and as he drove he was contemplating two new line possibilities for which he was being considered. He also had his mind on several other things. One of them was a difficult California phone conversation with Billy. The other had to do with some of Shoemaker's most recent and challenging perspectives about both marriage and faith. At a tiresome day's end he decided on something he only occasionally bothered to do while on the road. His hotel offered free health club access to a facility across the street from where he was staying. Since he had been missing his regular racquetball game for some weeks, he decided to combine a little exercise with recreation.

As he walked up to the wellness center's reception counter, his always-packed racquet and sneakers bag in hand, he showed the counter person his hotel key and said, "Any chance I might catch a pick-up game of racquetball?"

The young woman at the counter said, "Yes, sir. As a matter of fact a group of guys play every Monday night and they're usually open to walk-ons. The racquetball courts are on the other side of the basketball court."

Within minutes Wysong was warming up with a number of strangers in the two-court area. He asked one of them if he could join them in their challenge doubles games. "Perfect," the player said as he introduced himself and shook hands. "We're short a man, anyway. You can partner with me for the first game."

Wysong and his partner quickly won that game and by virtue of the group's rules, that qualified them to take on the winning doubles team from the adjacent court. His newly found partner said, "Good play, Pete. These next guys serve hard and run fast. Turn it up a notch, if you're able."

"Thanks. I will." And he did. But halfway through the game he put a few extra pounds of torque into a serve and as a result went down. He was unable to quickly get back onto his feet because of back pain. That was the end of his game and it was nearly a full hour before he could manage to shower, dress, rest a little and then get back across the street to the hotel.

The next morning he was still in pain, even after having downed over-the-counter pain killers as if they were peanuts. He was forced to cancel every one of his week's appointments by phone. As he was driving back to Atlanta in some pain he made a phone call to his primary care doctor who gave him the name of a specialty referral doc, along with a phone number.

Following his next morning's appointment with a neurosurgeon he was back home and in bed. He called his parents, who lived only twenty minutes away. He didn't have a particularly good relationship with them but he had nowhere else to turn. "Mom," he said, "I hurt my back. The specialist tells me I need back surgery. He says chances for success are very good because the x-rays show that the pieces of the disc pressing on the spinal column are large enough for removal. He says he can have me back on my feet in less than a month."

"A month? " she said, seeming less concerned for her son than for what it might mean for her. "Doesn't the doctor think your back was designed to use all of that disc?"

"I didn't ask that question, Mom. What are you now, a doctor?"

"No," she said, "a skeptic when it comes to surgery. A month's recovery is a long time. How is that going to work?"

"That's where you come in, Mom. Can I hang my hat over there for the next few weeks?"

"I don't know, son. Your father and I aren't in the greatest of health ourselves."

"Look," he said, "I really need your help. I don't have anyone else to turn to. Since Dannie left with Billy everything else has gone downhill as well. Right now I can't even get up and down stairs."

The mother again ignored her son's dilemma, saying, "You mean when you *ran* her off, don't you? We don't even get to see our grandson anymore."

"Okay, so I could have done a better job with my marriage. I can't change that, but I still need your help."

"Well," his mother said in a hesitant voice, "you know we don't have much space. We'd have to put a roll-away in the den, and . . ."

"Great, Mom," he said. "Thanks. I owe you. I'll be over there tonight." It was the week after Thanksgiving. He had *the* major trade show of the year to attend the first week of January and he absolutely had to be up to covering it.

After two weeks of complete bed rest he would give himself over to the neurosurgeon and then begin his recovery period. By e-mail he brought his supplier principals up-to-date and also advised them that they could count on him making the big show. Additionally, while at the show he hoped he could interview for a new line or two with several prospective suppliers who had previously contacted him in that regard.

Two days after the surgery, on a Friday afternoon, Will Shoemaker came to see Wysong at his parent's home. "Pete," he said as soon as he walked into the den where Wysong lay watching television, "it's good to see your sad self. Are you going to pull through, or is your mother out making hospice arrangements?"

"Will, come in! I appreciate your trouble to come over, if not your lack of sympathy."

"Well, my friend," an encouraging Shoemaker said, "I think all you need is time and rest. I've made arrangements with others at the church to help out by putting you on a hot meal delivery program three times a week for as long as you need. They'll bring enough food for your parents and for you."

Wysong winced as he struggled to raise himself up a bit from the recliner. "But I've never been to your church," he said. "Why would they put themselves out like that?"

"It's not complicated, Pete. They simply do it out of love for their fellow man. They seek to serve those in need. The reality is that they get as much out of helping as those receiving." Feeling that he was belaboring the point he said, "Look, I don't want to stay long, but if you think you're up to it we can resume our regular Friday afternoon meetings next week. I'll be happy to visit you here."

"Really?" he said, his face at first lighting up, but then reflecting pain as he tried to lean forward to shake hands. "Your generosity and that of your church is so cool. Thanks, man."

"You're welcome," Shoemaker said, "but we don't have anything God didn't give us. May I pray us out?"

"By all means."

"Almighty God, thank you for this day, thank you for our lives, and thank you for your grace and mercy. Father, I lift up my friend, Pete, and ask for his comfort at this time in his life. Oh. And Father, I also ask You to continue to draw him closer to You. It is in Christ's Holy name that I pray. Amen."

" I'll be better next week, Will. Once again, my friend, thank you."

CHAPTER 21

INTIMACY ON THE DOCKET

A week later Shoemaker was back visiting Pete in Wysong's parents' den. "How's the food at this boarding house?" he said as he was waved to a chair.

"Man," Pete said, "your church groups are bringing so much food that each visit carries the three of us for two days!"

"Great. I'll pass on your comments to the ministry leaders. Are you up for a session today?"

"I'm anxious for it," Wysong said with obvious enthusiasm. "Physically, I'm feeling some better, but a turtle could lap me getting to the bathroom."

"Congratulations on a right-attitude in this difficult situation," Shoemaker said.

"Thanks. I think I've come to realize that my head has been mis-threaded onto my neck for much of my life. Only lately has it seemed to be realigning a bit."

"Now that is what I call headway," Shoemaker said. Then he smiled and added, "Uh, no pun intended. Let me start by sharing with you something few divorced people ever hear from a marriage counselor, much less from the pulpit. You might be surprised."

Wysong grinned and said, "Hey, I know so little it isn't possible to surprise me."

"We'll see. But first, let me reiterate something. I think you'll recall from our initial meeting that we talked about Stephen Ministry being a *listening* relationship rather than a pro-active one. And you were very specific in asking me to also address the fundamental tenets of the Christian faith. I agreed to do so providing I could throw in the love and marriage thing as a bonus. Have I summed things up correctly?"

"Perfectly. Do we have a problem, Houston?"

"Not at all. I'm merely summarizing for both of our benefits. What you and I have is a recipe calling for one-third listening on my part and two thirds listening on your part. Would you agree?"

Wysong said, "Uh, let me qualify that a bit. Here I am, a grateful bed-ridden dude, regularly entertaining a visitor we'll call the host. But since I'm not *paying* this host, who simultaneously listens to my woes and teaches me about life, he isn't benefitting." At that, Shoemaker tried to interrupt, but Wysong waved him off and continued. "Therefore," he said, "our relationship cannot be said to be symbiotic, but parasitic. On that basis I yield the floor to the host."

"That's cute," Shoemaker said with an accompanying laugh. "Who writes your stuff? Your mother? No, don't answer that or she's liable to give me the heave-ho." He then added, "Time is short. Let's move on."

"Teach away," Wysong said, immensely enjoying the give-and-take.

"I will, but also remember that my giving is also my reward. So, then, let's take up the art of intimacy. Allow me to read a few verses from Solomon's attempt to set up the Shulamite maiden after whom he is panting."

"Jeez," Wysong said, holding up a hand in mock reaction. "I don't know about this. My mother has charge of the remote around here and she thinks Andy Griffith should be censored."

Shoemaker laughed and said, "Don't worry, I don't see her anywhere in the room! Anyway, the much-married King has come to Jerusalem in grandiose procession seeking to captivate the Shulamite maiden. But she is impervious to both his riches and his charm as she thinks only of her shepherd-lover and the day in which she will be reunited with him."

"Well, now," Wysong said, rubbing his hands together, "maybe I can learn something useful here."

"Then listen carefully. Solomon goes on and on in plying her with compliments meant to overcome her resistance. Here is a sampling of some of the entries:

> 'Your two breasts are like two fawns,
>
> Twins of a gazelle,
>
> Which feed among the lilies.'

and another entry reads;

> 'You are altogether beautiful, my darling,
>
> And there is no blemish in you.'

and another;

> 'Your lips, my bride, drip honey;
>
> Honey and milk are under your tongue,
>
> And the fragrance of your garments is like the fragrance of Lebanon.'

and yet one more;

> 'Awake, O north wind,
>
> And come, wind of the south;
>
> Make my garden breathe out fragrance,
>
> Let its spices be wafted abroad.
>
> May my beloved come into his garden
>
> and eat its choice fruits!'"

"Whew, slow down, man," Wysong said, and then added facetiously. "I need to catch all of this on paper."

Shoemaker paused for only a couple of seconds before continuing. "In spite of Solomon's silver tongue it turns out that the Shulamite maiden is impervious to his flattery. Now I want to touch on that more in a moment, but first let me ask if you're familiar with some often misquoted percentages about divorce."

Wysong nodded his head and said, "My divorce attorney saddled me with those surprising numbers as I was writing him a check, especially the one about those couples who read the Bible and pray together."

"Okay, then you know about the three 80%, 60% and 40% divorce categories, as well as the meager 1% divorce rate for those married couples in the category you just mentioned."

"Roger. But frankly, I find that last stat hard to believe."

"That you don't believe is fine," Shoemaker said, "but it doesn't change the well-documented facts. The point is such women want men who are strong in their character, who are consistent, and who are godly men. So here's the bottom line from the Shulamite woman's position: She didn't want to get involved physically before she married. In other words the message is to wait for God's time."

"Wait a minute," Wysong said. "I'm confused. No one goes directly from expressing ideal preferences in a mate, to the church. What about romance?" He had a look of chagrin as he added, "Not that I have anything going that remotely approaches the possibility of a romance."

"You're getting ahead of me," Shoemaker said. 'Romance' is coming up after we deal with 'conflict,' but since you *did* bring it up, can you recall the last thing you did that was actually romantic? Go back in time as far as you want."

"I think I have a case of amnesia here," he said tongue-in-cheek. "I fell pretty hard, you know."

"Okay, I'll throw you an easier one: If the right woman were to be romantic toward you, what would you want her to do?"

"You're embarrassing me, man," Wysong said. "Heck, I don't know. What are you looking for?"

"You said it yourself a minute ago. The first key to great sex is romance. There's a verse in chapter seven of 1st Corinthians that you might find interesting. It's the only verse in the Bible described by some as 'for the woman to memorize, but for the man to never quote.' Can you imagine its subject?"

"Not unless it has something to do with sex."

"Bingo. I'll quote you the verse and you tell me what it means. 'A woman does not have authority over her own body, but the man does.'"

Wysong absorbed that for a moment and said, "I think I understand. While the woman is to remember that the man takes the lead in sex, if he were to *tell* her that he may as well head for a cold shower."

"By George," Shoemaker said as he made a fist with his right hand and smartly pumped it into the palm of his left hand, "I believe you're getting it! And a corollary to that question is even better. Gird yourself for this one: In dating, it is not 'How far can I *go* in sex?' but 'How far can I stay *from* sex?'"

"Man," began Wysong, "as I've told you before, neither you nor the Bible think like most men."

"All I can tell you, Pete, is that I take my lessons from Scripture—from God—not from impulse. In a minute or so I want to wrap things up for this session, but before that I have one more tough question for you."

"Great," Wysong said. "Just what I was hoping for."

"Did you and your ex ever pray after you had sex?"

That the question surprised Wysong would be a stark understatement. "Are you kidding?" he said. "We didn't even talk."

"If you ever marry again," Shoemaker said, "I would ask you to commit to doing so. Since there are many blessed aspects of sex for a married couple it is therefore worth thanking God."

Wysong again shook his head, saying, "I can't believe you're okay talking so openly about such a thing. But since you brought up the subject, name a few of these 'aspects'—as you call them— aside from the obvious."

"Thank you," Shoemaker said. "You could easily come up with many yourself merely by thinking of associative words along the lines of gentleness, sharing, exhilaration, literal union, sensuousness, a form of holiness, responsiveness, emotional nourishment, etc. Pastor Nelson even suggests considering such an unlikely word as fright, like the first time you were on a roller coaster."

"And the point of all this is . . . ?" Wysong said.

"That in order for a married couple's sex life to be fulfilling for a lifetime, they must also share life fully. I don't mean merely sharing about each others' activities, but their hopes and their troubles–in other words—their very lives. To put it another way, they need to talk."

"Too much information, Will!"

"Why, Pete? What are you afraid of? Rather, you should fear the consequences of sex *outside* of God's will. After all, sex in marriage is pleasing to God."

CHAPTER 22

RECOVERY OF SORTS

Before another week had passed and as Wysong become increasingly able to get around, the surgeon approved him for the surgery. His father took him to the hospital and then picked him up following an overnight stay. After three days of recuperation at his parents' home he was able to drive himself back to his own home. Shoemaker helped by transporting Pete's clothes and personal items, but didn't stay long. "Will," Wysong said, "I'm just not up to speed, emotionally. Can I beg off of our usual visits for awhile?"

"Of course," Shoemaker said, "but I'm concerned. All you have to do is pick up the phone to let me know how I can help. Can you manage? I mean, the church can continue bringing you meals for awhile."

"No, thank you very much. Thanksgiving is coming up and Mom said she and Dad would see me through. I should be in pretty good shape before long."

Shoemaker called twice a week for the next four weeks, but every time he phoned he either got a recording or Wysong simply said he was getting stronger, but was struggling with some things and that they would get together again "before long."

The approaching Christmas was not a joyful time for Pete. Although he had made all of the arrangements for his attendance at the big upcoming show, he continued to find it difficult to focus on anything outside of his time off from work, his health, Billy, and his confusion over faith.

The day before Christmas Eve the 'Cobbler' had come to see him with an invitation to join his family for Christmas Day. "I appreciate the invitation very much," Wysong said, "but I'm still not up to it."

"Not up to *what*, Pete?" a concerned Shoemaker said. "I know you haven't been able to return to work yet, and you probably have some guilt with feelings of dalliance, but you'll be back into the swing of things in another week or two. It's Christmas. You have a son, a job, and a life to think about. For your own benefit you need to receive the peace of Christmas."

"What do you mean, *receive* Christmas?" Wysong said, the irritation in his voice being apparent. "Exactly what *else* is it that is coming to me?"

"Joy," Shoemaker said. "You have no joy, and that is sad."

"Joy!?" Wysong said, raising his voice. "What do I have to be joyful about?"

"Oh, a great deal," Shoemaker countered. "Listen. Joy doesn't come from knowing *where our journey has taken us* or *what* we have, but from *who* we are and *whose* we are. There is a wonderful verse in Hebrews that goes like this: *'For anyone who enters God's rest also rests from his own work, just as God did from his.'*"

"For crying out loud, Will," Wysong said, "resting is all I've been doing. How is that going to help me out of this mud hole?"

Shoemaker said, "That's just it. You need to stop digging and climb out. I know you don't actually have the strength to do that, but if you'll allow God to assist you, you can manage."

At that, Wysong *really* felt called to vent. "Is that right?' he said. "Well, I don't have a shred of evidence that God loves me. Look at me. I've lost my wife and son. Nearly half of my income has dwindled away. And I've been incapacitated ever since I was run over by the Ark. If God cares about me, how come I don't know it?"

Shoemaker accepted Wysong's challenge. "Look, Pete, all of us are called upon to go through the fires of life. God always sustains us if we allow Him to be a part of our lives. By that I mean He has not promised to keep us out of the furnace, but He *has* promised to meet us there and sustain us in its midst."

Wysong let out a deep sigh and said, "If I've heard that lame line once, I've heard it a dozen times over the past few months. I'm sick of hearing it. Heck, I don't even know what it means."

"I'm sorry," Shoemaker said, quickly seeing the need for empathy. "I understand your frustration. Many of us sometimes wonder why we must face many of the things that come into our lives. I know I have. And certainly *none* of us would choose these things. As a matter of fact . . . "

Wysong's boiler was still overheated and so he interrupted. "Wait a minute" he said, "exactly *when* has God personally met you in the 'furnace,' as you put it?"

As Wysong waited for a response he slowly began to realize something. *Why am I railing at the one man who cares most about me? Is it because I'm angry with myself or angry at the God of whom He speaks, as if he knows Him intimately? Which is it . . . or it is both?*

At the same time Shoemaker resolved to let Pete lean on him as much as he needed. "Let me tell you about someone I know well," he said. "This is a man who lost his wife of 34 years. He lost her to the Lord only a few years before they were both due to retire from the work they had done for many years. He took care of her for nearly two years as she slowly lost her battle to cancer. In all that time, however, each of them not only grew closer to each other, but also to God."

Shoemaker paused for a moment to keep from losing his composure. Continuing, he said, "Both the man and his wife took to heart a particular message as given to us by Christ Himself in the book of John. This was close to the time when Jesus would be put to death in taking on mankind's sins. In fact, they are words Jesus was speaking to his disciples in promising them that He would send the Holy Spirit to guide them. His words also spoke to the couple I'm telling you about. Let me share them with you."

Shoemaker reached for one of the two Bibles he always had with him whenever he traveled, especially if he was going to visit someone with whom he might be teaching or sharing. "Perhaps these verses will speak to you as well. I'll read it as written in contemporary language from John 14, verses 25-27."

"I'm telling you these things while I'm still living with you.

The Friend, the Holy Spirit, whom the Father will send at my request,

will make everything plain to you.

He will remind you of all the things I have told you.

I'm leaving you well and whole. That's my parting gift to you. Peace.

I don't leave you the way you're used to being left–feeling abandoned, bereft.

So don't be upset. Don't be distraught."

Wysong listened intently to all three of the verses and then focused on what had led Shoemaker to recite them. "Yet, the man's wife died," he said.

"Yes, but do you understand the point?"

"No, I don't."

"The woman died in faith, that she, too, would defeat death and continue to live in Christ's promises of eternal life. The bottom line for you and I is that in our hour of need we can draw on our heavenly resources."

"I'm hearing everything you're saying, Will, but the truth is I don't know what to do with it."

"That's okay. I understand that you haven't yet come to walk in strength with the Lord, but I'm convinced that you will, that He will reveal Himself to you. In the meantime, realize that nothing other than trials and afflictions would have ever led some of us to know Jesus Christ as we do, to trust Him as we have, and to draw from Him the measure of grace which our difficulties in life make indispensable."

"I appreciate everything you are trying to do for me," Wysong said, still feeling self-pity, "but I'm still struggling." Then, seeing that his mentor was moved by the story he had just shared, he added, "I'm sorry for your friend's wife having passed. Is he still living?"

"See for yourself," Shoemaker said as he wiped tears from his eyes.

The story suddenly resonated with Wysong. He blinked in comprehension. "I'm sorry, Will. I now remember your telling me when we first met that you had been happily married for 41 of your years. That was 34 years with your late wife and seven with Miss June. Is that right?"

"Yes" he said, "but, the point is not about me, it's about you. While you are perplexed, confused and disturbed at your current trials–amid thinking that your future appears bleak—this need not be the case. My advice is that you get alone with God as soon as possible. Be thankful, not *for* your tribulation, but *out* of it. That is the only way He can begin conforming you to His image."

CHAPTER 23

CONFLICT!

Wysong finally hit the road again, and when he did he stayed out for two straight weeks. As a part of that trip he did some territorial catching up before hooking up in Orlando for the year-opening trade show in Florida. With respect to the show itself, he managed pretty well after the first full day. By then he was able to toss the cane he had been relying upon until that point.

He had also talked at length by phone with Billy every couple of days of the two week trip. He had even sent Shoemaker an e-mail to the effect that he would be missing two consecutive Friday meetings. His mentor had sent him a cheery return e-mail wishing him success with his trips and that when they next met they would talk about what was perhaps the single most important aspect of any marriage relationship. Wysong replied enthusiastically in a return e-mail with, "What the heck could that be? We just finished dealing with intimacy!"

Shoemaker sent a brief, but enigmatic follow-up which read, "True, intimacy deals with about 25% of the book we're studying, but so, too, does conflict. All couples fight. Challenged couples fight dirty. Well-balanced couples fight clean. Have a great trip."

Wysong couldn't wait to both hear and share in that lesson. In fact, he wanted to take his own shots on the subject. He had been giving a lot of thought to the points Shoemaker had been making during the past month, especially some of those from their most recent session.

One of the questions that remained uppermost in his mind is the one that had sent him to the church and the Stephen Ministry resource in the first place: Exactly what does 'born again' mean? It was true that he wanted to understand what the term meant from a literal–call it, practical—perspective. But he was also curious about the role faith supposedly plays. Because he had been testy on so many points within Shoemaker's Biblical teaching, they hadn't been able to hone in on what Wysong considered to be the bottom line. In the end he decided not to push things when they got together, rather to let the subject fall where it may.

Thus, at their next meeting his first question was, "Okay, Cobbler, I admit I had plenty of thunderstorms during my failed marriage, but never a single one that ended with a rainbow. Talk to me about this so-called benefit of conflict in marriage."

Shoemaker laughed. "Good opening, Pete. But tell me, did you have any success in finding a new line at the big show?"

"As a matter of fact I did pick up a line, even though it's a small one. But that's a start. And I've been regularly talking with Billy, too. He seems to be doing pretty well since his start-up at a new school. I promised him I would come out there and spend a week with him during Spring break."

"That's good news all around," Shoemaker said. Then, acting on an impulse, he put his right hand up in the air for a high five. Wysong enthusiastically slapped his upraised hand. But as he did he felt his mentor wince at the blow, followed by his comment, "I think I'm through doing that bit!" Then, changing the subject Shoemaker said, "What do you think is the problem if there is zero conflict in a marriage?"

"That's pretty obvious," Wysong responded. "There is none. It's a perfect marriage."

"Not according to marriage counselors," Shoemaker said. "In fact, the total lack of conflict presents a serious problem. Either they don't communicate, or one person is dominating and one is subdued. Why do you suppose marriages without conflict are actually unhealthy?"

"I'm clueless."

"I was, too, a long time ago. That was before I came to walk with the Lord–when I was a pagan, an unbeliever. My first wife and I actually had no conflict for quite some time. I'm ashamed to say the reason is that I dominated her and she simply accepted it. I don't mean that I abused her. Heavens, no. But I made all the decisions and she chose not to voice her objections. The fact is that this sort of behavior is quite common."

Wysong was nodding in agreement. "I understand that it wouldn't necessarily be healthy," he said, "but what's the real problem?"

"Such marriages are fragile. Like china or crystal, they are subject to easy breakage."

Wysong wanted elaboration. "I'm curious about your own situation," he said. "How did that change for you?"

"Thank you for asking. I neither changed my late wife, nor did she change me. Rather, once we both accepted Christ as our Lord and Savior, the Holy Spirit changed both of us." Shoemaker thought about what he had just said and decided to back track. "Look. I know you're still having trouble with the concept of the Holy Spirit, so let me explain. In preparation for allowing the Holy Spirit to enter our lives I first showed humility in moving towards reconciliation with her. She quickly followed. That was after five years or so into our marriage. Prior to that time we had actually discussed divorce."

"Are you saying that once you began having conflict, your marriage grew stronger? I don't get that."

"Not exactly. Every couple has conflicts, whether they're serious ones or merely a matter of preferences in choosing a television program or a dinner restaurant. It's first a matter of self-sacrifice, but more basically it's a point of learning to press for a resolution rather than for a victory."

"Now that's an eye opener," Wysong said.

"It was for me, too. What I would like you to do now is take a step back for the rest of today's time. I encourage you to talk about anything that might be on your mind. I'll be out of town next Friday, so we'll miss that session, but in two weeks we're going to have a little fun dealing with some even deeper aspects of conflict in marriage. It is those which have been called the real 'art' of conflict. Okay. Game on. The ball is in your court."

Wysong was genuinely interested in what this 'art' aspect of conflict might produce. In the meantime what followed was the longest single moment of silence between them since they had first met. *What do I have to share here?* was his thought. After another few moments Wysong realized that Shoemaker had no intention of being the first to break the silence. He hesitated for yet another few moments, unsure as to how to begin with something that *had* increasingly been on his mind.

He began slowly. "You know, I was actually hoping we could open things up a little today, but I wasn't going to push it. Even with all the Bible reading assignments you've given me, I need you to address this 'born again' business for me. I mean, it seems that whenever the mainstream media use the term it's in connection with a put-down. And for the few times I have stayed more than five minutes with some televangelist's show, I become instantly turned off, either by some pathetic appeal for money from a vulnerable public, or by its circus-like atmosphere. What's the real deal?"

"Pete, the fact that you have questions at all, is evidence that the Holy Spirit is working within you."

"Now, don't misunderstand me, Will. Remember, my interest is primarily intellectual."

"Of course," Shoemaker said, grinning inwardly. "Then let me give you some food for thought over the next two weeks. Call it a short course on the ultimate good news/bad news."

Wysong leaned forward, pencil wobbling in his hand like a D-student realizing the need to pass an exam.

Shoemaker began: "God Himself not only tells us there is only one way to heaven, but He also tells us how we are to achieve entrance. For the moment I'll ask you to suspend judgment on the authority of the Bible because of your intellectual interest in the born again aspect."

"I can manage that," Wysong said, not certain but what his own disclaimer had just been subverted.

"First, the bad news," Shoemaker said. "You and I are both sinners of the first kind. You say, 'What does that mean?' It means that we, as a part of mankind, have missed the mark. The proof is there every time we lie, hate, lust, gossip, worship anyone or anything other than God, or simply refuse to accept His offer of forgiveness. When the Bible says *'All have sinned and fallen short of the glory of God,'* it simply means that we have all come short of God's standard of perfection. And understand that this refers not only to deeds, but to words and thoughts as well."

"You're saying that you and I and Aunt Jane were all in the same leaky boat when we first drifted away from the birthing dock?"

"I haven't heard it put that way before, but that's right, with one huge qualifier. You'll see what I mean by that in a minute. But the news gets worse before it gets better. There's a price to pay for sin. That price is death. We are told this in no uncertain terms, in fact in seven little words: *'For the wages of sin is death.'*"

"I know the phrase, " Wysong said, "but what does it mean?"

"It means that by sinning we have not only bought into death, but that we have actually *earned* death. By being in direct opposition to our Creator's will we thus not only deserve to die at some point, but also to be separated from God forever."

"What do you mean 'die at *some* point?' We all die, sooner or later."

"Man wasn't originally born to die as we are. Adam and Eve made their choice in being disobedient to God's specific will and thus sin and death came to us through their genes."

"Hey, wait a minute," Wysong said. "Now you're into creationism versus evolution."

"Hey, yourself," Shoemaker said, "did you not agree to suspend judgment for those things outside of this conversation's focus?"

"I did," Wysong said, a trace of 'you got me' in his voice.

"So," Shoemaker continued, "to use your own analogy, how could you and I—in our leaking boat—come to God before we drowned? That's rhetorical, obviously. Weighed down as we are with inherent sin, there is no way. So God decided to repair our boat. To do that He decided to come in person. I ask you, how could that happen?"

"Is that rhetorical also?"

"No. How could a spiritual God come to us?"

125

Wysong could give mental assent to what Shoemaker was driving at. "Is that the story of Jesus?" he said.

"Precisely. And as to confirmation from His Word, consider this: *'God demonstrates His own love toward us, in that while we were still sinners, Christ died for us.'* For some," Shoemaker said in continuing, "that's confusing. Let me give you a little different analogy than our leaking boat. Suppose you are in a hospital dying of cancer. I come to you and say, 'Let's take the cancer cells from *your* body and put them into *my* body.' If that were possible, what would happen to me?"

"You would die?"

"Yes. And what would happen to you?"

"I would live. Thank you very much."

"To be more precise, I would die *in your place*. I would die *instead of you*. The Bible says Christ took the penalty that we deserved for sin, placed it upon Himself, and *died in our place*. To me, this is absolutely incredible, not only for the Biblical fact, but because the Creator of the universe chose to send Himself to earth to live and die among us as a man. And He did it for one reason and one reason only. And that was?"

"Yet another pop quiz?" Wysong said, subconsciously looking for some way to put some distance between himself and account-ability to God. He knew he needed to answer the question, however, so he said, "According to your earlier Biblical quote, the reason must be because he loves us."

"Yes!" Shoemaker said with enthusiasm. "And just when the bad news gets worse, the good news gets better. That's because you and I can be saved through faith in Christ. By faith, Pete, not by sight. Salvation comes not by understanding, but by a personal rela-tionship. That has been your stumbling block to understanding what faith means. Faith is nothing more or less than trust. And it is that trust that renders one being saved, how we become born again."

Wysong was thinking. "I'm struggling," he said as his eyes wandered around a portion of the room, perhaps for some sort of clarification beyond the two of them. That didn't work so he tried restating what Shoemaker had said. "Let me get this straight. By simply trusting in a relationship with Christ God gifts us with delivery from our inherent sin. Is that it? I mean, we don't have to do anything beyond accepting the gift?"

"That's it," Shoemaker said. "Paul clarifies that very thing just in case someone should boast for thinking he had worked his way into God's favor." He paused before asking his next question. "Are the scales on your eyes and heart lifting?"

"I don't know if they are lifting so much as I'm becoming more aware that they were closed in the first place."

"That is very perceptive. Before Adam and Eve 'threw' the game in the Garden of Eden, they enjoyed the presence of God in their lives. I mean they had an intimate inborn relationship with God that permitted them an open and reciprocal communication. After they disobeyed Him they died spiritually."

"So what *was* their relationship with God at that point?" he said, still striving for logic to take over.

"It was external. Their communication came not from their hearts but from their lips. They lacked His internal presence and His peace. As I said, they were spiritually dead."

"And as for us?"

"Because of A & E's disobedience we are born physically alive but spiritually dead. Therefore, for us to have an intimate relationship with God we have to . . . what?"

"Be born again. But are those words actually Biblical?"

"Read it for yourself in John 3:3: '*I tell you the truth, no one can see the kingdom of God unless he is born again.*'"

"You know something?" Wysong said, "Maybe, just maybe, I may be seeing a little light. Thanks for dumbing things down for me."

Shoemaker could barely contain himself at Wysong's apparent proximity to revelation. Without betraying his excitement he managed to say, "On the contrary, sometimes I think I'm as dumb as a bump when it comes to explaining God's plan of salvation, but He always comes to my aid. That's the key, you know, trusting alone in Christ alone to both forgive us and give us eternal life."

"Point of clarification, professor," Wysong said. "When you use the word 'alone,' do you mean that literally?"

"I love that question," Shoemaker said. "First, let me qualify something. What does it mean to be a Bible literalist? It means taking literally what is *meant* to be taken literally. Jesus Himself uses the parable, intending to put his point in a form that would have been understood by the common man. But the answer to your question is 'yes.' If you're with me on that I'll tackle your actual question."

"Steady and ready," Wysong said.

"Okay. Here goes. What faith alone in Christ alone means is that the word 'alone' is exclusive in both instances. Let me give you an example. Think of the trust you place in a chair to hold you through no effort of your own. Faith alone is enough, not requiring anything to support it, just as that very faith is in Christ alone, with nothing else added."

"Okay," Wysong said, "I think I understand that, but help me with something else." Pete knew he was being dogged in his pursuit, but he wanted solid ground for what he viewed as mental assent on the subject. "The trust you're talking about is for the express purpose of what?"

"It's as simple as this," Shoemaker said. "Nothing less than Jesus Christ getting you into heaven through no effort of your own, other than to seek God and respond to His free offer."

Wysong's mind was whirring. He was trying to both follow and analyze at the same time. "For the sake of argument," he said, "let me take the defensive position for a moment. In this process let me ask you to suspend your explanation of original sin."

"Touché," Shoemaker said, grinning.

Wysong nodded and said, "Good. So check this out. I've gone to church in the past and I help the poor even now. I don't steal and I've never committed a felony, much less murder. I don't even curse. I admit to having lusted, but with an exception or two it was only for my wife. But that's in the past. As you can see, I'm basically a good person. So now, on balance, why would someone like me be denied entrance to heaven?"

"Those are all–well, mostly—good elements, Pete. It's the argument that's the problem. Good living or any other good thing you might do cannot get you to heaven, simply because neither you nor I *are* good people. We're *all* sinners. And as such we deserve to suffer."

"So God is going to send me to hell because unbelievers reject Jesus? I don't find that very compassionate."

"Compassionate?" Shoemaker said with a touch of emotion. "First of all, we all deserve the condemnation of God, but He *sends* no one to eternal punishment. We send ourselves because we suppress the truth of God. It is by grace that any of us are walking with the Lord. If we *were* good people, we would know no suffering."

"So what's the bottom line?"

"Trust in Jesus Christ alone. God will then give us eternal life as a gift." Shoemaker wanted to slow things down a bit, not wanting to overrun Wysong. "Let me get a grip on this horse's reins for a moment," he said. "If most of what I've shared with you this afternoon is galloping away, what I'm about to say is what counts most. Let me lead up to it by saying that when someone so places their trust and does their best to live to that trust, they become born again. Did you hear what I just said?"

"Yes," Wysong said. "What is your point?"

"Just this," Shoemaker said. "Whether or not you understand, Pete, this is what brought you to seek Him, which is what you are doing. We seek God with our head, but we find Him with our heart. Why? Because faith comes through revelation, not by intelligence."

Wysong was troubled. "Then how am I going to simply understand without believing?" he said.

"I honestly don't think you can do that," Shoemaker said, shaking his head. "You came to me wanting to know what being born again means. Being born again is a matter of what is in one's heart and not what one chooses to call himself." Shoemaker took out his handkerchief as if to wipe his brow, saying, "Man, I've been in this pulpit way too long. Is any of this making any sense to you?"

Wysong's mind was still in race mode. "Not totally," he said, "but I think I could pass a written test on the subject."

"By putting it that way I'm not so certain you could. Let me check you out. What does it take to become a believer?"

"Praying a special prayer?" Wysong said in a tentative tone.

Shoemaker was gentle but adamant. "No, sir," he said. "Praying, and even claiming to have accepted Christ doesn't make one a believer. Remember, it's all a matter of personal relationship. The Bible clearly tells us that assurance of eternal life always comes in the present, never from anything done in the past. Once we confess or repent of our sin, we ask forgiveness and ask Christ into our heart. Then we have to walk with Him the rest of our lives."

"The get-out-of-jail card isn't enough?"

A faint smile crossed Shoemaker's lips as he shook his head slowly and said, "Nope. He isn't only our Savior. We also have to make Him our Master. If we want to walk with Him, everything we do or think or feel has to do with that relationship."

"But I'm not seeking to accept the faith," Wysong demurred. "That was never my goal. Remember? I merely desired intellectual understanding."

Shoemaker fought to avoid a deep sigh as he said, "And that's perfectly okay at this point. Only God can convert and He is more than willing to work with you. I'll say it again. Salvation is a matter of revelation rather than intellectual apprehension. If you come to fully understand that, however, chances are revelation is not far behind." He paused for a moment and then held up one hand before adding, "I've gone to preaching, haven't I?"

Wysong nodded, saying, "I guess so, but I don't mind."

Shoemaker continued. "I admit that in my own enthusiasm I sometimes forget that but for the grace of God I would be headed for hell myself. But so that you understand with your head, if not your heart, Pete, realize that you can't be a Christian without being born again. By the same token, if you *are* a Christian, you *have* to have been born again. I feel certain there will come a time–perhaps in the near future–when you will cry out for Him."

"You acquit your case well, Will. I honestly don't know what to say. I wish I had everything under control as you seem to. Has that always been the case with you?"

Shoemaker was caught by surprise. "Hardly," he said. "The fact is only one man ever came out of the womb praising God, so to speak, much less me. I was past your age before I finally realized there was nothing more important than my need to trust Christ. That was quickly followed by my repentance."

Wysong glanced at his watch and said, "Time for you to go. You don't want to keep Miss June waiting. As always, thanks for coming. I appreciate your humility as well as your teaching, Will. I don't know when I've had so much to think about. See you in two weeks." He gripped Shoemaker's hand more warmly than he ever had before.

When Shoemaker got home the first thing his wife said was, "Did you ask Pete the question?"

"Which question is that?" he replied as he saw to hanging up his jacket.

"If he wanted to trust Jesus with his life," she said.

"No," he responded, "but I have no doubt that God is going to reveal Himself to young Mr. Wysong. And when He does, a host of angels will be singing in heaven."

CHAPTER 24

HIATUS

After a three-day territory trip to the low country of South Carolina, Wysong drove back to Atlanta and then flew to Pittsburgh for a week-ending sales meeting with his decorated drink ware supplier. Reps from each of the five independent rep territories nationwide assembled to learn about new products, upcoming promotional emphases, and performance reviews. On the second morning he went down for a hotel breakfast earlier than necessary, planning on catching up with a national newspaper's news of the day.

Within minutes of settling in with his omelette and the sports page, however, the west coast rep joined him, ending the solitary breakfast plan. He was older, Jewish, and had done a fine job in the short time he had been covering the western territory after a long period of the Company not having had a rep in the area. On four different national show occasions since then the three of them–the sales vice president, the western rep, and Wysong—had played some shoot-around basketball together in the adjacent wellness center during pre-show downtime. Only once–at the last get-together—had Pete managed to barely out-shoot both of them. Since then he had done his best to keep them from forgetting.

As the western rep sat down he said, "How's it going, sharpshooter?"

Wysong smiled and said, "Nothing but net, Paul. What's happening in your life outside of constant travel and drink ware presentations?"

"Hard to think outside of those lines, isn't it?" the rep said. "My wife and grown kids are doing well, but I lost a big line a month or so ago. What a jolt. I had represented them for more than 14 years."

"Wow. Sorry to hear that,"Wysong said. "I know what you're going through. I recently lost two lines in a single week, including a biggie. What is your story, if you don't mind my asking?"

"I don't mind at all," he said. "You'll be surprised, though. I lost the line because of my exuberant witness."

Wysong's mouth flew open. "Tell me about it," he said.

"Well, I guess I could have avoided it, but I don't regret doing what I did. Some months ago I e-mailed my usual bi-weekly call report to the sales manager. In closing, I simply added a postscript noting that God had blessed me with a successful road trip. Within a week I heard from the manager about that. He said he had shared my report with the vice president of sales and that he had been instructed to advise me that I was never to send another report into their office suggesting that God had anything to do with my sales success."

Wysong was riveted to his chair. "Was that an unusual thing for you to include on your report?" he said.

"Are you a believer, Pete?"

"Uh, yes," he said, granting himself grace. *I am seeking truth*, he told himself.

"Then you'll appreciate my story," the rep said. "I've only been walking with the Lord for two years and my witnessing courage up until that particular point had been suspect. To back up a little, shortly after I had accepted Yeshua–or Jesus—as my Messiah . . . I'm Jewish you know . . . I worked a show with the vice president who was a member of the Jewish family which owned the company. I mentioned to him about the Jewishness of Jesus, and that through studying the book of Isaiah I had come to realize He was the Jewish Messiah. Well, he took mild exception to my comments and I dropped the subject."

"But it ultimately got you fired?"

"No. Not really. The subject never came up again. Then, about a week after I took the call from the sales manager I got a second call. That was from the vice president himself, a man I had known for fourteen years. He said he wanted to make it clear that whatever work I did for them I accomplished on my own, that it wasn't due to God. He reiterated that I was not to send another statement into the office regarding my faith. All I could think to say was that I couldn't deny my relationship with the Messiah."

"How did that go over?"

"I don't know, but I assume what I said next put the millstone around my neck. I remember my exact words because I had read them in the Bible earlier in the day. I quoted the apostle Paul in 1st Corinthians where he says: 'Neither he who plants nor he who waters is anything, but only God, who makes things grow.' Three days later I got my pink slip in the mail. Years of my solid representation for them apparently severed through a fellow Jew's unwillingness to tolerate the truth of God's Word."

"Wow!" Wysong said. "I applaud your courage, but I can't help wondering if you pushed too hard. After all, he did rebuff your earlier, more subtle approach. I know that my own teacher-mentor-minister has come close at times to crowding me off of the faith trail with the pride that can come with knowledge."

Wysong's friend sat for a moment without replying, his mind apparently turning over what he had just heard. "Now that's an interesting point I frankly had not considered. In the zeal that always seems to go with a new convert to anything, I may have overlooked not having being invited to share. Mea culpa for my lack of humility. Thanks for your insight, Pete."

"Insight?" Wysong said in surprise. "That's something I've rarely been accused of."

"How long have you been walking with the Lord, Pete?"

Unlike the first time he had been asked that question, Wysong wasn't in a panic. "You know," he began, still searching for words, "under my friend's tutelage, I think I now have the head knowledge of what it's all about . . . but quite honestly, Christ is not yet in my heart." That was the best he could do.

"Thanks for being candid," Paul said. "I doubt that was very easy for you to say. It's obvious to me, however, that you are drawing nearer to Him. Your friend must think a lot of you, but not as much as God."

Curiosity overcame Wysong's reluctance to pursue the discussion in much detail. "That's a difficult notion for me to grasp. But tell me, how is it that you—a Jew—came to know Christ?"

"I love that question," Wysong's western counterpart said. "First, realize that all of Jesus' disciples and probably all but a very few of the first 500 of His followers were Jewish. Jesus was born a Jew, raised a Jew, crucified a Jew, and resurrected a Jew. Nowhere in the Bible does He say, 'I am no longer a Jew.' As the Messiah, He came first for the Jews and then for the Gentiles."

Wysong was again searching for words. This time he found them more quickly than the last. "As little as I know about either Judaism or Christianity, isn't Jesus-as-God blasphemous thinking for Jews? I mean, they certainly aren't looking for Him in the Second Coming."

His friend laughed. "Truth be known, most Jews weren't—and aren't—even looking for the *First* Coming. As a culture we're more secular than religious. As for me, a Christian neighbor had been witnessing to me for years through a combination of how he lived, what he did and what he shared. One day, I asked him about the Jewish Messiah. He began talking with me and before long challenged me with something. He said that if Jesus is not the Messiah, Jews and Gentiles alike should reject him. But if He *is* Messiah, all of us should consider believing in Him. He said that at the very least we should be willing to examine the evidence. I agreed, and began doing that very thing."

"So, with time you converted to Christianity."

"No. Not quite. Labels can be problematic. I consider myself to be Messianic, a member of a Jewish-and-Gentile congregation which focuses on Jesus as the center of our lives. As a Jew I simply came to accept Jesus–Yeshua in Hebrew–as the Messiah, the one of whom Acts 4:12 says–'*Salvation is found in no one else, for there is no other name under heaven given to man by which we must be saved.*'"

"I'll bet that didn't go over too well at home."

"*That*, my friend, has been interesting." The rep shook his head and smiled. " I'm 48 years old and was newly married at the time to a Gentile who was saved. And here I have to thank God that she had not thrown her faith into my face. She did pray for me, however. But as for my parents, that has been a different story. I shared my testimonial with them and even though they're secular, they haven't spoken to me in two years."

"That's powerful stuff, Paul. I'll be anxious to share this with my spiritual mentor when I get home. I guess you were what he refers to as being 'unequally yoked' at marriage. My ex and I didn't even *own* a yoke, much less know how to pull together in the harness."

At that point the sales vice president walked up to their breakfast table and said, "You boys talking about my jump shot?"

Wysong said, "That's all we *ever* talk about, boss!" Then he turned to his friend and said, "Thanks for sharing on that other matter, buddy."

Paul smiled and said, "Not at all, Pete. Thank *you*! Everyone *needs* grace, but not everyone accepts it."

CHAPTER 25

BACK TO THE SONG BOOK

After not having met with Shoemaker for two weeks, Wysong confirmed that they were indeed meeting that Friday. Following that conversation he called his ex-wife's California phone number. Billy answered with, "Wysong's. This is Billy." Pete broke into a smile so broad it nearly touched both ears. "Hi, son," he said enthusiastically, "It's daddy. How are you?"

" Daddy! "Billy exclaimed. "When are you coming to see me?"

With those few words, Wysong was moved to tears. After several moments he managed to say, "In a month or so, Billy-boo. We're going to have the grandest time, you and I. I think about you all the time. Are you helping your mother?"

"Yes, I dry some of the dishes . . . and make up my bed and . . ." he turned to his mother who was sitting nearby . . . "Mom, what else do I do to help?" There was a pause as Wysong could hear talking in the background, but couldn't make it out. "Oh, yeah," Billy said, "sometimes I scrub out the toilet bowl. Yukk." They talked for almost ten minutes, and after he had hung up Wysong didn't know which was greater: His guilt or Billy's need. They were probably equal.

At week's end Shoemaker arrived at Wysong's apartment and had barely settled in before Pete said, "You won't believe what happened during my trip to Pittsburgh!"

When he had finished sharing the breakfast story, Shoemaker said, "What a testimonial! I couldn't have scripted your friend's witness any better. When you get a chance, send me his e-mail address. I want to offer him some additional encouragement. Do you have any questions resulting from that encounter? I would like to finish sewing the last thread of conflict into the fabric of marriage, but at the same time I'm flexible according to your interests."

"As a matter of fact, I do," Wysong said, trying to reflect back to his thoughts during the trip home. "Something struck me about an article I read on the plane. It dealt with something called 'a difference of doctrines.' As I see it, a doctrinal clash actually led to my friend Paul's loss. That doesn't seem fair."

Shoemaker was nodding his head as Wysong was speaking. "I think you've been reading about someone's arguments against a belief in God in particular, and Christianity in general. First of all, a clash of doctrines is not a disaster–it is an opportunity. And from what you said about your friend he acquitted himself very well."

"But what about the hundreds–really, thousands–of different denominations in Christianity alone? Doesn't this suggest that interpretations of faith in God are literally arbitrary?"

Shoemaker said, "I'm glad you're open to investigating things,Pete. You're absolutely correct with respect to the diversity of interpretations, but the problem is not the number. It's more a matter of making interpretation *itself* a god."

"How is that?" Wysong said.

"Because God's existence does not hinge on a particular interpretation of one or more verses from the Bible. God still *is*, regardless of interpretation. Look. No amount of logic or evidence can prove faith in God to someone who will not believe, nor will the most devastating of personal circumstances deter someone who unconditionally places his or her trust *in* God."

"That's an earful," Wysong said. "Talk to me some more. Until you came along I never had occasion to spend time talking with anyone who . . . how is it that you always put it . . . 'walks by faith rather than by sight.'"

"Okay," Shoemaker said, animated by Wysong's surprising lead-off request. "Let's look at faith–or trust–in its simplest form. We know from the book of Hebrews that without faith it is impossible to please God. Why? Because anyone who comes to Him must believe that He exists and that He rewards those who earnestly seek Him. Because of my trust in Him, heaven for me is a given. As a result I'm much more interested in living *this* life according to His will."

"But what does that do for your ambition, your health, your prosperity?"

"I just described my ambition. As for my health, I watch myself, but it is what it is. And if I go to meet my maker with no more than the modest means I have now, I am far more anticipating the everlasting promises I have in Him than any possible material gain in this short life."

"Man, you're killing me!" Wysong said. "Let me hit on a different track. If the evidence of God is both everywhere and irrefutable, then why can't man come up with scientific validation?"

"You're saying you want *man's* version of validation to be the marker, rather than take God's Word. But it isn't so much that our intelligence separates us from lesser species, even if God *did* make us in His image. Rather it is our *spirituality*–our capacity and desire to believe in an after life. For someone to have an underlying faith in God, it does not require scientific validation. Further, he could never obtain it."

"Why not?"

"Because science can neither prove nor disprove God's existence."

"So what is faith's reward?" Wysong asked, still clinging to his perceived need of black and white answers.

"I can state that in one word: Understanding. A paraphrased Augustine said it something like this: 'Therefore, seek not to understand that you may believe, but believe that you may understand.'"

"Well, you've burned out what little brain I have, Will. Sometimes I bite into stuff that doesn't want to go down without some help."

Shoemaker couldn't resist using a non-Biblical phrase he had read early that morning. "No one has ever starved with food still in their mouth."

Wysong saw opportunity suddenly jump up so he capitalized on it. "So who is writing *your* stuff, these days?" he said. "Don't bother answering. Look, I want you to know I've been giving things a great deal of thought lately. In fact, I was listening to the radio on the way back from the airport–I think it was a Christian talk show–and I heard a couple of quotes by someone named C. S. Lewis. He said that 'if a man is *united* with God, how could he not live forever?' Then he added the flip side that 'if he *is* separated from God, how could he not wither and die?' Those thoughts have since gotten inside of my head and may even be nibbling at my heart."

Shoemaker blinked through suddenly dampened eyes. "Pete, you don't know how close you are drawing to Him. Keep it up. As for C. S. Lewis, he is one of the most read and quoted Christian lay men of the 20th century. You can't go wrong reading him, if you get a chance. In fact, since you brought it up, before you leave today I'm going to give you a copy of his little best seller called *Mere Christianity*."

"Thanks. I'll read it. Not to change the subject, but we're off on a rabbit trail, aren't we? When can we get back to the Marriage, Inc. track?"

"Rabbit trails are not off limits. In fact, they're often 'discover' trails. The only way to know we are right is to be willing to discover where we are wrong."

Wysong smiled and said, "The Song book, Will. The Song book. Where are we?"

"We're exactly where we left off," he said. "But we'll have to step it up. I have a date tonight with Mrs. Shoemaker."

Wysong laughed and said, "Well, what are you waiting for?"

"Roger!" Shoemaker said, wiping his still-damp eyes under the pretext of cleaning his glasses. "We're ready to deal with turning conflict into intimacy and joy. When you were first married to your ex, you each brought different thoughts, view, opinions, and other aspects together. Consider that you were like two blocks of granite, each barely seeing and knowing more than what was immediately in front of you. Marriage, with all of its joys and struggles allows the two rough blocks of granite—through the friction of close prox-imity–to wear down one another. With time and continued friction, more and more of each person is revealed to the other."

"I like that analogy," Wysong said. "I assume you're saying then that if there was no friction–no conflict—theirs would be an incon-sequential relationship."

"That's it, exactly. Their marriage would be superficial and stale, likely resulting in divorce."

"Bingo!" Wysong said. "That was us. We were like two blocks of granite, all right. But we were sitting at opposite ends of the boat. To make matters worse, the boat was leaking."

"I think you're about ready to teach the marriage class, Mr. Wysong," Shoemaker said as he leaned back in the chair with his hands open and raised. "At the very least, you're ready for some insightful lessons from the middle of Solomon's Song of Songs."

"Sing away!"

"Then accompany me, if you will," Shoemaker said, playing along. "When the Shulamite woman begins to extol to the ladies of the court of King Solomon—which is where she was currently residing against her desires—they were taken by her description of the missing shepherd-lover. They, too, wanted to see such a man."

Wysong scratched his head and said, "I may have missed something there. I've read that passage several times and I still come up short. See if I have this part straight. She has a shepherd-lover with whom she dreams of having a rendevous, but King Solomon has somehow spirited her away to his court and is trying to woo her affection. And even though the silver-tongued King has so far managed to corral something like 60 queens and 80 concubines, he nevertheless strikes out with the Shulamite maiden. What happened to his offensive game plan?"

"The defense, Peter, my lad," Shoemaker said. "Are you getting the message of the gentleness and tenderness of the relationship between the shepherd and the maiden? The young shepherd–call him a defensive lineman—arrives upon the scene at Solomon's court in Jerusalem and appeals to the maiden to dump the King and leave with him for the home they have planned in the country."

"How cool is that?" Wysong said. "She flat out chucks old Sol and all of his riches for the home boy."

"Is that all it sounds like to you?" Shoemaker said. "Listen closely to some of what she has to say about her lover:

'My beloved is dazzling and ruddy, Outstanding among ten thousand.

His eyes are like doves, Beside streams of water,
Bathed in milk,

And reposed in their setting.'

What do you think she means by the word 'reposed?'"

"How one lies in a casket?" Wysong said facetiously.

"Nope. She means his eyes rest, that they don't ever change. They never narrow in anger. She is saying that her shepherd-lover is gentle and unchanging in his love for her. Now, how would you describe the degree of tenderness from your own marriage? "

"That hurts," Wysong said, "but I have it coming. I'm beginning to recognize how poorly my ex-wife and I managed tenderness. On rare occasion I did actually use romance, but only to get sex. And she–probably as a result of my own tactic–used sex to get romance. How sad were we?"

"More importantly," Shoemaker said, "how beneficial that you now realize the mutual loss. I think you are now prepared to deal with romance, my quick-study friend. That's for the next time we meet. In closing today, you might appreciate a verse I long ago memorized from Ecclesiastes:

'Enjoy life with the woman whom you love all the days
of your fleeting life
which he has given to you under the sun;

for this is your reward in life,

and in your toil in which you have labored under the sun.'"

CHAPTER 26

BACK ISSUES

Wysong was working in the greater Atlanta metro area for a week, in addition to making his phone appointments for the following week in central Mississippi. At week's end he felt a twinge in his back while rearranging some things in his van. He wasn't concerned that he was being revisited by the herniated disc because it had been successfully treated. He had been literally pain free ever since. Still, his back was bothering him and since he was headed out of town in a couple of days he decided to pay his first visit to a chiropractor in more than ten years.

As an assistant ushered him into the chiropractor's office, she said, "Dr. Valentine will be with you in a few minutes." As Wysong sat waiting, he amused himself by scrutinizing the various items sitting on several bookcase shelves. One object was a desk-sized replica of the skeleton of a tyrannosaurus rex dinosaur. On the base was an engraved brass plate which read, "70 Million-Year-Old T. Rex" and "Thanks For Straightening Me Up, Doc."

When the chiropractor came in, Wysong pointed to the model and said, "That's clever."

"Yes. Very," she said matter-of-factly. "A client gave it to me."

"You know," Wysong said, "a good friend of mine tells me that the dinosaurs are really only a few thousand years old, not tens of millions of years. Do you have any thoughts about that?"

Wysong observed that the chiropractor seemed surprised at the question, if not a little irritated. He had made his comment merely to see what sort of response she might offer. She said, "My client is a geologist, actually a retired paleontologist. I suppose he should know. Why do you ask?"

Before she could shift to the subject of Wysong's back problem he said, "I've been trying to resolve some questions I have about evolution versus creationism. How did dinosaurs fit onto Noah's Ark, I wonder? What do you think, doc?"

"Sorry," she began, "I simply don't have any thoughts on that, Mr. Wysong. Now, what can I do for you?"

Wysong left the chiropractor's office feeling a bit better for the adjustment he received, although he declined the invitation to return for regular treatment for what he was told could be the remainder of his life. As for the dinosaur-and-ark question he had asked the chiropractor, he knew where he could take it with likely better results.

Later that day Wysong welcomed Shoemaker to his home and then proceeded to unload his latest Biblical challenge relative to post-modern accepted truths. "I'm bothered by a couple of things today, Will. One of them is about Biblical accuracy."

Shoemaker was certainly not anticipating that sort of session opening from the man whom he thought was beginning to absorb more than a few of the underlying principles of Christian faith. After a moment's contemplation, he reached into his brief case and withdrew a well-worn Bible. Handing it to Wysong, he said in dead-pan fashion, "Could you point out an error?"

Wysong said, "You have me there. But different people I've spoken with recently–in addition to some of my reading–have put some notions into my head. For example, how in the heck could the ark have either accommodated or managed such huge meat-eating giants as T.Rex? Surely both man and dinosaur could not have coexisted. And just to throw a little grease on top of the monkey wrench, tackle this one for me: Did the 'cave man' precede or follow God's flood?"

Shoemaker put down the Bible and said, "I can see we may not get around to dealing with 'romance in today's marriage,' but that's okay with me. Let's *do* tackle some of that baggage you brought along with you today. I grant you that I'm not a geologist, but I know something about several of these issues you've mentioned."

"I figured you might," Wysong said.

Shoemaker clicked the cap of his ball point pen twice before bringing his chin to rest on the hand holding the pen and saying, "You still seem to be seeking scientific evidence of selective points of the Bible, so let me camp where you are. Do you have any idea how many thousands–make it millions, perhaps hundreds of millions-of different things could go wrong with the human body if it hadn't been intelligently designed?"

Wysong didn't lose a beat before responding. "Based on how many little things have already gone wrong with this body of mine in fewer than 40 years," he said, "without some pretty clever engineering I would probably be toast by now."

"Worse," Shoemaker said. "You wouldn't have come to be in the first place. Look, the Bible was written as a history book, not as a science book. But if you want to proof text from scientific findings I can give you a couple of relevant Biblical bones you can chew on."

"Serve 'em up," Wysong said.

Shoemaker nodded and proceeded. "As recently as 2005, a noted biologist discovered soft tissue–including blood vessels and even whole cells–when it became necessary to break a T. Rex's huge thigh bone. The biologist said that not only were the vessels flexible, but some of them could even be squeezed. After extensive testing came confirmation that that particular T. Rex bone contained hemoglobin, that is, red blood cells."

"Meaning what?" Wysong said, prodding for more detail.

"Meaning that the presence of red blood cells in a T. Rex bone is unexplained by evolutionary thinking, which suggests that millions and millions of years have passed since big T and all its cousins met their demise. The biologist herself stated that she was puzzled and could not understand why the bone was not mineralized."

"I don't recall any news fuss along those lines," Wysong said.

"That figures, given the largely biased mainstream media," Shoemaker said in nodding. "I do recall a part of her quote for MSNBC at the time, however, because I found it so intriguing. The biologist said that the discovery flew in the face of everything they understood about how tissues and cells degrade. And a contemporary of hers was even more explicit in stating that the T. Rex bones couldn't be but a few thousand years old. The point is simply that dinosaurs could certainly have coexisted with man."

Wysong didn't want to give it up, saying, "But what about the millions and millions of years that science tells us have passed since the dinosaurs?"

Shoemaker was just as perseverant and a lot more factual. "What God clearly tells us in His Word," he said, "is that all land-based life, which includes dinosaurs, died in the Flood. All, that is, except for Noah and seven others of his family. As a result of the sudden, world-wide flood, many fish were buried alive and fossilized quickly. Evidence of the speed of such fossilization exists in wonderfully preserved specimens, including a marine reptile which was fossilized at the moment of giving birth to her baby."

Wysong scratched his head before rebutting. "H'mm," he mumbled. "Getting back to Noah, how could he have shooed even one of those behemoths aboard the ark?"

"Look," Shoemaker said, "people assume all dinosaurs were the size of T. Rex, but they weren't. The average dinosaur was about the size of a sheep. More importantly, Noah didn't do either the calling or the shooing. God did."

"Great answer to a question a lot of people probably ask," Wysong said, shrugging as if it weren't really important to him anyway, but that he was glad to hear the rebuttal. "That still leaves the cave man, though. Whose human bone structure contemporary of today were they?"

It was Shoemaker's turn to shrug. He said, "We don't know more about this than what God has told us in His Word, although speculation abounds. But since you asked the question, let me offer this. We often hear the word 'evolution,' but after Adam's fall to Satan, his temptation in the Garden, and then the birth of Cain and Abel and Seth and numerous other children of Adam and Eve, his sons 'devolved' at two different rates into two different people groups."

Wysong held up one hand as if it were a stop sign. "Seth?" he said. "The brothers Cain and Abel I know of, but I didn't know he had siblings."

"It's all in the book of Genesis, Pete, although some of the commentary is necessarily developed by inference and credible construction. Let me finish the point in response to your question. Whereas Adam was created in the image of God, Seth was born under the curse of sin."

"The 'curse' of sin?" Wysong said, his tone begging for detail.

Shoemaker was willing to oblige him to a point. "His parents' disobedience in the Garden," he said. "When Abel later died at Cain's hand, Cain's people subsequently devolved into what we today think of as 'cave man.' Cave man was full of violence and lacked the same light of God. Seth's people, however, devolved more slowly and did not retreat as far from man's former state simply because they walked more in the light of God. It was through Seth's line that Noah, then David, and ultimately the Messiah, would be born."

Wysong still didn't want to let go. "What, then," he said with a sense of 'Gotcha!' do we know of the description of the forward progress of men and his discovery of tools, metals, techniques for construction, and the like?"

Shoemaker didn't so much as blink. He was enjoying Wysong's line of questioning because he was displaying an attitude of 'I want to buy into this, but you have to help me.' "What we know for certain because of what Genesis tells us, is that the cave men did not come before Adam or after Noah."

"Very interesting," Wysong said. "I had no idea of such things. How did we get off onto this rabbit trail, anyway?"

"Your visit to the chiropractor. Remember?"

Wysong laughed. "Enough of that. Say, did I tell you that I found a great air fare from Atlanta to San Diego for my visit to see Billy? I booked it. From that point I can rent a car to drive the 80 or so miles to the little desert town of Borrego Springs where Billy lives with his mother and her parents. I'm really excited about it. Spring break can't get here fast enough."

"No, you didn't tell me, but that's good news. I know Billy will be beside himself to have his dad spend some time with him."

Wysong glanced at his watch. "Sorry," he said. "I've eaten up all of our time with my peripheral questions."

"They aren't peripheral at all. Your interests are the reason I'm here. The fact is, a time will come when you don't need someone like me with whom to share, but even then we'll continue to be friends. I'll always be interested in your life and growth. Now, let me give you a clue as to what we'll be dealing with after your return from seeing Billy. The key word is 'gardening.'"

"Gardening?" Wysong said, puzzled. "That has something to do with love, sex, romance and marriage?"

"Yup. Well, after a fashion. You'll see."

CHAPTER 27

SPRING BREAK

As Wysong was winging his way towards San Diego via a stop in Dallas, he re-read the last e-mail Danniele–his ex—had sent him. From the time she and Billy had left Atlanta nearly four months earlier, she had agreed to send him a weekly 'Billy Update' so long as the child support payments were timely. They had both done their part and that was about as close to anything mutually "civil" as they had managed in years.

On the drive to Borrego Springs he called the motel to confirm his week-long reservation and the fact that the swimming pool was fully operational. He knew how much Billy loved to be in the water. He then punched up the house number to advise that he was on the last leg of his trip. Danniele's father answered the phone. "Hi, Frank," Wysong said without asking if it was him. "How's Billy doing?"

"Oh. Pete, it's good to hear your voice. He's doing great, although I haven't been seeing as much of him the last month or so."

"What do you mean?" Wysong said.

"Well, since Dannie took up with her new boy friend, they're gone a lot with Billy."

Boyfriend? was Wysong's thought as he quickly made a judgement. He would have to check this guy out. He couldn't have Billy spending time with an unfit stranger.

He drove up to the house and had no sooner parked than Billy came racing out to the car and into his arms. It was all Pete could do to get all the way out of his seat before he found himself with an arm full of boy. He rubbed his son's head and kissed him, tears in his eyes. "Am I glad to see you, Billy-boy," he said as he reached into the back seat for a big package. "Look what I brought you!"

"What is it, daddy? Can I open it now?"

"Of course! But I'm not sure you're big enough to use it."

Billy ripped it open and said, "Wow! It's a Rip-Stik. I know how to ride this. I've seen it on TV. Let me try it."

Wysong said, "Wait a minute. You have to wear a helmet and elbow and knee guards. Do you have any of those?"

The boy looked disappointed, saying, "I used to. You gave them to me for my skateboard, but it got broken. I don't know where the stuff is."

"Don't worry," Wysong said. "I picked up everything at a sporting goods store in town. Go ahead and dig them out of the back seat. Are your mom and gramps and gram here?"

"Mom will be back for dinner. She's working."

Just then, the boy's grandparents came out of the house to greet him. "Hi, Pete," they said enthusiastically and nearly in unison. "Give us a hug," said Emma, the grandmother. "Dannie will be here a little later. Archie picks her up and takes her to work."

"I guess that's who Frank was referring to on the phone," Wysong said, and then added with more than a trace of sarcasm, "I suppose he's a fixture around here."

"Come on in and have something cold," the grandfather said, ignoring his ex son-in-law's comment.

Two and a half hours later, as Pete was watching Billy in the driveway trying yet more tricks with his Rip-Stik, a car drove up. He saw his ex-wife lean over and lightly kiss someone. She got out and he drove away. The pair greeted each other and Pete said, "Got your own limousine service now, huh?"

His ex-wife glanced at him and then in the direction of the departing truck, saying, "He's a lot more than that."

During each of the next several days as Wysong returned from town to pick up Billy for whatever activities were planned for the day away from the house, he saw little of the boy's mother. Finally, he asked the grandfather for more details about Archie.

"Well, beyond what little we told you when you got here, we don't know much about him. Dannie seems to like him, but he doesn't spend much time here. He drinks a little, but then so does Dannie. We do what we can for Billy. When they first got here we took him to church and Sunday school with us every week, but Archie put a stop to that about a month ago. Hey, that reminds me. Tomorrow is Sunday. You want to go to church with us? Billy, too? You'll have to clear it with Dannie."

Wysong wasn't expecting an invitation to go to church. For all his visits with Shoemaker he hadn't been to church once. He had been invited many times, but he always had an excuse. *For crying out loud, it's your eight-year old son you're being asked to take to church!* "Yes, Frank," he said. "I'd like that."

Dannie had no objection. The next morning Pete gathered up Billy and the grandparents and drove into town to visit their little church in the 2,500 population community. Frank took Billy into a Sunday school room with half a dozen children in his age range, while Pete and Emma took a seat in the sanctuary. She said to Pete, "You know, you and Dannie had a rocky marriage, but I am so sorry both of you didn't work harder at things. We love both our daughter and our grandson, but she hasn't grown a lick since the divorce, either spiritually or emotionally. And as for Archie, well, he's even sorrier." Frank returned at that point, just as the service began. Wysong nodded and smiled comfortingly at Emma as he took her hand for a quick squeeze and release.

Frank noticed the gesture and gave his wife a knowing glance, as if to say, "Everything will be all right."

Wysong was paying closer attention to the pastor's message than any he had ever heard. It was about how important it is for the head of a family to look to his own relationship to God if he is to instill such a trust for God in the rest of his family. *What family?* he thought. *I don't have a family. At least not one that I can bring together.*

On the way home from church Billy said to his father, "Daddy, I learned something in Sunday school this morning! Do you know about the *Christmas Carol?*"

"Well, I know the song itself," he said, "and I've even sung it a time or two. What about it, son?"

"We learned about those funny characters in the song. They each have secret meanings. Do you know what 'six geese a-laying' stands for?"

"No. I don't. Tell me."

"The six days of creation!" He laughed at his knowing something his father didn't. "And what about the 'four calling birds?'" he asked with the pride that comes with knowing the answer.

"No, again. What does it mean, oh wise one?"

This time Billy laughed before he sprung the answer. "The four gospels. I know what they are: Matthew, Mark, Luke and John."

Tears flooded Wysong's eyes as he realized that both he and his son were studying the Bible. His mind rushed to the big picture of what his mentor had been teaching him, thinking that Billy might have been paying closer attention than he had.

But Billy wasn't finished. "Oh, yeah, daddy, and this is the best one. Who is 'the partridge in a pear tree?'"

Wysong thought for a moment and knew the answer. He didn't know why, and no one had ever told him, but suddenly he knew. "Jesus Christ," he said.

"That's right, Daddy!" he exclaimed, jumping up and down as best he could considering that he was strapped into his car seat. "You get a gold star." Billy turned to his grandparents and said, "He gets a gold star, doesn't he, gramp and gram?"

Wysong's thoughts suddenly filled his mind with the knowledge that the second longest day of his life was already rushing at him. He and his son would shortly be departing one another for distant homes for the second time in their lives.

The next day, as he was preparing to leave, he walked Billy to his rental car and said, "Would you like to drive to the end of the driveway?"

"Wow, can I?" he said enthusiastically, but then added, "I don't know how to drive, Daddy."

"I'll teach you, Son. There's nothing to it. Here, I'll push the seat back and you can sit in my lap and drive." Billy climbed aboard as Wysong started the engine and engaged the transmission. The car was oriented towards the street and he applied the slightest touch to the accelerator. The car began inching forward as he said, "Keep the wheels of the car straight, just like on your video games. Ready and steady."

Billy began turning the steering wheel, first to the left and then to the right, utilizing the entire width of the two-lane driveway. He beamed as he said, "I'm driving. I'm driving! Ready and steady."

As Wysong stopped at the end of the driveway, he said, "You know what, Billy-boy, I just had an idea. Maybe you could come to visit me in Atlanta for a couple of weeks this Summer. What would you think of that?"

The boy squealed with delight. "Wow! Could I? That would be so cool. And you know what would be a lot of fun when I come?"

Wysong wondered what he had in mind. Maybe to go swimming or to a theme park, or both.

Instead, Billy said, "My Sunday School teacher told us to ask our parents if sometime the family could make sandwiches and take them to people who have nothing to eat. You and I will be a family then, won't we, daddy?"

This time tears not only formed, but streamed down Wysong's face, causing him to turn aside to wipe them away. His thought was simply, *When are my son and I ever going to be more than a part-time family?*

CHAPTER 28

TENDING THE GARDEN

Wysong called Shoemaker the day after he had returned from his California trip. "Are we on for the day after tomorrow? I have lots to share."

"Affirmative. I want to hear all about it."

Friday afternoon came and—as usual—Wysong began his update with little weather or other small talk preceding it. He gushed about the California geography, the climate and even the stars of the Borrego Springs area. "Will, you should have seen that desert sky, by day *or* by night. I have never seen anything to compare with its clarity, away from the fog, smog and burning logs of civilization. I know everyone refers to their home town region as 'God's country,' but boy, is that some special place. Following his Chamber of Commerce introduction he took a deep breath and said, " before we get down to today's business I have something else to share with you."

"By all means," Shoemaker said. I've been telling June since you left, that this trip was such a wonderful opportunity for you."

Wysong had come to feel that he could truly share his heart with this man. The trouble is, he wasn't certain of what he really had to say. He only knew that something had happened during the time he had been away.

"Where do I begin?" he said. "I realized some things this past week, some truths, as it were. In fact, there are perhaps three different ones. First of all, I grew closer to Billy during those few days than in all of his preceding years. You might wonder how that could possibly be. I honestly don't know, but it has been on my mind since I left him. The best I can come up with is that since he has been effectively removed from my life I worry about him growing up without his father. The next thing I can do about that is to fly him back here for a while this Summer."

"Now that sounds like a wonderful idea. June and I would love to meet him."

Wysong smiled. "That's one truth," he said. Secondly, I have come to better understand some of the things you have been teaching me about marriage. Isn't it odd that in observing life in the context of fresh thinking one can actually have a different take on the same people? I tried putting myself back in time in my ex's shoes and it hurt. If it hurts me now, it probably hurt her then."

"Praise God," Shoemaker exclaimed, "*that* is what I call growth. Someone a lot smarter than me once said that happiness is there for those who cry, for those who hurt, for those who seek, and for those who have tried, for only they can appreciate their trials. Thank you for sharing that, my friend. Now, what's your third truth?"

"This one is a little more difficult to articulate. Basically, I would say that my heart has been softened with respect to the faith message you've been preaching and teaching. I still have questions, but I'm not certain what they are."

Shoemaker could barely contain himself with how the Holy Spirit was obviously working on Wysong, but he knew he needed to stay low key. "That's perfectly okay, Pete," he said. "Everything in its time. Consider that God's commands provoked Pharoah to harden his own heart. He can provoke people in the other direction just as well. And as you soften your heart, so God further softens it."

"Thanks for that, Will. Now, what's up for today's session?"

"Did you bring your 'gardening' tools?"

"Aha! Now I remember," Wysong said. "No, but I have always enjoyed reaping the benefits of something I've had a hand in planting and raising, be it a tomato, an Azalea . . . or a lesson of some sort."

"Well put," Shoemaker said. "Tommy Nelson, the pastor-author friend I keep mentioning likens the art of romance to someone who decides to plant a garden. As you pointed out, there is the sense of the thrill of seeing how beautiful or delicious it will become. His point is that the appreciation and enjoyment of such gardening is for a season. Inevitably, however, weeds and other destructive forces begin to take their toll on plants of any kind."

"I know that from personal experience," Wysong said as he nodded in agreement.

"Then you know that the gardener can't sit back and watch it happen because he would be wishing for whatever is planted to die. Like a gardener, each partner must work to improve and protect their relationship. I get a kick out of how Nelson likes to introduce this subject for his audiences by saying, 'You may think you are Romeo, but you aren't marrying Juliet.' What do you think he means by that?"

"Well, our subject is romance, so it must have something to do with that."

"Exactly. Every woman has the desire to be 'romanced.' Consider how the wolf—our young King Solomon in the verses we've been studying—continued to romance the maiden, even though she was longing for her shepherd-lover and not for the King.

'How beautiful are your feet in sandals, O prince's daughter!

The curves of your hips are like jewels,

The work of the hands of an artist.'"

"That hits home," Wysong said. "I didn't understand either the purpose or the need for romance during my marriage. Since we were already married I figured I had a license. I admit that I often took her for granted simply by taking her."

Shoemaker nodded, saying, "You fell prone to a common mistake of many people in marriage. After the sweetness fades we can become too lazy to discipline ourselves to love and be committed to this person who is our wife or husband. Here's one way of pulling yourself up short in this sort of thinking. Put yourself in her position and be honest about how you would feel if someone really only desired your body instead of the person you are and your relationship to her. Wouldn't you feel 'prostituted?'"

"You know," Wysong said, "at first blush it's hard for a man to think that way because our natural inclination is to say, 'Bring it on!' But on second and third thought, it does make sense."

"Yes, and what about its opposite?" Shoemaker continued with his point. "This would be practicing passive behavior when your partner doesn't agree at all with your position. You know, rolling your eyes, sighing, ignoring the person, that sort of thing. How would that kind of behavior make you feel?"

Wysong gave the question a moment's thought before replying. "My ex and I treated each other that way on a regular basis. It felt terrible, yet we both continued doing it. I guess we were self-destructing from the get-go. We obviously didn't care about the effect we were having on one another."

Shoemaker further encouraged his student by saying, "I'll bet you can think of ways a couple could keep each other accountable to *not* practice either kinds of those behaviors."

"For sure. If nothing else you could at least try to open up awareness of the actual relationship, maybe even–gasp–get into discussion about it."

"Absolutely. Talking constructively is a lot more beneficial to a marriage than either taking a partner for granted or criticizing him or her. But enough on that point. Before we wrap up for today I want to touch on some guidelines to protecting a marriage from an affair. Even if someone has never come close to having an affair, the winds of temptation are always blowing. You need to understand how to stay out of that wind. And the best way to do this is through knowing the easiest ways people succumb."

Wysong blinked his eyes once, and then a second time, as if first having come to a decision he then affirmed his action. "I'd appreciate hearing that list," he said. "I've never told anyone this, but if I were charged on that count I would have to plead guilty. I'm been ashamed ever since, but especially now. I remember at the time I simply felt justified."

"Don't beat yourself up. It's time to forgive yourself and move on. For now, consider how easy it is to give yourself over if the following progression is allowed to develop:

1) You allow tenderness and respect to fade from your marriage.

2) You meet someone.

3) That person gives you the feelings your mate once gave you, then promised you, but over time cut you off from.

4) You make an effort to be in that person's presence, at first merely enjoying it from a distance.

5) You then begin fantasizing about being with him/her.

6) You communicate to the person how you feel.

7) You have an affair."

Wysong shook his head and looked down, saying, "I know what happens to the garden at that point. It dies. The marriage is dead."

"Yes, sir," Shoemaker said. "And do you know why it's so difficult for a person to change his or her attitudes towards another person on their own? And this applies whether it's an attitude or a habit."

"Not really."

"Generally speaking, people will only change when it becomes important to someone else. In other words, a person won't change for his own sake, but he might if he finds a reason outside of himself."

"That's a lot to chew on," Wysong said.

CHAPTER 29

REVELATION

Wysong was off to south Florida for a two-week territory trip. Before his marriage had begun to go sour, he hadn't liked this trip. It meant he would be away from home over a full weekend. He had certainly missed his weekend time with Billy, even as young as he was at the time, but he now realized he had even missed that time with Dannie. Now, of course, what difference did it make being away from his apartment? Home was wherever he finished his day.

He had acquired the product line for which he had recently interviewed, but even in combination with the other new line the two would barely replace the revenue of the smaller of the two lines he had lost some months ago. Would the levee hold back the water that was continuing to accumulate?

He left his rented beach-side apartment in Lauderdale-by-the-Sea early one morning to make the 45-minute drive to see one of his two largest accounts in Miami. This would be a much longer day than he had planned. The first call was to see one of only two distributors in his entire territory who had to be seen quite early in the day, or not at all. It was barely 6:00 in the morning. Daylight Savings Time was a week away so it was still dark at that hour. Pete pulled into a parking spot near the inside entrance of the poorly-lit multi-story parking deck fronting both the client's office and the adjacent low-price range motel.

He had just finished his presentation with the distributor principal when he heard two identical but fairly loud and sharp sounds coming from outside the front of the building. The two men looked at each other in puzzlement. Wysong's first thought: *Those weren't gun shots, were they?*

Within several minutes he had left. As he exited the building for the adjacent parking garage he heard police sirens. Then he saw two police cars barrel around the corner and slide sideways to a stop, just like in the movies. Police quickly blocked off the parking lot entrance and approached Wysong as he was crouched beside his two-wheeled cart piled four-high with sample cases. He stood up, not certain whether he should raise his hands or cover his eyes.

Guns drawn, two police officers approached him and one asked, "What's your business here, sir?"

Wysong nervously answered, "Seeing my customer, Pencil America. I just left the v.p.'s office. My car is parked over there." As he turned to point to it, he could see that the driver side window was broken out. *What is happening to my life?*

He sat down on one of his sample cases. Twenty minutes later the other of the two officers came over to take his statement. "Sorry, sir, but the car that was parked next to yours was stolen and several shots were fired by someone. One of them apparently hit your car. Did you witness anything?"

After Wysong had cleaned up the glass inside his car as best he could and obtained from the police the address of a nearby glass shop, he sat behind the wheel of his car. He was still parked and in deep thought. *What if I had arrived on the scene five minutes earlier? Would I be dead? Would Billy be without a father?* And then another, very different thought occurred to him. *Would I have gone to heaven or been damned to an eternity, separated from God? What is that short verse of Shoemaker's concerning troubling times? Ah! "To whom shall I turn?"*

When Wysong returned to his apartment at day's end he immediately began searching for— and quickly found—a thin Bible in one of the dresser drawers. The cover read *New Testament & Psalms.* As he opened it he saw on the very first line of the first page, the words *The Way of Salvation.* Turning, as directed, to Romans 10:9, he read,

"That if you confess with your mouth, 'Jesus is Lord,' and believe in your heart that God raised him from the dead, you will be saved.'"

Wysong closed the Bible and sat back, thinking. After a full minute he knew what he must do. Dialing a number on his cell phone, he waited for an answer.

"Hello," began the recorded message, "you have reached the Shoemakers. No one is in at the moment. Please leave your name and number and one of us will return your call as quickly as possible. May God mightily bless your day."

Great. Just when I need the Cobbler most, he's gone fishing. "Will," he said, speaking into the receiver, "I need your help, man. Please call me on my cell. You have the number." Within five minutes of hanging up, his cell phone rang out. He anxiously pressed the receive button and answered. "Will?"

Shoemaker said, "Yes. It's me, Pete. I just got home from a grocery run with June. What's up? Are you still in Florida?"

"I am," Wysong said. "I nearly had my car stolen. They settled for shooting out one of my windows. Probably didn't like the mileage number. Anyway, I've had the crap scared out of me. I'm like one of those Old Testament guys whose lament was 'Woe is me.' Listen to my litany: My family is broken. My business is in the dumpster. I've barely begun regaining my health. And right now I'm sitting here in this stupid rented apartment all by myself and wondering about my purpose in life. You know better than anyone that until recently I never gave God so much as a thought, much less acknowledged Him. Now, all of a sudden I find myself becoming a philosopher."

"A philosopher?" Shoemaker said.

"Yeah. I find myself plagued by personal loss on all fronts and right away I figure God is playing favorites and I'm not one of them."

"And where is that leading you?" Shoemaker said, giving Wysong all the slack he needed.

"That's the upside," he said in an even more excited voice. "I've also been thinking about this from another angle. After all, why *should* I be favored? God doesn't know me because I don't know Him. Listen, Will, I'm ready to change that."

"You are?" Shoemaker said, hearing what he had only hoped to hear. "Give me a second," he said. He quickly cupped his hand over the speaker and caught his wife's attention. She was sitting in a nearby chair, looking expectantly at her husband. He said excitedly, "I think revelation has come to Pete!"

"Are you still there, Will?" Wysong said anxiously.

"I'm here. I'm here. Sorry. Where were we?"

"I have a Bible in my hands and I'm ready to turn myself in."

"You mean you're ready to let *Him* in, don't you?"

"That's it. That's what I want to do. How do I go about it?"

"Take it easy, Pete," Shoemaker said. "First, I have some news for you. God is not only with us at this very moment, but if that shooter is still anywhere around and decides to take you out after all, you'll be in paradise with Jesus as surely as the thief on the cross who asked to be remembered by Him."

"I will?"

"Absolutely," Shoemaker said. "Repentance and faith are the only two requisites. God will do the rest. It's time for you to pray about your conviction. Speak to God from your heart. I'm here to help if you should need it."

"Okay," Wysong said, tears rolling down his cheeks. "Can I put you on speaker while I go to my knees?"

"Of course."

"Here goes. Dear Lord, I'm such a stubborn doofus." There was a pause and Shoemaker could tell that his friend's emotions had been unleashed. Shoemaker waited quietly in prayer. Wysong continued in a shaky voice. "I visited your house when I was a boy, even a few times as an adult, but I may as well have been playing hooky. Anyway, for some reason You must think I'm worth your time and trouble. Forgive me and help me more clearly see the light." A short pause followed, and then this: "I hereby accept the precious gift of grace that your servant, Will, has been letting seep into this thick head and cold heart of mine. I don't know what else to say now. In the name of Jesus Christ, Amen."

Shoemaker weighed in with, "Praise Him indeed. I know you said that from the heart, brother, but do you know what just happened?"

"No, sir. I don't."

"You have been put right with God. Your sin has been taken away. But it is through nothing you have done. God does this on the

basis of what Jesus Christ has done for us in His death and resurrection, *and*, on the basis of our faith. Now, when you get back home
I'll tell you more about what's ahead for you in your relationship
with Him."

"Works for me. Can I get up now?"

Shoemaker laughed. "How else are you going to make a very
important phone call?"

"Oh, wow. Yeah! Thanks for reminding me. I'll see you when I
get back. I owe you my life."

"No, you don't," Shoemaker said. "You owe it to Christ."

CHAPTER 30

MOVING ALONG

A few days later Wysong returned to Atlanta. It was mid-afternoon on Friday and he lost no time in calling his spiritual mentor and asking him to come to his apartment in their usual meeting slot. When Shoemaker arrived he quickly gave his friend a bear hug and said, "Talk to me! I'm dying to know how things developed that led you to your decision for Christ." Wysong quickly briefed him on the particulars of the shooting/stolen car/police happening. Then he turned to relating the details of his thinking immediately prior to the call he had made from the Florida apartment.

In response to the story, Shoemaker said, "Brother, talk about how mysteriously the Lord works." He stood up and gave his friend a second big hug. To lighten the moment he added, "You know, I think there's a book in this for you somewhere." Then, in a more serious tone he said, "You've talked with Billy. Right?"

"Oh, man, have I! I called him right after I hung up with you. He didn't quite understand, but he knew from my voice how excited I was. Neither of us can hardly wait for his trip back here."

"Again," Shoemaker said, "I can't tell you how happy I am for your decision. You are now a 'new man.' You have been regenerated. As you'll soon discover, part of that process is instantaneous, while other parts are gradual. Allow yourself to grow through the inspiration and workings of the Holy Spirit that is within all believers. Not only are we given the power to do the will of God, He defines success in our lives as walking with Him *thorugh* our journey, regardless of the journey itself."

"I have a lot to learn," Wysong said. "I *do* have one question, however. How can I truly know that I'm saved? I mean, I don't feel any different."

"Good question for a new believer. You'll begin to understand it by the evidence of your words and deeds, not to mention through the inspiration, support, and encouragement of your brothers and sisters in the fellowship of the church. Reading the Word daily and talking with Him through prayer is how you continue to develop your relationship with God."

Wysong suddenly remembered a phrase he had read in one of the books Shoemaker had given him. He said, "Don't worry. I won't let Him go until He's blessed my socks off."

Shoemaker blinked as if something relevant had come to mind. It had. "Let me tell you about that 'worry' word," he said. "If you worry, you haven't prayed. If you pray, don't worry."

Wysong thought that through for a moment before saying, "It may take me a while to learn that one."

"Then let's get you off the dime on another matter as well," Shoemaker said. "Do you have any plans for Sunday?"

"Nice segue, Mr. Shoemaker," Wysong said. "You've invited me to attend church with you many times, but I always had a ready excuse. May I join you and June for church this Sunday?"

"We'll pick you up at 9:00 A. M."

"Done."

"Okay, that's settled," Shoemaker said. "Now, are you ready to tackle part two of the *romance* of marriage?"

"I've been waiting for this," Wysong said. "I'm not too old to marry again, you know."

"Well . . . maybe marginal," Shoemaker said, joking, "but miracles still happen. Hey, of course you aren't. I have friends who have remarried at twice your age. Speaking of that, there's a corollary to the notion of age in romance and marriage."

"Yet another good segue, Cobbler," Wysong said.

"Thanks. It goes like this. The younger a person is the more likely he or she is to think of romance relative to 'things,' like bringing or getting flowers or chocolates or some other little things. Those are important, of course, but there are many other aspects that add to the deepening of an intimate relationship. Does anything come to your mind in that regard?"

"Well," Wysong began, now enjoying more than ever Shoemaker's interactive teaching style, "from the hindsight of my own negative experience, I would say it's important that a couple doesn't get bored with one another."

"Score an 'A' for the new man's thinking!" Shoemaker said as he raised his right forefinger and pointed towards Wysong. "A husband's appreciation of his wife is a constant process, just as her respect for him should grow greater every day. Let me read you from two verses of chapter seven of the Song. Now, keeping in mind that successful romance is always in the eye of the beholder, what do you suppose this verse meant to the maiden when her shepherd-lover spoke this catchy little gem?

'Your nose is like the tower of Lebanon.'"

Wysong laughed and said, "If I were to tell that to my lady I believe I would be on the receiving end of a blunt–if not a sharp—instrument."

"Probably, but to a lady in King Solomon's day it referred to the fact that the tower of Lebanon faced the enemy, towards Damascus. As long as the tower was there, protecting the people, they knew they were safe. Therefore, he was saying that her countenance is just as trusting as the tower. Perhaps more romantic than you would have guessed, eh?"

"Yeah. Right."

"Then maybe you'll like this compliment from Solomon better:

'Your head crowns you like Carmel.'"

"Meaning?" Wysong said.

"Carmel was Israel's 'postcard.' It's where the great rolling hills were, where the cattle would gather in great number. His admiration deepened for her. Anyway, I think you get the point that his verses were intended to convey things such as 'I love being with you,' or 'I can trust you,' or 'You are the most lovely thing I know.'"

"I understand." Wysong said. "Romantic times are not going to happen every day."

"That's right," Shoemaker affirmed, "but a marriage without romance is like a sinking ship."

Wysong nodded vigorously and said, "Mine went down before it could get out of the harbor."

"Well, you know how to keep the next one afloat. And when that happens, you can pray every day that God will make you a more romantic partner. I prayed for June this morning, as I do every day. This is how I prayed: "Loving Father, let me love my wife as you loved the church. Let me give myself up for her. Let me honor her with my words, and present her to you holy and cherished. Let me love her as I love myself."

"Man," Wysong said, shaking his head, "you are something else. How do you come up with a prayer like that?"

"I'm not the author. I found it in Ephesians. Tell you what, I'll give you a little 40-card file with such prayers on them for your second 'hope chest.'" They both laughed.

CHAPTER 31

SUMMERTIME

The first week of July Wysong drove to the airport to meet Billy's flight. Dealing with the airline's safety-focused procedures for picking up an unaccompanied minor was much simpler than it had been during the early years following 9/11, but still required negotiating some red tape. His son was among the last few passengers to exit the plane, in the company of a flight attendant. He ran wildly towards his father, exclaiming for all to hear, "Daddy, daddy, I'm here! I'm really here!"

On their way to the house Billy was nearly non-stop in relating everything he could think of that had happened to him since his father had been out to see him during Spring Break. Wysong finally interrupted, saying, "I have a question for you. It's a tough one. Are you ready?"

Billy broke out in a grin that betrayed his missing two front teeth, which he considered to be a badge of pride since all of his same-age friends were missing a few teeth as well. "Steady and ready," he said, laughing.

"Okay. For one million dollars, what's the answer to this *Christmas Carol* question: Who were the eight maids a-milking?"

Billy laughed again as he said, "That's easy. The 'Beatles.' You owe me, dad!"

Wysong cracked up and reached over the seat back to rough up Billy's hair. "You mean the Beatitudes, don't you?"

"That's what I said. Do I get the money?"

"What you get is dinner at our old burger place. Is that okay?"

During dinner at Billy's favorite fast-food restaurant, Pete said, "Well, big boy, what would you like to do tomorrow? Go swimming?"

"Oh, boy!" he said. "Mommie packed my swim suit." He was thoughtful for a moment and then added, "But don't forget your promise."

"Promise?" Pete didn't remember any particular promise.

"You know, about the sandwiches," Billy said.

Still not understanding, Wysong said, "Oh. You mean to take to the swimming pool?"

"No," Billy said. "Remember, you said we could make sandwiches for the hungry."

Wysong felt as if he had taken a slap on the head. He now clearly remembered what Billy had asked him more than three months ago, but he was taken aback that a boy so young would be so perseverant about doing something so unselfish. He hadn't learned that from either his father or his mother. Then it came to him. *Of course, the church! Sunday School has taken over the role* I *should be playing.*

The next morning they went to the grocery store and bought two loaves of bread, one jar of peanut butter, a jar of seedless red raspberry jam, and a box of sandwich bags. Together, they made two dozen sandwiches, placing two PB & J sandwiches into each zipped sandwich bag. Then they drove into Atlanta to one of the largest of the inner city parks. A few apparently homeless people were scattered here and there during the lunch hour.

Pete watched from close by as Billy boldly walked up to the first small cluster of people. He offered them the sandwiches, saying "My daddy and I made these for you." Pete teared up, not only for the pride and love he had for his son, but also for the thought of the Scripture that Will had quoted to him many times in making a point about helping others in need: *"Whatever you have done for the least of them, you have done for me."*

Billy stayed with Pete for the next six weeks as he took much of that time off, only working day trips several days a week, but taking his boy with him everywhere. Father and son did everything a visiting family would do if they had never been to Atlanta, including trips to Stone Mountain, the Aquarium, a zoo, a water park, and a theme park. During the first few days, Pete also took Billy to meet the Shoemakers. At Will's home Pete said, "Will, I want you to meet my son, Billy, the handsome little guy I have told you so much about. Billy, shake hands with Mr. Shoemaker, daddy's best friend in the Lord."

The two men had agreed to take a break during the Summer in terms of their weekly meetings, but would start back again the first Friday after Labor Day. As father and son were walked to their car, Pete said to Will, "I haven't told you until now, but next week I'm not only planning to join the church, but both Billy and I going to be baptized. Will you stand up with us?"

Shoemaker froze in his tracks and said, "Praise God. What a day that will be. Cantankerous crocodiles couldn't keep us away!" He hugged Wysong for only the third or fourth time in their relationship. Pete had often joked about not being a 'hugger.'"

Half-way through Billy's stay, Wysong said to him, "How would you like to visit a kangaroo ranch?"

"You mean the zoo? We did that. But I don't remember seeing any kangaroos."

"No, not the zoo. I'm talking about a ranch just for kangaroos. Its location is a secret of sorts. You might even get to throw a boomarang."

"For sure?" he squealed. "Cool!"

And so the balance of Billy's visit went. There was plenty of time for fun, games and talk. Wysong didn't actually tell his son that he was giving serious consideration to giving up his territory and moving to Los Angeles. In essence, he would be starting over as a west coast multi-line rep.

Aside from the downside of the increased cost of living he knew the territory had much greater revenue potential than the southeast, simply because of the greater population.

If he were going to effect such a change, however, he would want to make the move in early December. In the meantime, he had to work out the logistics, not the least of which included advising his current supplier lines, most of which he would not likely be able to retain. He would then begin lobbying for new ones out west. Of course he would also have to list his condo, but it was a seller's market and he didn't foresee big problems there.

On the way to the airport, both of them were quiet. Wysong wanted desperately to share the idea of the move to join his son, but he thought it would be safer to wait a month to be certain he could line up at least some of his ducks. That way he could also give him an exact date. "Tell you what, Billy," he said, "When I come out to see you for Christmas, we'll check out all the big zoos in San Diego."

"But I don't want to go back there," he said." Billy's eyes were filled with tears as he looked up at his father. "I want to stay here with you."

"I know," Wysong said, "but your mother needs you out there, and gramp and gram do as well. I promise to call you every other day."

"*Every* day!" Billy said.

CHAPTER 32

RE-ENGAGING

"Will, is it okay if we meet at your place?" Wysong said over the phone. "I've decided to relocate to southern California sometime before Christmas–to be nearer Billy. In the meantime, some fix-up people are going to be coming and going."

"That's great news for both of you, Pete. Let's do that. I'll see you here this Friday. We should be able to wrap things up with our study over the next two or three sessions."

That Friday afternoon Wysong settled in at the Shoemaker's comfortable home as June popped into the room for a minute to say hello. "Hi, Pete. Will told me you wouldn't mind if he told me about your plans to move nearer Billy. He's always careful about the 'confidential' thing, you know. I think you're doing a wonderful thing."

"Thanks, Mrs. Shoemaker. I appreciate your support."

"June. Remember?" she said as she smiled in leaving the room.

"Of course I remember. Thank you." With that, he turned to his mentor and said, It's been a while, Will. Where are we?"

"We're right where we need to be, but I want to mention a couple of things before we get under way."

"Great. Call me 'rabbit ears.'"

"Hey," Shoemaker said with a twinkle in his eyes, "that's fresh stuff. New writer?"

"Yeah. My son!"

"Okay. Three things, actually. First of all, I want to extend an invitation to you to join my Saturday morning Bible study group. About a dozen men meet at the church for the purpose of both Bible study and fellowship. We've been on hiatus for the last month and are just starting up again. We call ourselves Men of the Way. Even if you can only join us off and on for a couple of months before you leave. All Christians need to be part of a small group. This will give you a sense of what small groups can be like for when you establish yourself in a church in California. Christianity doesn't thrive in a vacuum."

"Thanks," Wysong said. "Count me in. What else is on your pre-agenda?"

"The timing of your plan to go west. I have been serving in this Stephen Ministry for the past five years and I'll actually be closing out my active role right about the same time you leave. Of course, I'll continue with my teaching ministry."

Until now Wysong hadn't thought through the changing nature of their relationship, perhaps because he considered it so vital and personal. He was suddenly forced to do so. "I can't tell you how much your caring and teaching have meant to me," he said. "In fact, I won't try at this time. Not only is it too soon, but we still have work to do together."

"It has been my privilege," Shoemaker said, "but first, the third item on my laundry list. It has to do with something called the Walk to Emmaus, a wonderful men's weekend Christian retreat in which our church and many others participate a number of times a year. Have you heard of it?"

"You know," Wysong said, "I have seen it mentioned in the church bulletin and I've wondered what that's all about. In fact, just last Sunday one of the guys in the Singles Sunday School class mentioned it. He even said he would sponsor me if I wanted to go. If you recommend it, then maybe I can squeeze it in at the end of this month."

"Do I recommend it? All I can say is that my own Walk–which was ten years ago–turned out to be the single most meaningful three-day period of my entire life!"

"So, how do you *really* feel about the Emmaus Walk, Mr. Shoemaker?" Wysong said, laughing. Now, what else do you have to sell?"

"Nothing. Let's get down to business. Open your Bible to chapter eight of the Song. Here is what I would like to do. This last chapter is especially important and I want to split it up into two sessions. The first part is not going to make nearly as much sense as when part two is complete. This chapter of Song of Songs is like the Bible itself from the perspective of its two parts being inseparable."

"Fine with me."

"Okay, please read aloud for us verses five through nine."

Wysong read:

"Who is this coming up from the desert,

leaning on her lover?

Under the apple tree I roused you;

there your mother conceived you,

there she who was in labor gave you birth.

Place me like a seal over your heart,

like a seal on your arm;

for love is as strong as death,

its jealously unyielding as the grave.

It burns like blazing fire,

like a mighty flame.

Many rivers cannot wash it away.

If one were to give

all the wealth of his house for love,

it would be utterly scorned.

We have a young sister,

and her breasts are not yet grown.

What shall we do for our sister

for the day she is spoken for?

If she is a wall,

we will build towers of silver on her.

If she is a door,

we will enclose her with panels of cedar."

"Did you get all of that?" Shoemaker said as Wysong finished reading.

"Oh, yeah. But if you can hold off on the pop quiz until next time, I'll bring you an apple."

"This chapter is all about commitment, Pete. Frankly, it, too, is an art. Tommy Nelson expresses this notion by saying that commitment is having the perseverance and perspective to make your marriage last a lifetime."

"Well, I've already failed at that."

"That's history. It can't be changed. But there are lessons that can be learned for the future, and that's what we're talking about. When a person goes into a marriage it is critical to consider divorce not to be an option. Why? Because, if divorce is an option, people will take it. If you see marriage as Christ intended and stay committed for a lifetime, He will give you and your partner abundant joy."

"How can two people commit to the unknown?"

"That's a fair question," Shoemaker said. "Let's deal with that. I'm going to give you a commentary on what you just read and see if it makes more sense. Again, as I said when we first began this study, the interpretation I like for this book is with three main characters, not two, as some prefer."

"Before you launch into the guts of these verses, I need a little review. Explain the book's setting one last time. I'm a slow study."

"Not at all. Solomon, with his many wives, seeks to woo a young Shulamite maiden. But she has a shepherd-lover to whom she is faithful and true. She does not yield to the efforts of Solomon. Every time he flatters her, she begins to speak about her own lover. At the close of the book–which is the chapter we're now dealing with— she is seen united with her shepherd-lover and resting in her love. Remember, in a marriage the wedding is only a ceremony which comes *after* love, not before."

"This is such a beautiful story," Wysong said. "I don't mean to digress, but why do you favor this interpretation versus other interpretations, which cut the shepherd out of it altogether?"

"Because most verse references to Solomon have the city and palace as background whereas references to the shepherd picture him appropriately in a rural setting. In other words, the sharp geographic contrast reinforces the idea that there are two male characters in this poignant drama, not just the polygamist, Solomon."

"But Solomon wrote the poem, Wysong said. "Why would he make himself out to be the bad guy?"

"Ah," Shoemaker said. "But he wrote it at the inspiration of God."

"The prosecution withdraws its motion," Wysong said. "On another point, God's order for His people was monogamy?"

"Not quite," Shoemaker said. "God was actually fine with polygamy for the Old Testament fallen man, but you're right about his order for the redeemed man. That very fact brings into play one other item relative to this interpretation, which is wonderfully made in the Believer's Bible Commentary. The point is that the nation of Israel has been unfaithful to Jehovah (God), running after other lovers. In the Song of Songs we read of the beauty of faithful love."

"I get it," Wysong said as he tightened his lips. "Sad but prophetic. Okay, begin the commentary."

"What do you make of the verse,

'If she is a wall, we shall build on her a battlement of silver?"

"What I read into this is that her brothers are saying they will affirm their sister if she is strong."

"Right on," Shoemaker said. "In other words, if she is a 'wall,' she is sexually closed off to men. She is not immoral. She is pure. She can say no. She will not sell out her virginity."

"Hm'm. That smarts," Wysong said. "I was guilty of *helping* my ex sell out."

"So you have learned. And speaking of how we are to respect our mate, is our loving treatment of our spouse of a higher call than that of saying 'I'm sorry?'"

"No. And sadly, in my own case, I don't recall *ever* saying 'I'm sorry' to Dannie."

"Then when you read the lines,

'Put me like a seal over your heart, like a seal on your arm,'

what do you think the maiden meant?"

"Giving herself over to him?"

"Yes. Ownership. She was saying, 'I don't want any other woman in your heart and I don't want your arm around any other woman. She immediately goes on to say, *'For love is as strong as death, its jealousy unyielding as the grave.'* Now that's a little more cryptic. Its meaning is that once you die you never come back. Love is as severe as death."

"Then what," Wysong said, "is meant by saying love is permanent?"

"That love is a Divine institution," Shoemaker responded. "Just as salvation is of God, so is marriage."

Once again Wysong took the meaning of the verses Shoemaker was dissecting for him personally. "And for someone like me," he said, "who has violated God's trust in that respect, you're simply saying, 'Go, but sin no more.'"

"I don't say it. Christ said it. He said it for everyone. Now, let me wrap things up for this section. God is saying to let nothing quench our love for our mate. He even goes so far as to give us an example in the book of Hosea. Hosea's wife left him to become a temple prostitute, yet, he stayed faithful to God's request and continued to love her. This is a perfect example of the extreme love Christ has for *us*. How have we prostituted His love for us?"

"I now understand such a question" Wysong said. "We have breached the dam. I mean there has been no end to our release of those waters."

"You have that right," Shoemaker affirmed. " Many lives could be changed if the statement I'm about to make were recognized for what it means to a man, as well as to a woman: A girl is ready to be married only when . . . now hear this . . . she is willing to stay single before she will disobey God."

"Whew. I need to loosen my collar. It's getting hot in here."

Shoemaker laughed. "I understand," he said. "It's also time to close out this session. Some of my grandchildren are en route this very minute. We're kid-sitting for our date night."

CHAPTER 33

WYSONG'S WALK

Wysong chose Shoemaker to be his sponsor for his Walk to Emmaus, and the first thing Pete-the-pilgrim did was to attempt to seek out answers as to the details of the weekend retreat. This, even though Shoemaker's advice had been "don't anticipate." He bought several booklets and even went on line, trying to satisfy his curiosity. It was all to no avail, however, in terms of his coming up with anything substantive. When he mentioned his failed exercise in a passing comment to Shoemaker he received a good-natured, yet fatherly rebuke, "Son, you need to stop demanding patience and begin preparing for it."

Chagrinned, Wysong soon came to the conclusion that the retreat would be a special time for reading, relaxation and contemplation. To that end he decided to pack several books he had recently acquired but hadn't yet found time to open. Several days before the start of the Walk, Shoemaker e-mailed him, saying "The location of the Walk's site is on the far side of the county and over a pretty convoluted route, so I'll drive you and we'll stop for a little dinner en route on Thursday evening."

When he picked him up, Wysong's first question was, "How will I get back on Sunday afternoon? This isn't a Snipe Hunt, is it?" He was only half-joking.

"Tell you what," Shoemaker said, " if I'm not there for you by Tuesday, then, 'yeah,' it was a Snipe Hunt." Both of them laughed, but Wysong remained surprisingly anxious.

Once they had arrived at the rural retreat site they were joined by another 30 or so pilgrims and their sponsors for a short devotional time with singing, followed by a time of dessert held in the facility's large kitchen and hosted by the Walk's enthusiastic team of volunteers. Shoemaker and the other sponsors then took their leave.

The lay leader briefly described the agenda for the next three days, as well as certain procedures. The pilgrims were then dismissed to return to their assigned barracks-type rooms with an admonition that they would observe complete silence from that point until after chapel the next morning. *What the heck is this all about?* was the first of Wysong's reactionary thoughts. *So much for my reading agenda. I hope this isn't some sort of cult gathering. No, Will wouldn't do that to me. But, if I had my car here, I might bolt for home and ask for forgiveness later.*

Friday morning was well underway and he still wasn't totally convinced of the wisdom of his decision to attend. He caused himself to think about Shoemaker's comments concerning his own anticipatory experience of the Walk many years earlier. Someone had told him to read what had taken place between Jesus and the two disciples He had joined in walking towards the village of Emmaus the day after Christ's resurrection. Wysong now clearly recalled what Shoemaker had said about that strange event.

His spiritual mentor said the two men walking with Jesus were not able to recognize Him as they had continued to talk of the day's incredible report of the empty tomb. When they stopped at an inn for supper at day's end, Jesus sat down with them. Taking the bread, he blessed and broke and gave it to them. At that moment, wide-eyed, they recognized Him. And then Jesus disappeared. As Wysong was into his recall of Shoemaker's words it was at that moment that he realized the point of it all. During the disciples' walk to Emmaus with the risen-but-unrecognizable Christ, they truly came to *know* Jesus. A short time later they not only received revelation, but also understood the implication of His resurrection. Wysong now needed to apply that message to his own circumstances.

Saturday morning came, and with it Wysong's complete turn-around. Before he knew it, Sunday's late afternoon closing ceremony was underway. It was then that he spotted both Will and June among the crowd of sponsors. The sponsors and friends were all there to hear the testimonies of each of the pilgrims. Each took his turn alphabetically. Wysong was last, of course.

As he stepped up to the microphone he looked directly at Shoemaker. He pointed to him and said, "There he is, folks, right there! The guy I thought on Thursday night had shanghied me into a Jim Jones type cult gathering." The house shook with laughter. "I was scared to even take a drink until the next morning." Again, laughter, none harder than Will's.

"But let me tell you, ladies and gentlemen," Wysong continued, "I have just spent the single most important and meaningful three day period of my entire life. And I thank God that I was able to experience this weekend with such fine fellow pilgrims and this incredibly caring servant team." He looked intently around the room for a moment or two, saying nothing but making eye contact with many, including both Shoemaker and the Walk's lay director.

He continued his comments. "During this weekend I not only placed a huge bag of what I thought were rightful personal worries at the foot of the cross, but I truly surrendered myself to Him. We were told early in the week that we would have the opportunity to tell you what this experience has meant to us. I recall a number of lines from one hymn among many that we sang this week. They so moved me and so reflect the feelings I'll take away from here, that I want to share them once again in a special way."

With that, Wysong motioned to the Walk's music director-and-momentary accomplice seated close to him. The co-conspirator hoisted a guitar from his lap as Wysong said, "Join me in singing, if you will." Everyone was caught by surprise as Wysong's hand came down and his partner began strumming. Microphone in hand, Wysong began to sing in a full-throated and on-key — if unpracticed — voice. At the same time he beckoned the audience to participate.

"In Christ alone my hope is found.

He is my light, my strength, my song.

For ev'ry sin on Him was laid; here in the death of Christ I live.

For I am His and He is mine, bought with the precious blood of Christ.

Till He returns, or calls me home; Here in the power of Christ I'll stand.

Here in the power of Christ I'll stand."

With that, the entire wet-eyed crowd stood as one, clapping their hands and either nodding or slapping the person next to them on the back. Pete sat down and the Walk's lay director took the microphone, saying "And all God's people said . . . "

The crowd responded with "Amen."

Many rushed up to shake Wysong's hand and congratulate him, as well as each of the other pilgrims. Shoemaker quickly found Pete and said, "That was some turnaround, your weekend. From near-desertion to super-witness! Grab your stuff and let's go. June and I are hungry. You can fill us in with the details on the way home."

CHAPTER 34

POLITICS AND RELIGION

Wysong was making sales calls in the Atlanta area the week following his Walk, full of enthusiasm for the experience as well as having found the Lord. He decided to try sharing some of his excitement with several distributors selected for their business and personal relationship rather than for what he thought might be their spiritual beliefs. In the first instance his comments had been met with a shrug and no consequential response. Undeterred, he tried again. In the second instance with an older customer, the interchange following Wysong's brief sharing went like this: "Pete, there are two things I never talk about with either customers or suppliers. The first one is politics and the second one is religion. Now football, that's a different story."

"Why is that?" Wysong said.

"Because with the first two I end up either being the offended or the offendor. I don't like either."

"Well," Wysong said, "I can't speak very knowledgeably to politics, but when it comes to talking about the single most influential person in history, I would have to say He . . . "

The distributor interrupted. "Now you're talking football, the Green Bay Packers, right? Vince Lombardi! Or maybe Bart Starr, or even Bret Favre! Yeah, Favre. I told my wife just the other day that if I knew of something memorable Favre had ever said in an interview–before he left Green Bay—I would put it on my office wall."

Wysong laughed and said, "Gordon, I was talking about Jesus Christ."

Pete's customer's face fell as he said, "Of course you were. That's exactly what I meant by talking religion. You'll offend someone. In this case, me."

"Does what I said really offend you?" Wysong said. "You know, I used to feel the same way, but then I began questioning the lack of satisfaction with my life. As a result I began to investigate the Bible and what Christ had to say about the things of eternity. The bottom line is that I came to realize that if I were on my deathbed and there were any chance whatsoever of Jesus being God, I would want to know that."

"There you go," Wysong's customer said. "The Bible says Jesus came not to unite us, but to divide us. I say you're doing a fine job of that. If you don't mind, I would rather see what new products you have."

Wysong felt the sharp sting of rejection, but something else was speaking to him as well. *Maybe the problem lies with my tactics.*

On the third sales call to see a mother-daughter ownership team whom he had often heard mention their church, he tried a totally different approach. After a minute or so of greeting he said, "I've just returned from a weekend Christian retreat and I'm wondering if you've ever heard the song, 'Everybody talkin' 'bout heaven ain't goin' there?"

Surprised at both the subject and the question, the two women looked at each other and then at Wysong before the mother responded in a serious tone, saying "Indeed I have. As for my daughter and I, we expect to go straight to heaven. Our consciences are clean. What else do you have?"

Wysong's on-the-job evangelistic training obviously wasn't working. He wanted to respond by saying something about what he had learned the previous week, which had to do with self-judgment regarding the purity of one's soul not being the criterion for one's heaven-deserving character. Fortunately, he hadn't the courage to say it.

The morning's efforts with his questions had been a gut-check. He knew full well–from a business perspective–his need to avoid controversial subjects with customers, but he had wanted to examine himself. He gave himself a grade of "A" for enthusiasm, but an "F" for effectiveness. His consolation was something Shoemaker said about Christians' responsibility being to merely *carry* the message, that it was God's job to convict. But there was something more. His thoughts rummaged through some mental files. *Oh, yeah. It was a newspaper article's evangelistic comment by Billy Graham: "God's revelation to believers is not a license to kill."* Wysong knew there had to be a better way.

The next day he again tried something different. Recalling a story the Cobbler had told him during their drive home from his Walk, Wysong planned to share it over lunch with a long-time distributor friend whom he knew had been churched at one time, but had fallen away from God. He let his friend talk about himself for a while before he got around to sharing his idea for moving to the west coast in order to be closer to his young son, even if it meant a complete rep start-over.

"What?" his friend said. "That's pretty risky. But I certainly admire you for doing it."

"Thanks," Wysong said, "but I also wanted to talk to you about another matter. You're a bright guy, Ted. Tell me what you think of the following true story. A man earned a Ph.D. in physical chemistry at Yale and then entered medical school. During his training at a North Carolina hospital, a dying woman often talked to him about her faith in Christ. The man had long rejected the existence of God and thus the call to be accountable to a Creator, but he couldn't ignore the woman's serenity. One day, she asked him, "Doctor, what do you believe?"

At that point Wysong's friend shifted his position at the table as his lunch benefactor continued. "Caught off guard," Wysong said, "the doctor's face turned red as he stammered, 'I'm not really sure.' A few days later the woman died. The young doc became both curious and uneasy about the woman's question. As he did so he realized he had rejected God without adequately examining the evidence."

The friend interrupted, saying "Pete, is this story your way of punctuating the news of your new-found faith?"

"Absolutely," Wysong said as he bulldogged to the finish of his story. "By now," he said, "the young doc had become both curious and uneasy and he began reading the Bible as well as the writings of former atheist-turned-believer C.S. Lewis. A year later the doctor fell to his knees and gave his life to Jesus Christ."

Wysong looked his friend in the eye and said, "Ted, my point is that the catalyst in this story was nothing more than a sincere question from an elderly woman whose heart was failing, but whose concern for others was strong. Why the story, you wonder? It has only been a short time ago that the son of this same doctor helped me find what was missing in my own life."

"Well, "said Wysong's friend, "that's a nice story, but I think religion is a very personal thing. I can see that your faith is good for you, but it's not for me."

As Wysong walked to his car his thoughts were self-examining. *I tried four different approaches to witnessing and none of them were effective, so far as I know. I think I'm beginning to understand something. My enthusiasm and new knowledge have led me to pride, whereas my revelation from God should be leading me to humility. In none of these instances was I actually invited to share.*

CHAPTER 35

CLOSING ON COMMITMENT

The following week Wysong was talking with Shoemaker during their usual Friday session when he said, "Man, did I get shot down this week every time I tried to share my enthusiasm for Christ. I even shared with a friend the story of your father's conversion." Pete laughed and then added, "My customer was more impressed with the joke I had told him earlier about how I used to juggle four clubs and three balls, but that I had given it up because I didn't know what to do with my other hand."

Will smiled and said, "What you did was done from your heart, and you did fine, but only God can change people's hearts. Continue to allow yourself to grow in His Word and mature in your faith and you'll be better able to utilize your gifts by picking both your tools and your battles, so to speak. In the meantime, *live* your newfound faith and don't be hesitant to give your short personal testimony, rather than that of others. As for the juggling jokes, don't give up your repping job."

"Wait a minute," Wysong said in an animated fashion. " What you just said about giving my personal testimony is resonating with me. You're saying that my best witness is how *I* happened to come to the Lord."

"Yes, given someone's interest. Keep it to a minute or two. You know, a relatively few sentences that describe how it was with you before you found Christ, how that happened, and what was different for you after the fact. If you try giving someone medicine who doesn't want it, all they'll do is gag."

"But if God has hardened someone's heart, how can a person overcome it?"

"God doesn't harden anyone's heart," Shoemaker said. "Take the Egyptian Pharaoh, for example. For four hundred years the descendants of Abraham in Egypt had grown to something like two million in number. Pharaoh, the king of Egypt, saw the Israelites as foreigners and upsetting his balance of power. Enslaving them, however, would turn out to be the biggest 'oops'of his career."

"That's when God joined Pharaoh's game of hard-ball?"

"He did, but not until after the Israelites prayed for deliverance from their ordeal. In the process of Pharaoh's refusal to honor Moses' repeated requests to free God's people he hardened his own heart . . . repeatedly. After that, God simply turned him over to his own sins, thus having the effect of Pharaoh's hardening his heart yet further. God does that today when people reject the Holy Spirit. And sometimes–like Pharaoh–they take plague after plague upon themselves."

"Isn't that the unpardonable sin, rejecting the Holy Spirit?"

"It is. But we digress and although this subject is important, why don't we get back to Solomon's Song? I want to give you a little more background on the cunning King before closing out our lessons."

"Okay by me," Wysong said.

Shoemaker launched into the subject. "There was a point at which God gave Solomon the choice of any one thing he wanted. The King wisely decided to ask for the wisdom to discern good from evil so that he might lead God's people well. In the book of Kings we are told that God not only granted Solomon's request, but even promised to give him riches and honor, as well."

Pete recognized the story , saying, "And that spilled down through the generations to 'the wisdom and wealth of Solomon.'"

Shoemaker nodded in the affirmative and continued, saying, "He began his rule with devotion to wisdom and a deep ambition to build a magnificent temple to honor God, something his father, David, had wanted to do but was denied the opportunity by God. Yet something happened on the way to the temple. His passion for living by God's wisdom was displaced by a non-Biblical cliche: 'Power corrupts and absolute power corrupts absolutely.' In other words, Solomon simply wandered from his wisdom."

"I'm curious about something," Wysong said. "What happened to Solomon and his ideals of personally wooing an innocent maiden like the Shulamite, given that he already had a stable of some 80 consorts and 60 queens? Worse, with time didn't he garner a total of something like 700 wives and 300 concubines?"

"It's quite simple," Shoemaker said. "His marriage to foreign women who worshiped pagan gods eventually led him–and ultimately the nation–into idolatry. The lesson for us and also the lesson that leads us to finishing up about commitment in marriage is the same: Keeping our love for Christ and his wisdom preeminent is a primary objective for those who want to live to satisfy God throughout the course of both their marriage and their lives."

"Great segue, Cobbler," Wysong said. "Let me add something to that. As my thoughts of the Lord have begun to permeate everything I do and say, and even think–although not yet continuously–something occurs to me. I can now understand how an unbeliever who is doing well in life nevertheless reaches a point when he knows something is missing. But he still has to be honest with himself and say, as I did, "If you're there, God, show me.""

"That's well stated," Shoemaker said. Then with a wry smile he added, "And, by the way, your use of the nickname 'Cobbler' is actually right on. I never told you, but that was my nickname right up until I finished college. In fact I am honored. Let me share with you a relevant side story about a poor cobbler in the writings of Leo Tolstoy, the Russian literary giant."

Shoemaker continued, saying, "While reading the Gospels the aging shoemaker, who earnestly sought God, heard the Lord say, '*I will come for you tomorrow. Look for me on the street.*' Day came and the old man received a procession of three visitors. First, he invited an old man in from the freezing snow and gave him tea. Then he found a poor mother and her baby outside with no jacket. He gave her a warm coat. Finally, a hungry boy stole an apple, was caught and faced severe punishment. The shoemaker paid for the fruit and defended the lad."

Wysong was intently listening. "That night," Shoemaker said, "the man 'saw' each of the three visitors in the dark corner of his tiny room. They each laughed. As they were disappearing, the shoemaker asked, *'Who are you?'* Then he heard the voice of the Lord. *'It is I,'* the Lord told him. *'For where love is, God is.'*"

Wysong smiled broadly. First of all, he was relieved he hadn't offended his mentor. Secondly, he understood the message.

"Okay," Shoemaker said, "away we go with our final installment of this incredible love story. You know by now that in order to have a Godly marriage, Jesus Christ must be your Lord *as well as* your Savior. Here we want to deal with being committed to God and then to one another. Now, if you would, Pete, read aloud these final five verses of the Song."

"Will do. I've read them before but a lot of it is still 'Hebrew' to me.

'I am a wall, and my breasts are like towers.

Thus I have become in his eyes like one bringing contentment.

Solomon had a vineyard in Baal Hamon;

he let out his vineyard to tenants.

Each was to bring for its fruit a thousand shekels of silver.

But my own vineyard is mine to give;

the thousand shekels is for you, O Solomon,

and two hundred are for those who tend its fruit.

You who dwell in the gardens with friends in attendance,

let me hear your voice!

Come away, my lover!

and be like a gazelle or like a young stag

on the spice-laden mountains.'"

Shoemaker said as he looked at Wysong, "I know, I know. But bear with me. It's worth taking a look at the thread of this rich fabric of verses. For starters, we have the maiden's assurance to her brothers that since she is now of marriageable age, she has been steadfast as a wall. Her lover knows that. Further, she tells them of Solomon's vineyard with its many tenants but then, in a surprise, shares what she thinks of his—Solomon's—offer. And what *is* that?"

"This is so cool," Wysong said. "I'd laugh except that it hits too close to home. She tells him to 'take a hike.'"

"Right. She says she has her *own* vineyard, which is where?"

"As I read it and now hear it, it's not 'where' at all."

"Precisely," Shoemaker said. "Her 'vineyard' is her shepherd-lover. Then, amid the presence of witnesses, the shepherd-lover asks the Shulamite maiden to commit herself to him in marriage, to say, 'I do.' And how did her lover respond?"

Wysong felt led to jump to his feet as if a fan at a football game, cheering for his team. As he did so he shouted—right arm raised in enthusiasm—'Come and claim me, sweetheart. And be quick about it!'" He sat back down, saying, "Man, you gotta love it!"

Shoemaker nodded his head and said, "Thus the book closes. To quote my favorite commentary, this has been called the Old Testament's endorsement of monogamy in the face of the most glaring example of polygamy to be found in the Scriptures. Now you can better understand why I prefer the interpretation of the two males versus the single voice of Solomon, the polygamist. For what it's worth on that note, the otherwise much more beneficent younger King Solomon became spiritually bankrupt in his later years, to which you earlier alluded. In any event, don't you see how this is a powerful plea to Israel of Solomon's day to return to the God-given ideal of love and marriage?"

"I do." Wysong said, "And in all humility I have to say you have done a fine triple-threat job in reaching this former pagan. That includes effectively conveying to me the holy meaning of the institution of marriage, leading me to God's saving grace, and taking a personal interest in ministering to me at a time when I didn't know where to turn."

"You are too generous, my boy, but I appreciate that very much. We are nearly finished with our study of the Song of Songs, but we still have a couple of very important points to establish for the commitment in marriage. These are extremely well illustrated in Nelson's study. Here's his first one: What do you make of the Shulamite maiden's phrase . . . '*thus I became in his eyes like one bringing contentment?*'"

Wysong thought about that for a few seconds before commenting. "She found peace in her shepherd-lover's eyes?"

Shoemaker nodded and said, "There is that. But she also believed that God had placed her in his path. In fact, there is a corollary to that statement and it goes like this: 'Get in the path that a woman is in as she is looking for that kind of man.' Think about that for a minute. That's the way I felt about my late wife as well as I do of June. God surely placed each of them in my path."

"I hope that will yet happen to me," said Wysong. "I never gave my first marriage a chance, and neither did my ex-wife. I'm ashamed of that, but as you have said many times, 'That is history.'"

Shoemaker was ready to wrap things up. He said, "Then you're ripe for understanding how to apply these verses to your relationship with any future prospective mate. And if I were to give you a 'pop' quiz on the subject of how you should address such a relationship, what would be your answer?"

"To give oneself totally and completely to one another?"

"That's half of it,"Shoemaker said. "But for how long?"

"Until the day you die."

"You're clear, brother. Let me close both this session and our study of this special book with a verse from another book, Matthew 19:6. It is one I have repeated *three* times in my life.

'So they are no longer two, but one.

Therefore what God has joined together, let man not separate.'"

Wysong furrowed his brow and said, "*Three* times? Didn't you say you have only been married twice?"

"You're correct. In addition, my late wife and I repeated our vows on our 30ᵗʰ anniversary, six months before the Lord called her home."

"I'm sorry," Pete said, wishing he hadn't asked the question. "But the way you stated that verse does raise one last question. You said 'let not man separate.' I've always heard that phrase stated as 'let *no* man separate.' What's different?"

Shoemaker looked up at Wysong in surprise. "Do you know, I've never had anyone ask that question before. You are absolutely correct in your observation. The reality is that what was once common usage isn't used at all any more. But the verse isn't suggesting that someone might actually object to the marriage–even with reason— or that someone could somehow cause a split between a man and his wife. What is meant is that God intended marriage to be permanent, therefore *mankind* should understand God's will in that respect."

CHAPTER 36

WYSONG'S TESTIMONIAL

Months earlier Wysong had secured a ticket to his alma mater's homecoming game in Tallahassee. He hadn't been to a Florida State University football game in more than ten years and he was really looking forward to the Saturday afternoon game, as well as the weekend with old school friends. He had been calling on accounts in Jacksonville all week and immediately after a quick lunch on Friday he headed west and the 200 mile drive to Tallahassee.

He was talking on his cell phone with Wally Barneveld, his pal from college days, and the man whom he still considered to be his all-around best friend. Barneveld had gotten tickets for Wysong as well as for himself and his wife. Pete would be staying at their home for the weekend. "Wally," he said, " just read off the top five things you have lined up for me the weekend, other than the game. I want to review them."

"Uh, I didn't realize you were coming *this* weekend," Barneveld said, not wanting to be one-upped.

"Okay, wise guy," Pete said, remembering that his good friend could return service as well as serve, "let's get serious for a moment. There *are* two specific things I would like to do."

"Let me guess," Wally said. "A visit to the one place on campus you have never been–the library—and a frantic search for some woman who would be willing to lower her standards by going to the game with you. Pretty close, huh?"

"Look, buddy . . . " Wysong began and then paused for a moment as he waved at the occupants of two cars in passing them. Both cars had 'Go, Seminoles!' flags flying from their radio antennas, ". . . okay," he said, "I'm back. I know for a fact you couldn't find the library with a map. As for a date, well, I think it's a little late into the week for that. No, what I would like is to go to church with you and Sherry on Sunday morning."

Wally was taken aback. "Are you serious?" he said.

"I know. I know. Pete Wysong-and-faith, an oxymoronic statement. Used to be, for certain. People change. I'll share my testimony with you tonight."

"Great. I can't wait to hear it, brother. But what's your other wish?"

"Oh. Yeah. Remember when we created our 'Flying Fools' routine for the Circus? You, the clumsy catcher, and me the fearless flyer? Do you think we could visit the Flying High big top? The FSU Circus is still active, isn't it?"

"Of course," Barneveld said. "They even perform out of state on occasion, as well as in Europe and Canada. This is November, though, and I don't know if the circus tent is still up or not, but we'll check it out. I guess you've forgotten that the Flying Fools act lasted exactly two weeks before the flyer crashed and burned and was reduced to juggling in order to get his one-hour elective credit."

"Yeah, well, I can still juggle. How's your 'catching' career working out?"

"Enough of this banter," Barneveld said. "See you for dinner."

That evening, Wysong and the Barnevelds regaled each other with both common and familiar stories, as well as getting caught up with their lives. At Pete's insistence, the couple had first shared with their guest. "Now it's your turn," they said in sing-song unison as they glanced at each other before turning to face Wysong.

"Where do I start?" he said. "You knew that my ex-wife and I were on a rocky road almost from the beginning. We literally slugged it out through marriage, separations, and reconciliations. At least until we finally decided to take off the gloves and spurs in arriving at a divorce settlement. She got the house and the little car. I took the big car and most of our debt. And as for Billy, we split up the weekends until a year ago when she took our son and moved to California."

"California?" Wally said. "That couldn't have been good news."

"No kidding," Wysong said, sarcastically. "She moved to be near her parents but it wasn't long before she began chasing after some hard luck building contractor she met at a trade show. Neither I nor my divorce attorney were smart enough to address the possibility that she might leave town and take Billy with her. Well," he added as he slapped one knee, "that's the downside to my life."

"Sorry about that, Pete," Wally said. "We didn't know the particulars."

"Get to the upside," Sherry chimed in. We're dying to know about your coming to the Lord."

"You know," Wysong began, "I've never really put it all together for anyone. For quite a while following the divorce I was wallowing in a pit of anger, unhappiness and self-pity, desperately wanting someone to climb into the pit with me. I actually went to a church once out of that attitude, even though I didn't really have a clue as to what to expect. It wasn't that I hated God because of my circumstances, it's just that I had never known him to either hate *or* love."

"And did you find help there?" Sherry asked.

"That came a little later," he said, "but shortly after my one-time visit to the church I met a wonderful woman through a Christian dating service. I took her to lunch but it didn't take long before she saw through my 'fellow-Christian' story. She took me to task for lying to her about my faith and then she dumped me before we could get to desert. The really sad part of this is that I was smitten by her from the get-go. But I never got up to bat a second time."

"I have news for you, All-Star," Barneveld said. "You don't get a second at-bat once you're been ejected from the game."

"I know. Don't remind me. But that's what sent me looking for help. I remembered the Stephen Ministry inquiry I had made at the church and I called them. I was surprised when they assigned someone to me. A wonderful man, a Stephen Minister by the name of Will Shoemaker, took me under his spiritual wing."

"That had to be a positive step forward," Sherry said.

203

"But things didn't start well," he said. "I took a poor attitude to the first few meetings. I think all I really wanted at the time was someone to commiserate with me over getting the shaft in life."

"Stephen Ministry," Wally said, emphasizing the name as he glanced at his wife. "We have that lay ministry program at our church. Sherry and I have yet to sign up for training, but we have talked about it. So what happened after you got over your snit?"

"Snit?" Wysong said. "I can't argue with that description. In any event, he wouldn't punch my card. Funny thing is he was more than happy to listen. Turns out he was also a lay Bible teacher."

"Whoa!" Barneveld said. "You got a two-fer."

"It was actually a three-fer. I'll tell you why. First of all, I shared with him about wanting to understand what the born again thing was all about. Surprisingly, after I told him more of my background and marriage than I had planned I found him to be totally sympathetic, even offering to give me a short course on Biblical marriage. What was I going to do, turn him down?"

Wally shook his head and said, "Man, did he take on a load!"

"Yeah. I know. But in short order I began to understand I had gone about my marriage all wrong and that God has very different—and specific—ideas in that regard."

"You know," said an encouraging Barneveld, "most men in your shoes hang out at the school of blaming their ex rather than going in for some self-examination. Good on you, mate."

"Thanks," Wysong said, "but I can tell you that I was conflicted about what I was doing. Sure, I had invited his teaching along with his ear, but at the same time I challenged him on both his marriage and faith perspectives. Remember, all I wanted was ammunition for another shot at the woman who saw through me before we could get to dessert. "

Wally and Sherry looked at each other and shook their heads as they chortled disrespectfully.

Wysong ignored them and said, "Believe it or not, the Cobbler—that's what I call Shoemaker—started me off in the Old Testament book of Songs. I mean Solomon's Song of Songs. One of Shoemaker's goals was to convey God's message to me about the sanctity of marriage. As I said, I didn't buy it at first. But after a while I realized that I had subconsciously bought into my own father's warped ideas of marriage. My dad left sacrificial love totally out of his marriage to my mother."

"You mean," Barneveld said, "now we no longer have to hide the women and children when you come around?"

"Now that hurts," Wysong said, " but it isn't the half of things. In the bargain the Cobbler led me to Christ." Wysong paused, a thought catching his attention. "Or, now that I think about it, it might have been the other way around. I mean, my understanding of Christ's teaching began to allow me to grasp what marriage is all about. Why Jesus could love me was a totally alien concept for this good-time-Pete."

"Keep talking," Sherry said. "Wally and I are once again amazed at how mysteriously the Lord works."

Wysong was reveling in the first-time detailed sharing of his growth, this time having been asked. "You know," he said, "I think the hardest thing of all for me to learn was that as Christians we're not here for our own purpose at all. We're here for the purpose of God. The two are not the same. One of the first things I came to learn from Shoemaker is that if a man does not believe that Jesus is God in flesh, he does not believe in His name."

"Wow, that was a good start," Wally said.

"Yes, it was. But I grasped the idea intellectually long before I took it to heart. Listen to me," Wysong said. "I'm preaching to the choir. You guys have known for a long time what it has taken me 36 years to learn. No, that isn't right. Actually, it has taken me less than a year, because for 35 years I barely knew *about* Him, let alone *knew* Him."

As Barneveld had been listening to Wysong an idea began edging itself into his head. As the notion continued to press on him he could no longer resist. Finally, he jumped in with it. "Pete, why don't you share your story with our Sunday School class tomorrow? We'll meet for an hour at 9:30 and then the three of us can make it to the 11:00 sanctuary service. We usually have about 40 or so folks in attendance at the Sunday school class. I know our teacher will be glad to give you 15 minutes or so. What do you say?"

"Whoa, whoa, Catcher. I've never done that before. I'm not sure I'm ready for prime time. Besides, your teacher might not go along with it."

"What do you mean you're not ready?" Barneveld said indignantly. "You just finished rehearsing your witness. All you have to do is tell it again. Besides, you'll have a little time early tomorrow morning to think it through. As for the teacher, I have a little pull."

CHAPTER 37

SUNDAY SCHOOL

The next morning the two friends drove off to the campus to inspect what they could of the Flying High unit during the off-performance season. Sherry saw to cleaning house and cooking for the evening meal to follow the big Saturday afternoon game.

Driving to the campus interior they quickly spotted the huge tent and parked close by. As they approached the entrance, they saw someone exiting and locking the main entrance door. Both of the men recognized him and Wally shouted, "Hey, Coach, can you use a couple of 'Fools' for a headliner act?"

Coach turned around and looked at the pair for several seconds before responding in recognition. "Let's see, now. Yeah, Barneveld, you can clean up after the elephant act we don't have. And, Wysong, I don't recall that you ever passed the juggling final." Then he laughed and greeted them with bear hugs, saying "Good to see you, boys. I don't see many former 'Flying High' troupers once they go out into the real world. I'll bet Wysong is here for the homecoming game, huh? You still live in town, don't you, Barneveld?"

Wally said, "Right on both counts. I didn't think you would recognize Pete, but he's also going to visit our Sunday School class tomorrow." Looking at Wysong, but speaking to Coach, he said, "I haven't told him you're the teacher, but the 'juggler' has recently come to the Lord and he might be willing to share his witness with the class."

Wysong looked surprised, but didn't say anything. Coach said, "Now *that's* what I call good news, son." He clapped Pete on his shoulder and added, "See you tomorrow morning, boys. Sorry, but I have to run. Enjoy the football game even though it's not 'The Greatest Collegiate Show On Earth!'" The rest of the day went well for Wysong, especially with the drubbing his team gave the visitors.

The next morning, at Wally's Sunday School class Coach introduced Pete as a former Flying High Circus member. He added that, along with Barneveld, they were the only pair of 'Fools' he had ever passed out of his course. He then qualified his teasing of Wysong by saying, "Welcome a man who just this year discovered that the Ultimate Coach had been hiding in plain sight all of his life." The class roared with laughter as they shouted 'Hallelujahs.'

Pete stepped forward and after thanking both Coach and the Barnevelds for their hospitality, began recounting in some detail how the Lord had revealed Himself to him. Towards the end of his fifteen-minute witness–and in a surprise move for all but one other person in the room—he reached under the podium and pulled out three juggling clubs. At Wysong's request Coach had placed them there earlier that morning. Someone in the class said, "Throw 'em high, Seminole!"

Wysong immediately began juggling the three clubs as he continued his testimonial. "Let me tell you about one of the most important lessons I have learned in my coming to the Lord." At that point he moved from single spins to double-spinning each club. He continued speaking. "Imagine, if you will, a paying audience watching a Flying High juggling performer who suddenly makes a drop in the middle of his act." He punctuated his statement by dropping one of the clubs out of his routine. Quickly picking it up he resumed juggling as well as continuing with his message.

"As the juggler regains his composure," Wysong said, "and proceeds with his act, he nevertheless drops a second time, and then a third." At that point Wysong made two more deliberate drops followed by smooth transition pick-ups in illustrating his point. He even threw in a gratuitous drop-line in saying, "You know, my business is really picking up." At Coach's lead, everyone groaned.

Wysong ignored the reaction and continued his club juggling. "So," he said, "the performer's sloppy routine continues until a few moments later he finds his audience becoming restless. In fact, because several of them were especially short on forgiveness, they begin booing him." Wysong stopped juggling and said something guaranteed to bring a cheer from the class, "Must have been some University of Florida fans in the crowd."

The class laughed and Wysong resumed juggling, this time giving each club triple spins. He then caught each of them in turn and took a quick bow. The class began to applaud, but he quickly put up the palm of one hand to indicate he hadn't finished.

"Now," he said, "consider how sharp a contrast that sort of human response to others' mistakes is to Almighty God . . . who *never* fails to forgive us our mistakes. All we have to do is ask for that forgiveness. . . and then go forth, spending more time correctly practicing life's routines. Now before I wrap this up let me say that until I became *hungry* for Christ, I could not find satisfaction with life. His glory took me to Christ. That grace took me to the cross. And truth took me to the Word of God, salvation, and redemption. I now stand before you a satisfied man."

He paused and looked around the room, letting the comment sink in before adding, "But there is more. Until I became *thirsty* for Him, my soul remained parched. Not until I sought the Lord did I realize that the primary reason for the failure of my marriage was because I had not let Him into my life." The class wanted to applaud but restrained themselves for the moment as Wysong again looked around the room.

"In closing," he said, "let me paraphrase the message God gave to His people through the prophet Amos: 'God wants only one thing. He wants you. That's *all* He wants.' Thank you."

On that note Coach came forward to hug his former pupil as the class erupted with the applause it had been holding in abeyance.

The church service itself followed. As the three of them left the sanctuary, Wysong said, "Wow! How appropriate was the pastor's sermon, preaching about the importance of allowing God to use others to both encourage us and hold us accountable. I thank you guys for your hospitality, your support and your sharing. It has truly been great!" Wally and Sherry were equally appreciative of both Pete and the events of the weekend, and said so.

CHAPTER 38

BILLY

Wysong drove back to his Atlanta area home in a little over six hours. Weary from the day and about to retire at nearly 10:00 P.M., the phone rang. "Pete," said the voice on the other end, "this is Frank, Dannie's father."

"Hey, Frank!" Pete said, certain the call had to be to congratulate him on the Seminole's televised win. In the back of his mind, however, his thoughts were, *Frank doesn't care about college football. He rarely calls for any reason. And he never calls late at night.*

"Pete," Frank said in a halting voice, "I have some terrible news. Archie and Dannie were headed back from Escondido from an auto race—across the mountains on highway 78. A drunken driver missed a curve and plowed, head-on, into their pick-up." At that point, Frank broke down.

Wysong said, "Frank, what happened?" His voice betrayed his fear at what might yet be coming.

"Their truck went off the road and rolled . . . and they . . . and Billy . . . well, they're all hurt bad and in the hospital." Frank broke down a second time.

"When did it happen, Frank? Which hospital? How badly is Billy hurt?"

Wysong could hear Frank take in a big gulp of air as he tried his best to finish the story. "It happened almost two hours ago. It took an hour for the ambulance and a fire truck to get to them after a witness called 911. They're in Escondido Methodist."

Wysong was beside himself. "Frank, what about Billy! How bad is he?" Then he caught himself. "I'm sorry, you have a daughter in this also."

"That's okay," Frank said, but Wysong could tell from his voice that things weren't okay. "Both Dannie and Archie have broken limbs and facial cuts. They'll recover, but Billy . . ." He broke down a third time before managing to say, "Billy has a punctured lung. He's in Intensive Care. You'd better get out here. I'll give you the ICU phone number. I'm so sorry."

CHAPTER 39

CALAMITY

After a seemingly endless red-eye flight and a short rental car drive from the San Diego airport to Escondido, Wysong burst into the second floor ICU waiting room where Frank and Emma were sitting, trying to comfort one another. They both rushed to hug Pete. He had been on the cell phone with Frank a number of times during the previous nine hours since the initial phone call. "I need to see Billy," he said. "Where is he?"

"I alerted the ICU duty nurse that you were coming," Frank said. "She'll take you to him, but they only allow one visitor in the room at a time." The grandfather looked down the hallway. "There she comes now. We'll be right here."

The nurse said, "You must be Billy's father. I'll escort you to the ICU room."

As she led him down the hall he said, "What's his status?"

"He's critical," she said. "I'll call the doctor for you."

Wysong entered the intensive care room to see tubes and monitors connected all about the eight-year old. "Billy," he said softly, bending down to touch his son's forehead. "Daddy's here. If you can hear me, son, know that I won't be leaving your side." He glanced at the attending nurse, hoping for some sort of reassurance. The nurse's only response was a tight-lipped nod.

Wysong continued his apologetic monologue. "I'm moving out here to be near you, son. You've got to get well. Hang on. Hang on, son," he pleaded." With that he fell to his knees at the bedside. "Almighty God," he said, lightly clutching one of Billy's arms, "hear my prayer. My son has done nothing to deserve this. It's all my fault. I lift him up before you, Father. Please spare his life." He paused a moment to think before resuming his prayer. "Dear God, I don't know what else to say. I'm new at this. Thank you, Lord, for my new life. Now I ask you for my son's." He tried to think of something else to say. Instead he ended with, "In Jesus' name. Amen."

As he opened his eyes and then stood he saw a white-jacketed doctor rush through the doorway followed by two orderlies. As the orderlies quickly took hold of the bed to move it through the door, the doctor said, "Mr. Wysong, follow us. They just brought your son back from radiology. We're going to have to open him up again. We performed surgery on his lung an hour ago, but he's still bleeding internally."

Wysong was walking alongside his son's bed while doing his best to speak coherently to the doctor. "How could he have suffered a punctured lung?" he said. "I understand his seat belt was fastened."

The doc glanced at him and shrugged his shoulders. "Who knows?" he said. "If he was in the back seat, which is what I was told, he wouldn't likely have had an air bag to cushion him as would those in the front seats. When the truck rolled, he could have sustained the injury to his lung any number of ways."

Pete persevered, saying, "What about his other lung? Won't that carry him?"

"Not if he continues to bleed internally."

Pete dropped back as they rushed through the 'Staff Only' door to the operating room area. A nurse put up one hand saying, "Please, sir. Remain in the waiting room back down the hall." She pointed back to where Pete had first seen Frank. "Either I or a volunteer at the desk will relay updates to you. We may need some blood from you."

"I understand," Wysong said. "Do everything you can, please. He's my son." He repeated his plea, no louder, but with greater emotion. "He's my son." By then he was standing alone outside the operating room. With that he headed back to the waiting room, hands enfolding the sides of his head, tears streaming down his cheeks.

His ex-wife's parents were still in the waiting room. Pete hugged them both again as he began peppering them with statements and questions. "I don't know if he'll make it. I'm going crazy. Who was driving? Dannie or her boy friend? Isn't it a law to have side air bags in the back seat? How old a truck is it? How many times did the truck roll?"

"I don't know the answers to most of those questions, Pete," Frank said as gently as he could. "I think the best thing we can do right now is pray."

Pete lifted his head out of his hands, eyes still streaming tears, his emotions tumbling. "All I'm feeling is numbness. Billy is only a little boy. Why him? Is this my baptism for becoming a Christian late in life?"

"I'm an old man, Pete," Frank began, "and not very smart at that. But what I do know is that God can handle your anger. Go ahead and tell Him how you feel."

That's exactly what Pete did. For several minutes he let his emotions run, alternately pleading with God and blaming Him as well as blaming himself. An interminable thirty minutes followed, during which Wysong simply sat, his eyes glazed over. Every few minutes his former in-laws tried talking to him, but he would not respond. As they were trying one more time the nurse who had received Pete when he first arrived entered the room. He searched her face, hoping for a clue, but he couldn't force himself to interpret anything.

"Mr. Wysong," she said in a sympathetic tone, "would you come down the hall? The doctor would like to talk with you."

Frank said, "Go ahead, son. If we're not here when you return, we'll be checking on Dannie. She's been admitted to a room on the third floor."

The nurse led Pete to an alcove off the main hallway. The same doctor he had raced down the hallway with was sitting there. He stood as Pete entered the area and said, "I'm sorry Mr. Wysong. Three of us worked on Billy. We couldn't stop the bleeding. It was massive. Two different blood vessels had ruptured."

Pete said, "What do you mean? They're still working on him, aren't they? He isn't going to die, is he?"

"Mr. Wysong," the doctor said, as tenderly as he knew how, "There was nothing further we could do. Once the aorta gave out, the heart had no resource for blood and the boy's brain became deprived of oxygen. I'm so very sorry. I will try to answer any questions you have."

Pete slumped onto a chair, wailing, his head pitching forward into his hands. After a moment the doctor placed a hand on his shoulders without saying a word. Pete looked up at him and shook his head as he tried to stem the tears. "I have no family," he said. "I lost my wife. My son has just died. I may as well be dead, myself."

The doctor said, "I'll be happy to call the hospital chaplain for you, Mr. Wysong, but I'm confused about something. You said you lost your wife. I understood that her injuries weren't life threatening."

Pete looked at him forlornly and said, "We divorced almost a year ago. If I had kept our marriage intact, as God intended, Billy would be alive today." He caught his breath, wiped his eyes for the hundredth time during the past few hours, and forced himself into some degree of coherency. "Thank you for doing all you could, doctor. I'll break the news now to my son's mother." He got up to leave, but hesitated. Turning back to the doctor he said, "Could I meet with the chaplain?"

CHAPTER 40

COMFORT

A balding man in his mid fifties entered the small but adequate chapel in which Pete was sitting with his head held in his hands. "Mr. Wysong," he said, "my name is Ron. I'm the hospital chaplain. I'm so sorry to hear about your son. May I sit down?"

"It's your chapel," an emotionally conflicted Wysong said. "I don't even know why I asked the doctor to see you. I don't know which is my greater emotion right now: sadness or anger."

"I can understand that," the chaplain said, reaching out to put a hand on Pete's shoulder.

At that, Wysong shrank back, his nostrils suddenly flaring against tear-soaked cheeks, "No you don't!" he all but screamed. "You have *no* idea. I've only recently accepted Jesus Christ as my Lord and Savior and *this* is what I get in return! I don't know whether to regret having placed my trust in Him, or pray that he take me out right here and now."

The chaplain's response was to gently say, "I *do* understand, Mr. Wysong. I understand that your loss is so great that you don't know where to place your feelings. But be assured that God can handle whatever you decide to deposit with Him." He hesitated for a moment and then added, " I'm glad to hear that you know Jesus. I know this sounds hollow at the moment, but Christ Himself encourages us with these words: "Blessed are those who mourn for they will be comforted.""

Wysong tried to reach down inside himself for that comfort, but he couldn't do it. Instead, with a momentary sense of bitterness, he asked the chaplain, "Where was God when my son died?"

Softly and compassionately the chaplain responded. "The same place He was when His own Son died."

With barely a moment's hesitation tears again fell from Wysong's eyes, realizing his misplaced reaction. He looked up at the chaplain and shook his head in saying, "I'm mourning, but I have no comfort."

The chaplain was up to the moment and said, "To that I can only tell you that when I lost a close family member I turned away from myself and to the One who suffered on my behalf. Whenever I would grieve with Christ I always found comfort. In fact, He would dry up my tears almost instantly, although they would return many times."

Uncharacteristically, Wysong reached for another man's shoulder. Amidst his sobs he said, "I'm lost. Isn't it also right for me to be angry?"

The chaplain hugged him and affirmed understanding by patting him several times on the back. Drawing back a little he said, "That's a very good question. God allows things in our lives that are often not to our liking or apparent benefit, for the purpose of our becoming more dependent upon Him. I know that's hard to understand, and you probably won't understand today or even tomorrow. But if you let it, that time will come."

Wysong wiped his eyes again and said, "But I don't know how to deal with my grief. I feel like I'm dying."

"Then go ahead and share those feelings with Him. He's a big God."

"I want to, but I'm not sure how to do that."

"Maybe it will help to know this, brother. Christ is now in you, and you in Him. The Maker of the universe is in this with you if you simply open up and allow him to wrap His arms around you."

Wysong looked up, blinked once, and quietly nodded, indicating that he had some understanding. "You know," he said, "I'm not the only one who needs comfort at this time. But my grief is too great to be of help to her at this moment. Would you speak to Billy's mother about her loss? She's in room 3027. Please tell her I'll see her shortly. And thank you so much for your help."

CHAPTER 41

STILL REELING

"Will," Wysong was saying to Shoemaker at his home several days after his return, "thank you for your phone calls to comfort me while I was in California." He had wanted to come to the Shoemaker home rather than having him see the mess that had accumulated in his apartment.

"Of course," Shoemaker said as he gestured towards the chair in which Pete always sat during his visits. "I can't imagine the difficulty of the past week or so. Laying a child to rest is surely the most agonizing thing a parent could ever go through. Tell me about how you're doing."

"I don't know how I'm doing," he said, "except that I have been crying rivers of tears for the entire time. I can't seem to come to grips with the reality of never seeing Billy again." At that, he pulled his hands together inside of his legs and leaned forward in his chair, his emotions suddenly letting go.

Will was facing him at the time and he reached out, putting a hand on each of Pete's shoulders as he said, "It's okay. Just let it out. God hears your cries and he will comfort you."

After a moment Pete said, "You're right, and I know it. He has and He is. Thank you, my friend."

Shoemaker's wife came into the room with a plate of cookies she had just baked, offering them to Pete. "It's good to see you, son," she said. "Please, take two or three. Otherwise I'll have to set a mousetrap near them to keep Will at bay."

Wysong smiled and said, "You know him pretty well, don't you?"

"Don't I?" she said. "But that's the responsibility that goes with marriage. Working at understanding your spouse is what keeps married life both interesting and stretching."

At that point Will couldn't resist jumping in, saying, "You know, she never ceases to surprise me. In fact, once she even qualified the comment she just made by saying, 'Your job is to figure me out, and my job is to keep you guessing!'"

Wysong laughed and shook his head, saying, "You two are a hoot. Thank you, June. Don't mind if I do have a couple of these delicious looking low-calorie treats."

"You're entirely welcome," she said, "but you're way too young to be worrying about calories." She winked at her husband and added, "Now, if you'll excuse me I have some work to do in the kitchen."

Shoemaker nodded and said, "Thank you, sweetheart." Then, as his wife left the room he turned to Wysong and said, "I found her whom my soul loves."

Pete chewed on that for a moment and said, "You build her up even when she isn't in the room. That beats the dickens out of how I treated Dannie, not to mention how I defrauded Marlene the first time I met her, always seeking to get what I wanted."

"Well said, my friend. But don't keep beating yourself up over that. You're on a new path now." Shoemaker paused and said, "Look, you have a great deal on your mind. Are you certain you wouldn't like to talk a little more about things? I know everything is terribly painful, but talking about things at this stage is better than bottling them up."

Wysong nodded and said, "If I'm able. It was so sad. I did talk with Dannie that night but there wasn't much we could say to one another. I apologized for my shortcomings during our marriage. I'm glad she has someone to help her through her loss. That is, if the relationship with her boy friend holds. Obviously there was no point to my staying around any longer than necessary. She was discharged the next day, and Billy was cremated three days later. A pastor at the grandparents' church conducted the memorial service. We each have an urn of his ashes."

"Any particular thoughts about the service itself," Shoemaker said.

"It's interesting that you should ask. There was. The pastor offered the sacrament of communion, and as he prepared us for that he made a connection between the Old Testament's sacrifice of an unblemished Passover Lamb and the sacrifice of Jesus' unblemished, righteous life. His point being that without the shedding of blood there is no forgiveness."

"What was the significance of that moment for you, Pete?"

"That's the really interesting part. As I prepared to participate in the Lord's Supper I had an image of Billy and I together last Summer—out in that beautiful field of grass—as he was learning to throw a boomerang. I value that positive image and memory. Then, as I took the bread and juice at the service I recalled how Jesus painted a memory picture for His disciples as He served them at His last Passover meal. What binds everything together for me now is the picture of Christ's sacrificial love, of His broken body and shed blood. You have told me more than once that if we share that image often we will never lose it. I don't want to lose the connection between my son and God the Father's."

"That is a wonderful association," Shoemaker said. "Taking communion should always serve to remind us of the memory of the greatest love the world has ever known, as well as Jesus' assurance of our unearned blessings."

Wysong nodded and said, "You know, after the service I spoke with the pastor and he said something else that I'll never forget. He told me to consider allowing the memory of Billy's life to be a special reminder of the kindling of the hope of a joyous reunion."

At that, Shoemaker looked pensive and said, "You have just described a humble and examined heart, my friend. I am so blessed that you have come to this."

"Thanks, Will. Your saying that means a great deal to me. I find that I still require a lot of time alone, however. I suppose because I have so many regrets."

Shoemaker nodded. "I understand," he said, "and I'm so sorry. If you'll pardon my sharing something I once read concerning regret, it is this by Henry David Thoreau. I have obviously never let it go. What he said is so simple and yet so profound: 'Make the most of your regrets. To regret deeply is to live afresh.' Does that make any sense to you?"

"H'mm. I'm not certain. If it means that the hard-earned lessons of our sins and slip-ups are making us who we are, it does make sense. But I hate the process."

"Of course you do," Shoemaker said. He wrinkled his face as if he were pondering something. "Tell me," he said, "how were things left with everyone out there."

"Not very good," Wysong admitted. "I blamed myself. My ex blamed her boy friend. He blamed the drunken driver. Only the grandparents–God bless them–refused to assign blame. Do you know what their position was?"

"I would be interested to know."

"It's close to your point about regrets. That God sometimes uses catastrophe to teach us greater dependance upon Him. I still don't get that. All I feel is grief, loss, and more grief. For me, focus is a stranger."

"I know. I know. Grieve away. It's important to do so. If you don't work through it now, you'll only have to do so later. Know, however, that you will be comforted in your grief."

"That's the second time I've heard that," Wysong said. "Both you and the hospital chaplain must be working from the same book, but it still sounds contradictory."

"The Bible is very clear on this," Shoemaker said. "It tells us that those who mourn will be blessed through comfort because of their faith. You know that Billy is in heaven, in God's presence. And because of that he is no longer hurting or broken. Now here's another way to look at this: At the same time he faded from your sight, those on the other side were welcoming him."

"What a beautiful thought," Wysong said, finding it difficult to speak through fresh tears. "Not only to I need to believe that, I need to remember it."

"First of all," Shoemaker responded, "you need to believe that God is in control of your life. Consider that both you *and* God can't be in control of your life. If you think *you're* in control, then God is *not* in control."

Pete pondered Shoemaker's comment for a moment before saying, "Since the Lord has reached down and touched me–through your caring ministry–I *do* believe He is in control, even though I continue to struggle with the loss itself."

"And you *will* manage," Shoemaker added. "How can I be so certain? When Jesus gave John the Baptist's eulogy, He said of him, 'No man born only of woman was ever greater than John, but the least of those who are born again are *greater* than he.' That's you, Pete."

"Now *that* is strong medicine," Wysong said, "but difficult to understand."

"I know. But consider that He was referring to those on whom the Holy Spirit has descended and remained. That never happened to anyone in the Old Testament. Not until the Holy Spirit came at Pentecost. Before that, the Spirit came and went, but never remained."

"That's too deep for me," Wysong said.

"Okay, but think of it another way. As you pass through your time of deep personal mourning prepare to become obedient to God's will. Remember that by virtue of your having accepted Jesus Christ as your Lord and Savior, so also have you received the Holy Spirit. Prepare to change your thinking."

"But why is obedience so important?"

"That's another good question. I once read something by a scholar named Landis who puts the answer better than anything else I have ever seen. He said: 'If even the stars and elements that God created obey His voice, should not we obey Him as well?'"

Wysong had been sitting, but now he stood. Eyes ever wet, he placed the locked fingers of his two hands on top of his head and then slowly pulled the hands apart as he slid them down around the sides of his face, saying nothing. After a moment or two he spoke softly and slowly. "All of what you're saying makes sense to me, but my pain is still unbearable. I've heard people say you're only as happy as your unhappiest child. But I only had one child and now I have none. Where do I find *my* happiness?"

Seemingly ever-patient and genuinely sympathetic, Shoemaker said, "First of all, Pete, that's nothing more than a cliché. Don't give it more weight than it deserves because it doesn't hold up under scrutiny. At least it doesn't for those of us who *know* God is in control. Believe it or not, happiness is not what life is all about."

"What's wrong with being happy?"

"Not a thing, but here's the situation. Happiness depends upon circumstances. Again, what God really wants from us is obedience. Out of that obedience comes joy with life in Christ. We simply cannot lose our joy as long as we trust in God. As for happiness, both it and *un*happiness are part of life."

Wysong nodded at his friend's wisdom. He was beginning to recognize that their extended talk was precisely the therapy he needed. Upon impulse, he said, "How did you handle things when you lost your late wife?"

Surprised at the question, Shoemaker sat back and took a moment before responding. "Truth be known, at first I was inconsolable in my grief, just as you have been. But I never lost my joy. That came with my faith in God and His promise that life would not only . . . somehow . . . go on, but that I could actually take comfort and joy in Him."

"But you still mourned her loss," Wysong said.

"Of course, but there is more to that notion. I knew she would not have wanted me to deeply mourn her indefinitely." Then something occurred to Shoemaker and he said, "Suppose, for example, that Billy had lost *you*. Would you not want him to recover and go on with his life—after a reasonable time of grieving for his father?"

The notion fully registered with Wysong, but it was simply too soon for him to project his heart being healed. All he could manage was to slowly shake his head.

Shoemaker put his hand on the shoulder of his care receiver/ spiritual student/friend and said, "Pete, listen to me. In this past week you have witnessed to others about your faith for the first time, flown back and forth across the entire country, put to final rest your only child, and engaged in difficult interactions with others. All that while you've been dealing with some of man's greatest emotions. Now, with all of that behind you, grief remains as your constant companion. You naturally want to withdraw from everything. That is okay to a point, but you can't allow it to cripple you."

"I know. I know," he said, "but how do I stop the flow of these endless tears?"

"You don't. Let them come. You may find yourself standing in the middle of a room—or maybe in the shower—and wailing at God. You may need to pour out your heartache as if God were seated at your side. Whatever it takes, don't be afraid to begin the journey. Without a beginning there can be no ending."

Wysong raised his head and looked squarely at Shoemaker. He said, "It helps to know that you, too, my friend, have born an unbearable loss."

"Yes, thank you, but my cross won't lesson your own loss. It's true that you will no longer hear the voice or wipe away a tear from Billy's little face, but it is also true that with time God will wipe away your tears and ease your pain. Pray for God's grace to enfold you."

"The peace that passes all understanding?" Wysong said, recalling a phrase from a verse he had now read many times.

"Yes," Shoemaker said. "The peace the world cannot give. The faith that comes from Him will one day inexplicably lighten your heart. The scar will still be there, but to touch it will hurt less."

"I have to say that I'm humbled, Will." Wysong was listening like he had never before listened. He said, "Maybe it is beginning to dawn on me that if we can take comfort in His very words, there is nothing God cannot give us."

"Not only that," Shoemaker added, " but there is also nothing He cannot ask of us."

"I have never thought of that," Wysong said. "Tell me, what did you think when God called your late wife home? I mean, didn't you feel he had possibly asked too much of you, not to mention of your late wife?"

"No," he said. "I really wasn't thinking that way. At first, I prayed through my tears asking God to take away the pain of my loss. I actually thought I might die from love. But I didn't. I finally understood that life is made up of the greatest joys the human heart can hold as well as the most painful experiences the human heart can endure. But within the vulnerability we feel when bad things happen, we also have the opportunity to let go, and to let God be and do what God is and does."

Thinking he knew the answer, yet wanting to hear Will affirm it, Pete said, "And what is that?"

"Love," he said.

CHAPTER 42

SHOW TIME

W eeks passed, then two months. Although he had been working all of that time, Wysong found his once-trademark enthusiasm finally returning to both business and life. True to the Cobbler's reminder, while God had not spared Pete the fire of Billy's loss, He had met him in the furnace. He had said to Will only the day before as he hugged him goodbye at the conclusion of their Friday's visit, "Brother, I'm going to make it. Thank you for your encouragement. I don't think I could have managed without your counsel and support."

A few days later the phone rang early in the morning. "Pete Wysong," the voice on the other end of the line said, "this is Hunter Clark with American Awards. I have your e-mailed resume here regarding your interest in taking on our line of awards. I've checked you out with several distributors, as well as with some of your supplier accounts. We would like to offer you the southeastern territory. Are you still interested?"

Was he! It was a top line with a solid reputation for service. It would easily be equivalent to the line he had lost more than six months ago when his prize horse had fled the stable. Gathering his racing thoughts, he said, "Yes, sir! I can see myself running with your line from day one. I also appreciate your revenue plan of retainer-plus-bonus. One of my new business cards is going to read 'American's Rep. Have Awards. Will Travel.'"

"Great," Wysong's new supplier principal said. "Welcome aboard. We'll send your samples and catalogs today so you can acquaint yourself with the line. We want you in our booth at the Las Vegas show in two weeks, and we trust you'll be joining us there for a sales meeting with the rest of our reps."

Two weeks flew by and Wysong arrived at his Las Vegas hotel on Sunday afternoon. He immediately called the room of his friend, Sam Sampson, who was staying at the same casino hotel. "Sammy, you dog. When did you get in?"

"Couple of hours ago," Sampson said. "Man, thanks for agreeing to speak to the fellowship group on Tuesday, especially on the heels of the terrible tragedy with Billy. I appreciate your having kept me up to date via e-mail. When I called you last week about our scheduled speaker unavoidably bailing and asked you to fill in for us, I was afraid it might be too soon. I owe you. I've also spread the word."

"I'm a little nervous about this, Sammy, but I'm just going to tell it like it happened and trust in the Lord."

"Great. You'll have 20-25 minutes. See you at about 6:45 on Tuesday morning, if I don't see you elsewhere between now and then." Almost as if he had overlooked something Sampson hesitated and then said, "You're okay, right?"

"Yes," Wysong said, "all things considered, I'm actually doing quite well. All I need is to work through one other little item between now and then."

No sooner had he hung up but what he punched up Shoemaker's number in Atlanta. "Will," he said, his voice betraying his enthusiasm. "I need to talk to you. Do you have a couple of minutes?"

"Of course," he said. Why don't you come on over. June and I were planning an early dinner. Would you like to join us?" At the same time he issued the invitation he caught his wife's eye and mouthed Pete's name for her.

"Oh. No, thanks," Wysong said. "I'm in Las Vegas. Remember? It's the mother-of-all trade shows. I think I mentioned it to you."

"Of course," Shoemaker said. "Another premature senior moment on my part. You're giving your testimony, right?"

"Yes, I am. I'm both excited and nervous. This is going to be my second testimonial to a group, but it won't be to a Sunday school class. This is a non-sanctioned Christian group, made up of industry distributors, suppliers, and fellow reps. They only meet once a year, at this show. But that isn't why I'm calling."

"It isn't?"

"No. On the plane out here I got to thinking more and more about Marlene."

"The woman who sent you packing more than a year ago?"

"Yup. I've really never stopped thinking about her since we met. And as you began pounding into my head and heart about the beauty of commitment between a man and a woman, I found myself having flashbacks to that single date."

"So?" Shoemaker said while gesturing to June as if to say, 'You said this might happen.'"

"Don't you get it?" Wysong said, thinking that his mentor wasn't following his drift.

Shoemaker stopped playing coy and said, "You mean you want a second chance at selling her on your charms?"

At that summary Wysong blinked. "Well, yes and no," he said. "I mean, yes I want another chance, but more importantly I want her to see that the Lord has changed my heart."

"I know you didn't call for my permission," Shoemaker said. "How can I help?"

"I want your honest reaction. Am I looney?"

"That wouldn't be my guess. Look, June and I have been praying for this very thing because we think it's what has been driving you to seek the Lord. But I *do* think you need a plan. Given that first date, I doubt your name is going to recommend you. Don't forget to pray about it."

"Thanks for the encouraging word. That's why I called."

"We'll be praying for you, both for success in a new romantic adventure and for your testimony on Tuesday." Before he hung up he added, "I love you like a son, Pete."

Wysong couldn't keep tears from welling up. He couldn't keep from thinking about this man who had literally taught him more about truth, grace, and life in the past year than he had learned in all the 35 years which had preceded it. And through all of that his mentor had been willing to put up with a too-often impertinent personality.

CHAPTER 43

TESTIMONIAL REVISITED

It was early in the morning on the day of Wysong's talk. He knelt beside his bed and prayed, asking God to give him not only the strength and the words to share, but to truly communicate what was on his heart.

An hour later—after the meeting had been opened with prayer—Sam was introducing him to the audience, many of whom had been in the same room together a year earlier. "Good morning, everyone," Sampson said. "We have a real treat for you this morning. As you know, our scheduled speaker had a last minute family emergency and couldn't be with us today. My friend, Pete Wysong, graciously agreed to fill in. His is an amazing story. Some of you will recall that he first visited our group a year ago. At that time he was not walking with the Lord. In fact, he didn't even know he was seeking the Lord. But God revealed Himself to Pete in a mysterious way, and here he is today to share his story with us. Please make him welcome!"

Wysong took the microphone along with a deep breath and enthusiastically began his message. "Good morning! What a privilege to address fellow industry practitioners with my testimony. Let me give you a little background and then I'll flesh out the story for you. I know Sam won't hesitate to use a neck hook on me if I run too long." The audience of nearly seventy laughed.

"Ten years ago," he began, "I married a woman out of lust and looks, rather than out of love. Seven mostly miserable years later we divorced. And while I admit that I was unfaithful to her on several occasions, that wasn't the worst of things. I hadn't the least notion that marriage not only involves undying commitment, but that it is instituted by God Himself. The full truth is that I didn't acknowledge God for anything. This, in spite of His presence being evident all around us."

Wysong looked around the room, wondering if people were already judging him or if they were interested in the lessons he may have learned. "Out of the marriage came our handsome son, Billy," he continued, " but not much else. My ex-wife thought I was merely a life-of-the-party type of guy when in fact my focus was merely on my own needs. Between us we had absolutely no spiritual foundation and it didn't take long for the ground over the sink hole beneath us to give way. There may be some here today who know what I'm talking about."

Wysong looked around the room in a second effort to gauge his audience's initial reaction. From their attention it seemed they were at least following him. "Not long after the divorce," he said, "I signed up with a popular dating service, but over time I came up with no one of interest, even though I dated something like twenty-five different women in a year's time. I didn't know *what* the problem was, unless it was the purple Mohawk haircut I had at the time." The audience laughed and exchanged amused glances with one another.

"I'm kidding, of course," he said, shaking his head. "Then, one day—almost on a whim—I decided to try a Christian-dating service. Since I didn't know the Lord, however, you can imagine how poorly that was destined to work out." Again, laughter.

"Let me tell you about that. The first and only date to come of the profile matching was someone to whom I was immediately attracted. In short order we agreed to meet at a restaurant. In the course of some in-depth conversation over dinner, however, she quickly found out that with respect to my faith I was a liar and a fraud. Because she had set such a high and honest standard for herself, however, I was impressed. I apologized and asked for a second date, but she wouldn't hear of it. In fact, she walked out on me before we could even get to desert." He could tell that the audience wanted to laugh at that, but out of politeness declined to do so.

"What to do?" Wysong continued. "I sought to discover head knowledge of the subject that had gotten me torpedoed. I needed to know what my date had meant by her reference to having been born again. Unfortunately, I was merely interested in the knowledge, rather than its effect. I reasoned that if I could be armed with the proper 'code' words, I could reasonably engage a given Christian date in conversation. In other words I aspired to be a legalist." At that 'inside' joke the Christian crowd roared with laughter.

"Emboldened towards that end," he continued, "I went to a nearby church's advertised outreach talk. I thought it might shed some light on some of the 'code' words I didn't understand. In the process I learned about a lay ministry whose purpose was to listen to folks who had a need to share. They're called Stephen Ministers. I imagine many of you know someone who has benefitted from that ministry. Anyway, I was assigned a care giver who also happened to be a Bible teacher. I was hoping that my care giver-teacher would be able to coach me back into the game.

"Well, once again things didn't turn out the way I had them figured." He paused for a moment and released an audible sigh. "When I first met Will Shoemaker, I was very candid with him about both my story and my goals. As I think about it now, for him to even accept the assignment he must of had to reach down inside of himself. He said he would be happy to counsel me concerning what being a Christian was all about, even though I stated I was only interested from an intellectual perspective."

Wysong took a drink of water before continuing. "And then ," he said, "the minister/teacher surprised me by saying it was obvious to him that I didn't have a clue as to what marriage was about, but that he was willing to tackle that shortcoming as well." Another laugh from the audience.

He glanced in Sam's direction and received a broad smile along with a discrete thumbs up. He continued. "At the first of what would become months of weekly meetings with the 'Cobbler' — as I called my friend whose name was Shoemaker–he said the lessons were going to take me through the study of a book of the Bible I had never heard of: Song of Songs. I'm sure all of you study that book on a regular basis." Once again, laughter.

"Anyway," Wysong said, smiling and feeling more relaxed with each point, "during the course of studying the essence of all eight chapters of that book about love, sex, marriage and romance from a Biblical perspective, he also pumped me full of the message of the gospel. Early on, I only saw all of that as research for my project of dating some Christian women, if not a second chance with the one who had dumped me for being an imposter. Did I tell you that I tried to cover up my deceit with a lie?" Several in the audience said 'yes.'

Pete acted surprised and said, "Thank you. I trust that was the sound of grace." He paused for the laughter which came. "Now I know that some of you are probably thinking at this point that as a human being I was no better than a suck-egg mule." At that the audience only murmured, so he said, "Work with me, here. Let's see a show of hands of those who think I was worse than a total jerk." Laughter amid a strong showing of hands.

Wysong was not only feeling comfortable in telling his story, but was again realizing how often Marlene had come into his mind over the past year. His thought of her was not merely for the purpose of apologizing, but for the woman she was. And the more he thought about that notion the more he was drawn to even greater thought of her.

Snapping out of his momentary reverie, he took another drink of water and returned his attention to his audience. "To continue with my summary," he said, "although I think my notion of a summary has somehow raced off on a rabbit trail. Maybe I should ask you something at this point. Do you really want to hear the end of this story?" A loud chorus of 'yeses' was heard.

"Okay," he said. "After several months into regular weekly meetings with my minister/teacher, things began going south for me. I lost two solid product lines and my ex-wife moved to California in search of a new boyfriend. Of course she took Billy–our son—with her and left me in charge of our considerable credit card debt. The divorce attorney turned out to successful for his primary client–my ex—and somewhat less so for his secondary client, me.

"After that I found myself asking all kinds of people about the things I kept finding challenging in my spiritual mentor's sharing. As a result I was getting a lot of negative, even erroneous input from secular friends. But the Cobbler hung in there and we actually completed his teaching. In that process I digested his words about how wonderful are the blessings of a committed marriage."

At that moment Wysong realized where he was in his testimony and what was shortly coming up. He wasn't certain how he would be able to handle telling of Billy's loss. Maybe he could capsulize events.

"In order to save some time" he said, "let me use some bullet points. I began attending Will's church. Shortly after that I accepted Christ as my Lord and Savior. I then joined with both the local body of Christ and with all of you who share your faith in Him. I took a Walk to Emmaus where I laid down most of my hurt and confusion at the foot of the cross, and then I became active in small groups. I had gained salvation and was beginning to prepare my heart and resources to more closely follow and grow in Christ's image when the worst imaginable tragedy struck."

Wysong took a deep breath before continuing. "A little more than a month ago my son was killed in an automobile accident. Billy was barely eight years old, but the Lord saw fit to call him home." The audience's sympathetic murmuring could be readily heard.

"My first reaction was to call out God. Not call out *for* Him, understand, but in my anger and confusion, to call Him *out*, however one does that. But in spending time in prayer, in sharing with my new-found friends at church, in reading His word, and in continuing encouragement from my minister/mentor I slowly began to understand that God was still in control.

"It was then that my friend the Cobbler made a profound point . . . which is that I could not invest *only* in human life. He said that I needed to focus on something greater. And that what I had been learning was all about something much more lasting. He was speaking of one's relationship with God. Why? Because all salvation is based in relationship, not in knowledge. And all relationship is based in what? Trust. Trust in Whom? Trust in God."

Wysong was relieved to have gotten through that portion of his testimony without breaking down and said, "As I wrap things up, I'm not only doing okay, I'm doing quite well. I will always hurt from the loss of my son, but I know where he is. And I know that I will see him again one day."

Wysong paused. "And I have learned another thing, ladies and gentlemen. And that is this: Your marriage is on loan to you from God. You must treat it properly for His–for God's—sake. Why? Because marriage is nothing more than an expression of your relationship with Him.

"Now, in closing, allow me share with you what I'm going to do about all of this. And frankly, I have only today come to this decision. I'm going to find that Christian woman who started all of this and tell her what I think about things. Why? Because she may well be my one-in-a-million mate. Only she doesn't yet know it. Thank you."

Everyone in the audience instantly stood and applauded enthusiastically. Someone even whistled. As Wysong stood at the door while people filed out, each one shook his hand and thanked him for both his testimony and its message. When everyone had left, Sam said, "Wow! What a blessing. Brother, you might have another career in you if you choose to either hit the rubber chicken circuit or go to seminary."

CHAPTER 44

SEARCHING ANEW

U pon Wysong's return from Las Vegas he visited Shoemaker
and apprised him of both the trip and the talk. "What a conclusion to a combination business, personal, and spiritual year, my
friend," Shoemaker said. "Now, 'Solomon,' do you really think it
wise to pursue your unrequited female interest?"

"That, sir, is a very good point," Wysong said. Then, in a serious
vein he added, "I'm not absolutely certain how *I* feel. And it's even
possible that if I should get within twenty feet of her she might
decide to whistle up the fraud squad."

"You'll have to get closer than that if she's to learn you have
become a new person," Shoemaker responded, grinning.

"You think?" Wysong said. "Well, while I'm trying to figure all
this out, I have a job that needs some attention."

On Monday morning Wysong headed out on what he labeled
a territory "milk run." By that he meant the week would be one
of more driving than of making presentations. As he was driving
the nearly day-long stretch to North Carolina's southwestern coastal
area he found himself plotting his opening lines to Marlene should
he make contact. He even found himself saying the lines aloud, but
everything he tried fell flat. Finally, he simply dismissed the effort
as premature.

He knew it wouldn't do him any good to directly contact
the dating service because they wouldn't divulge confidential

information, even if he again signed up for their services. Even though he had her e-mail address from more than a year ago he reasoned that such an attempt at contact would probably be treated as junk mail. As for phoning her, he had already checked for a listing only to discover there was none. His first thought following that bit of information was that she might have married, but he dismissed the notion as needless speculation.

He had even tried to Google her. For whatever reason that also proved unsuccessful, which once again caused him to think her name might have changed. He plowed ahead, figuring if that turned out to be the case, so be it. Negatives four, positives zero. He liked the odds.

As Wysong pulled up to the Morehead City door of one of his special accounts, he vividly recalled that the owner had lost his wife to cancer only a few years earlier. It had been a year since the last call and he was interested in how things were going with him as well as the opportunity to stimulate some new business. He also had a special question. "Steve!" he greeted his friend and distributor customer enthusiastically. "How are you?"

"Hi, Pete. I'm actually doing pretty well, all things considered. I'm so sorry about the tragic loss of your little boy."

"I'm making it," he said, "and work is a good recovery tonic."

His friend nodded. "You're right about that. You'll always be hurting, but for what it's worth, time has not only lessened my own hurt, but also the frequency of it."

"Thanks," said Wysong. "That's insightful. I appreciate that as well as your fine business this past year. I'm anxious to talk to your salespeople in a few minutes, but first I would like your opinion on a personal matter."

"I'm flattered."

"You're someone I respect as being both a doer *and* a creative-type. I'm trying to track down a woman I once met who brushed me off for good reason. I know that sounds goofy, but without going into details, what would you do if you couldn't find any information on someone through standard sources. First, I need to locate her, then I'll deal with whatever I find."

Wysong's friend said, "I'm assuming you want a do-over. That's cool. Given what little you've told me I think I would start with mutual friends."

"No good," Wysong said. "I met her through a dating service."

"Then let's begin with what you *might* know: The name of a school or church, her workplace, maybe even a hobby. You must have some kind of clue rattling around in that 'rep' brain of yours."

"Good thinking!" Wysong said. Who says you get what you pay for?"

"Thanks, but I think I would reserve the word 'great' for positive results. Keep me posted. Now, are you ready to wow us with some money-making ideas?"

An hour and a half later Wysong was back on the road. From then until the final day of the week's road trip he shook and rattled his memory banks along the lines of what his friend has suggested. It was to no avail, however. Off the top of his head he couldn't recall Marlene having mentioned a specific name for a college, church, or employment.

Then, as he crossed the Georgia state line he tried a slightly different approach to the problem. Clearing his mind of the week's business as well as all of his dead end thoughts, he prayed. "Lord, I need your help. You know I'm a new creation in Christ. I want to attempt to make a new start with Marlene, but I can't locate her. All I want is to recall something–anything—she may have told me that would help me find her. Thank you. In Jesus' name. Amen."

As he continued driving his mind minutely retraced the conversation of that abbreviated luncheon date. Suddenly, new thoughts began rushing in on him. *Focus, dummy. Hobby interests. Didn't she mention something about old movies? She did. She said she liked old movies. We even had a short discussion about that. Sure! I named my favorite film classic and she did the same. What was hers? Let's see. Something with the word 'time' in it. What was it about? I don't know, but it was unusual. Aha! She said something about 'a man sacrificing his life to find happiness. That's a start. Where the heck can I go with that?* Aloud, he said, "Thank you, Father."

CHAPTER 45

LOST IN TIME

U pon Wysong's return home he immediately began research for the name of Marlene's favorite film. On line he turned up what appeared to be a thousand movie titles with the word 'time' in them. He needed some help.

"Wally!" he said as his Tallahassee friend answered the phone. "It's Pete. You having any luck finding a replacement 'flyer'?"

"Hey, Pete," he said, laughing. "Thanks for the call. We're doing way better than we deserve. How about you? I know it's been tough, but you mentioned something in an e-mail about an upcoming second testimonial at your trade show. How did that go?"

"Thanks for asking. Man, was I blessed there. And I picked up a solid new line as well. I'll tell you more about both a little later. But look, I need your finger tips and eyes for an hour or so. I'm trying to chase down a new chapter in the ever-growing saga of 'Peter Applefaith.'"

"I have no idea what you're talking about," Wally said, "but spit it out and I'll do what I can."

"Okay. Here goes. I have a list of what looks like a million movie names with the word 'time' in them, along with one-sentence descriptions. If I forward half the list to you, would you take a little time over the weekend to hunt for one that might relate to a particular promotional line?" Without waiting for either argument or agreement Wysong gave him a few more details of what had been going on and then said, "Here's the key line to the film. Write it down: 'A man who sacrifices his life for happiness.'"

"Whoa, whoa, my boy," Wally said. "What are *you* doing this weekend that's so important you can't manage this assignment yourself?"

"I already told you. Half a mountain of titles. I have to leave town Sunday morning for some traveling road shows. Look, I'm going crazy over trying to find Marlene. The only possible lead I have is a movie without a name. You surely owe me, don't you?"

"Owe you for what?"

"I don't know. For making you 'Star Catcher of the Flying High Circus' during the second week of April, 1995."

"Yeah, that's right. How stupid of me. Okay, send me your dumb list."

Within the hour Wysong saw to that task. That afternoon he spent several hours scouring his half of the list, but found nothing even close. At the dinner hour Tallahassee called. Pete glanced at the caller ID, clicked on 'receive,' and said, "Wally! You found it. Tell me you did!"

Wally said, "You mean *you* don't have anything? That's why I called, to see how *you* did."

"Nuts," said Wysong.

"Well," his friend said in a tantalizing tone, "I did find *something*. Your promo line was a little off. It reads this way: 'A man sacrifices his life in the present to find happiness in the future.'"

"Whatever," Wysong said, excitedly.

"Okay. But all I have is a film with the title, *'Back To Somewhere In Time.'* The bad news is it's not a chick flick. It's a documentary. How does that help?"

"I don't know. At least I have a lead. Thanks, man. Now I owe *you*. 'Bye!'"

"Wait a minute, bonehead," Wally shouted into the phone. How could finding the name of a film help you?"

"Oh, that," Wysong said. "Marlene said she was a member of the movie's fan club. If I can contact them they might be willing to share her whereabouts with me."

"I wouldn't count on it, but anything is possible."

CHAPTER 46

SOMEWHERE IN TIME

Wysong found a Web site called INSITE, an acronym for International Network of Somewhere In Time Enthusiasts. The film's actual title–*Somewhere In Time*—was quickly apparent, SIT for short. From there he garnered an e-mail address of the fan club and inquired if they could confirm a member by the name of Marlene Neuman. After a two-day wait and no reply, he went back to the Web site and joined the fan society along with ordering back copies of their quarterly journal. Once his payment had cleared he called a second time. This time he verified his own new membership and then asked the person on the line if she could confirm member-ship by a friend of his. Surprise! She could and would. "Neuman, Marlene?" she repeated, mispronouncing the last name but pronouncing the first name–Mar-lana, long second 'a'—correctly. She wouldn't, however, give him any information concerning an address. He had made a positive start.

"Thank you!" he said, barely managing to keep his response to a modest level of enthusiasm. Even better was the news that she was apparently still single.

He immediately located the film title on line and ordered a copy of the movie. Two days later it arrived and he was about to settle in and view it. The whole idea had merely been to acquire knowledge of some special mutual interest. He figured he needed a plausible reason to be contacting her—along with the news of his conversion, of course–if he should be successful in reaching her. *Am I being obsessed with a woman I've only met once for thirty minutes?* he wondered. He answered himself. *No. Not obsessed, but intrigued. No, that's not being honest. It's much more than that. I'm smitten. Okay, I'm gutted. But that's a full step below obsessed.*

One hour and forty-four minutes later he sat back and sighed, having watched what he could honestly say was the most romantic film he had ever seen. He said aloud, "Marlene–German pronunciation–no wonder you're a fan." Not only was he taken by the film's plot, its characters and production, but he had found the music so haunting that every time the melody rose in highlighting a scene, he teared up. No wonder she had called it her ultimate classic.

Next, he watched a bonus feature on the DVD which turned out to be the documentary Wally had actually found. Thus he spent yet another hour in watching captivating interviews with the film's actors, including Christopher Reeve and Jane Seymour. Following all of that he pondered how much closer he was to finding her than before.

Allowing his mind to ruminate on everything he had heard and viewed for the last several hours, he suddenly had an Aha! moment. Throwing the palms of his hands up and open, he then focused his thinking on the setting of the movie's final scene and how he might be able to use it to his advantage. Two things came quickly to mind. "Where" wasn't as important as "what." "Where" was the Grand Hotel on Michigan's Mackinac Island, but "what" was the fan society's annual *Somewhere In Time* weekend events. *Maybe she attends them!* he thought. *Yeah. What if I show up at the next one and somehow meet her, unannounced?* Then doubts interrupted his vision. *But what if she doesn't attend? Of course she would. She's a member of the fan club, isn't she? I need some support for the idea.*

He called the Cobbler. No sooner had Wysong blurted out his idea than Shoemaker said, "That's the most cockamamie thing I've ever heard!" Almost as quickly he qualified his statement. "But you know something? I like it. In fact, I want to see this *Somewhere In Time* film with June. I've never heard of it either. This 'buttinsky' friend of yours, however, suggests you go back to that same Web site and find out when the next event is scheduled. Who knows, if it isn't too far off they might be willing to confirm whether or not she's registered."

Wysong was excited about that possibility and immediately followed up. His spirits quickly sank, however, when he noted the next annual weekend event's date. It was in late September. It was now only early February. Nearly eight months away. Too long? What better idea or choice did he have?

"Wally. It's Pete again," he said over the phone. "I'm screwed. I can't put my grand plan into effect for eight months. But I may have a solution to the bigger problem. Now follow me on this. I need to approach Marlene in some more dramatic way than either an e-mail or a phone call. If she bounces me before I can get in a word there is no way I'll get a third shot. I figure I have three options. Plan A is to wait and work while I bank a few bucks and shore up my approach lines for when I do meet her. Plan B is forget about her altogether. Plan C is to run away and join the circus. What do you think, pal?"

Barneveld laughed through a sigh. "Okay, in response to your confession I am going to confirm a few things at which you have no doubt already arrived. We can rule out plan C because you have neither a circus skill nor motivation for swamping out elephant stalls. As for plan B, there is no way you are going to entertain abandoning your quest at this stage of the game. Plan A is your only genuine option. The only advice I can offer is that you pray about it. Have you done that?"

Wysong said, "Sadly, no. I'm still a novice at this faith thing. How do I go about it?"

"Open your heart to God," Wally said. "Tell Him what's going on. Talk with him about your goal as well and what you think is the best option for achieving it. You will thus find yourself laying it all out very clearly, perhaps for the first time. Through all of that ask for guidance. Then listen quietly. Listen for that soft inner voice that tells you something is best or right."

"You know something, not only have I done that once before, but it worked!" Pete said. "Thanks, man."

"And here's one more word of advice," Barneveld said in the way only a best friend can. "Assuming your lady *hasn't* registered, find out if she has *ever* attended your corn ball event."

"I was going to do that," came Wysong's mock indignant reply.

"Sure you were. Oh. One other thing that a Catcher would naturally think of, but unlikely a Flyer. If your dream girl friend is still yearning and hoping for her dream man to come along, chances are pretty good it would not likely be someone she has already rejected. In other words, 'Buckwheat,' give some creative thought to how you're going to address that issue."

"Ah, cheap consultants," Wysong said. "There's nothing like 'em."

CHAPTER 47

SOMEWHERE IN MICHIGAN

Wysong went back to his rep work with purpose well beyond either money or responsibility. He was trying to fill his days, weeks and months by being productively busy. It worked. The next six-month period had him well on his way towards the best earnings year of his life. If his supplier accounts were more than happy with his efforts, his distributors were also satisfied with his attention to their needs. Perhaps what surprised him more than anything was the fact that in tithing to a church for the first time in his life, contributions to his self-employment plan also grew, even in the face of increased expenses in other areas of his business. When he shared that revelation with Shoemaker, Will said, "Don't ever forget to thank the Lord in good times. Believers sometimes tend to forget God until things go south."

Developments with respect to the *Somewhere In Time* event had also taken some interesting turns. Wysong ascertained that Marlene had attended the event every *other* year for the past six year period. Since she had not attended the previous year, he decided to go forward in faith and book his own room at the Grand Hotel. He also made reservations for his flight to and from Detroit as well as a rental car for the five+ hour drive to the Upper Peninsula area of Lake Huron. He had even seen to being measured for a tuxedo since the dress code for the hotel's evening events was formal.

He was again on the phone to a particular customer service person at the hotel. Given the number of times he had already spoken with her they had become fairly well acquainted. "Susan, my friend!" he said enthusiastically. "It's Pete from Atlanta. Has my friend Marlene made her reservation yet? It's been a week since I last called."

"Oh. Hi, Mr. Wysong. Let me check. No, nothing under Neuman."

"What *is* the matter with that woman," he said, rhetorically. "Oh, well. I'm sure she'll get around to it soon. One thing I want to ask of you. When she does make her reservation it is very important that neither my name nor my inquiry about her is mentioned. She doesn't know I plan to attend. Is there any problem with that?"

"Of course not, Mr. Wysong. But you know we have more than a hundred rooms already booked, and the reservation cut-off is only one week away."

"This is really frustrating," he said. "Here I am planning a big surprise. I don't dare question her closely about her trip." Wysong was fabricating what he considered to be a half-lie, but one which he judged excusable, given the circumstances.

"Susan," he said, "I have to ask you for a favor. Give me a week's grace on that deadline sign up. If you'll do that I'll go ahead and book a second room, preferably adjacent to my first one. Then, when she calls to book her reservation, put her in that room under her own name and cancel my second room reservation. That way, you're covered. If none of this works by the deadline, I guess I'll have to flat out ask her." He knew full well he couldn't do that. Another light-lie.

"I'll do that for you, Mr. Wysong," the administrator said, "but if she's a no-show or you don't cancel by the end of the grace period you'll be on the hook for the second $1,000.00 weekend fee."

"Ouch," he said. "Okay. Let's do it. I'll leave the details up to the Lord."

Two days before the drop dead date Wysong received a call. "Mr. Wysong? This is Susan with the Grand Hotel. I have good news."

"Oh. Wow!" he said. " Talk to me. I was just about to call you one last time."

" I knew you were up against it so I checked the records very carefully. A high school 'temp' clerk on the front desk apparently took Marlene's e-mailed reservation a month before your last call, but entered it in the computer under M. Newman rather than Marlene Neuman. I apologize and I'm also embarrassed about this. Anyway, your girl friend is aboard. Are you happy?"

"Happy? You made my day, girl. Maybe my life. Did you get her into the adjacent room?"

"No, I wasn't able to do that, but you're on the same floor."

"No problem. Thanks again. See you in about a month."

Thirty days later Wysong was en route to the Grand Hotel. He realized that the island was hardly a stop-over location where one airport and a limousine could get the job done. What he hadn't realized is that getting to such an isolated domestic locale as Mackinac Island is really more like a time-travel trip. After the big-distance air leg from Atlanta to Detroit he hopped aboard a smaller plane for a nearly 300 mile flight North to a regional airport in a community with a population of fewer than 1,000. Then came a half-hour van ride to the ferry dock at Mackinaw City, followed by a carriage taxi to Mackinac Island in Lake Huron.

Following his nearly day-long travel and the particularly beautiful northern Michigan countryside he arrived at the stylish turn-of-the-century Grand Hotel. Just for the fun of it—and also because of the SIT's event literature suggestion—he changed into his tux prior to the ferry ride. He strode self-consciously into the hotel lobby but quickly relaxed when it was obvious that others had done the same, although his tux was definitely not a period costume as were most of the other guest's outfits. Upon checking in he asked for the customer service person, Susan.

The clerk said, "You mean the general manager, don't you, sir?"

"General manager?" said a surprised Wysong. "I thought she was a customer service rep."

"She was the customer service manager until her promotion a month ago. I'll ring her for you. Please pick up on that extension right over there, sir. And enjoy your stay."

"Susan Miller here. How may I help you?"

"Susan. Pete Wysong. I just arrived at your fabulous hotel. Could I see you for a moment?"

"Oh, hello, Mr. Wysong," she said enthusiastically. "We're so glad you're here. I'll be at the front desk in two minutes and escort you to my office."

As she approached the desk, she offered her hand to Pete, saying, "I hope everything is all right. Have you seen your room yet?" She was a woman in her late forties and had been with the hotel in various capacities for more than fifteen years, starting on the front desk and working her way up to sales and then head of customer service before her recent promotion with this mega-star hotel.

As he turned to follow her to the office he said, " No, I haven't seen the room, but I know everything will be wonderful. I appreciate all that you've done for me. And congratulations on your recent promotion. I didn't know I was being helped by the top banana. I'll bet that's a part of why you're where you are."

"Thank you for the compliment," she said. "Now, how can I help you?"

"Help is *exactly* what I need," he said.

The manager was always amused by the enthusiasm of first-time SIT event attendees. This person's story, however, promised to be exceptionally interesting, although she would not have violated hotel policy by inquiring.

"Here's the scoop," he said as he took the chair offered him. He proceeded to tell her the bare bones story of both his quest to meet Marlene for the second time in his life, and his coming to faith in Christ. He also shared with her his exercise in tracking down Marlene's interest in *Somewhere In Time,* plus his subsequent decision to stage their unannounced second meeting at the Grand Hotel. He hadn't figured out when, where, or even how he would approach her, however, and that was the help for which he needed suggestions.

"Wow!" she said in response to his chronicle. "I've heard a lot of SIT stories, but never one anything like yours. The Grand Hotel would be delighted to have a role. Let me first say by way of disclaimer that although I am personally a believer in our Lord, Jesus Christ, I cannot and will not place the hotel in a position of endorsing any one faith." Almost apologetically, she quickly added, "That said, let me see what we can do to help you as a paying customer. The weather is to be exceptionally cooperative for this time of year, so I think your personal meeting should be outside. How would you like to do a sort of re-enactment of Jane Seymour's and Christopher Reeve's famous first meeting near the beach?"

"You're kidding!" he said.

"Not at all. We have often staged various scenes as a part of our entertainment during the weekend. I could talk to Marlene and tell her we would like her help in framing a new presentation for consideration by the next SIT event's promotional committee. Let's see . . . I could tell her that in order to add to the presentation's mystique she won't actually meet the person playing the role of Chris until she utters the famous line. She'll buy that because she knows in the actual filming that's the way Christopher Reeve treated seeing Jane's character's photo in the museum for the first time. Chris wanted genuine reaction to the story's happenstance viewing. In fact I think she'll fully appreciate that particular point. What do you think?"

Pete slumped into his chair, blown away. "Man!" he said, "If I didn't have my cap set for Marlene, I'd ask *you* to marry me."

"Sorry," she said, laughing and adding, "I'm flattered, but taken. If you want to enjoy the weekend with her, however, we should probably do this yet today, before the dinner hour. I can find out if she's available. Are you up for it on such short notice?"

"Boy, am I! Nerves aside, though, I just thought of something. I had in mind my saying the film's trademark line–'Is it you?'—to *her*, but if you could get her to say it to *me*, as in the film . . . that would be incredible. What an opening that would then give me. Of course she won't likely recognize me at first, but I can handle it. Can you sell her on doing that?"

"I don't know," she said, "but I like the idea very much."

"Then it's all in your hands. Let me know any details. I'll plan to approach her through the trees to the beach, just like Chris did. Oh, one other thing. Will this tux be okay?"

"Hardly," the manager said. "But don't worry. The hotel has a period tux I think will fit you well enough. We have several in storage on the premises. I'll have it sent to your room. Also, I'm thinking that to better sell the scheme I can have a sham camera positioned near where the two of you will actually meet." At that point, she suddenly stopped talking and cupped her hand to her mouth, elbow on her desk, staring at Wysong.

He didn't miss the look. "You're wondering if I'm legitimate, aren't you?"

"The thought," she said, "is more along the lines of whether the hotel could be sued for aiding and abetting a would-be stalker. You aren't going to cost me my job, are you, Mr. Wysong?"

CHAPTER 48

BOY GETS GIRL

S usan had just finished sketching out for Marlene the impromptu screening idea for a future SIT weekend promotion. She had explained they wanted to use actual event clients in a mimicked setting of the famous beach meeting. They were still in the general manager's office and Susan was saying, "You're perfect for the part and I really appreciate your willingness to help on such short notice. I just spoke with our camera man and he's all set. As I was working this up earlier today I remembered your having told me that you had some acting experience through your mega-church's dramatic performances. This is going to be fun."

"Well, it *does* sound like fun," Marlene said. "Will there be anyone watching the filming?"

"No," Susan said. "Only the cameraman. But remember to ignore him and react naturally with the guy who will be playing Christopher Reeve's part. Then, once you have said your line, the cameraman will switch off the camera and leave. Everything will be in the 'can' and I can do the editing at a later time. What will make the clip effective for this 'reality' promotion is a combination of two actual weekend event hotel guests recreating the first meeting of Chris and Jane in their classic beach scene. Of course your one line–'Is it you?' is the killer closer for the promo."

"Who is playing Chris' role?" a curious Marlene asked. "I mean, shouldn't I at least meet him beforehand?"

"No," the manager said, almost a little too quickly. "That would lessen the effect. We want an element of genuine surprise. And we also want to make that point in promoting the clip. Remember how Chris preferred not seeing the beautiful young Jane Seymour's picture in the museum until the actual filming of the scene?"

"Of course. But who is this guy? Has he been to an SIT weekend before?"

"No. He's a newbie." Susan changed the subject. "Why don't you wear that beautiful outfit you always bring, the one that imitates Jane's costume from the beach scene itself? That's your call, but I have to run now. If you can come dressed to the beach near the far end of the trees in precisely one hour, we'll be ready to shoot. I have to run now. Again, thanks for your help, Marlene."

As quickly as Marlene had left her office Susan called Pete and asked him to meet her in the dining room, which was closed until dinner. She didn't want to chance Marlene's seeing them together.

"Are we on?" Wysong said, greeting her like a teenage boy asking if dinner was ready.

"We are," she said. "Your suit should be in your room by now. You'll have to wear the shoes you brought, but the spats should easily fit over them. Dress and meet me at the beach house, but make certain Marlene doesn't see you. She's due to meet both me and the cameraman out under the trees at the beach's far end at three o'clock sharp. That's only about 45 minutes from now."

Wysong was wringing his hands in nervousness as he went back to his room to change. *What will I say in response to Marlene's line? What if she doesn't even know who I am? What if she's mad about being set-up? What if . . . ? Stop it, you doofus . . . this is the moment you've been thinking about and planning for months. This is all about redemption with the woman you haven't been able to forget. Since you came to the Lord, you're a new creation. Start acting like it!*

Susan joined Wysong at the appointed time on the beach and positioned him for his walk. In the film's story—as earlier noted—a young writer sacrifices his life in the present to find happiness in the past. Richard Collier (played by Christopher Reeve) is approached at a college graduation party by an elderly woman who gives him an antique gold watch and says quite simply, "Come back for me." A picture of this woman in her later years reveals to him that she is the same woman who gave him the gold watch. Collier then becomes obsessed with returning to 1912 and the beautiful young woman (Elise McKenna, played by Jane Seymour), who awaits him there.

In visiting the hotel of history , Collier/Reeve comes across a mysterious scientist who tells him of his discovery of a time-travel method involving "intentional dreaming." Not really understanding anything except his unabated desire to meet the object of his pursuit, Collier/Reeve prevails upon the eccentric scientist to reveal his method, which turns out to be an intense and painstaking procedure of focus while in a dream state.

Believing in and then determinedly attempting the arduous process actually leads Collier/Reeve to successfully return to the young woman's time and location at the Grand Hotel. The film's young writer then begins looking everywhere on the grounds for her. Someone tells him he may have seen the woman he is looking for on the beach.

That explanation brings us back to real time. As for Wysong, all he hoped for was to make use of a special moment in the same beach setting where Collier/Reeve finally meets the young woman. He would attempt to capture for himself a magical second chance in life. Before literally going forward, however, he opened his heart to God and prayed, "Father, if this be Your will, it will happen."

Susan met with Marlene at a different point on the rocky beach, perhaps only a hundred yards away from where Wysong was quietly standing among trees unique to windswept lake beach areas like Mackinac Island. She said to Marlene, "Meet our front desk team leader and part-time company photographer, Joel. Joel, this is your ingenue, Marlene."

At that description, Marlene laughed and said, "I'm a little old for that title."

"Phooey, Joel," Susan said, "she's a knock-out with talent. Anyway, our other guest actor will be coming along in his role in fewer than five minutes. You can begin shooting as soon as you see him, but remember to keep Marlene between you and her unknown lover. Any questions, either of you?"

Both heads shook. No sooner had Susan left them than Marlene said, "Tell me, Joel, who is this guy Susan drafted to work opposite me, but wouldn't let me meet?"

"You know, I haven't met him either," the bogus cameraman said, although it was the truth. "Susan did tell me that this is his first trip to an SIT event and that he only viewed the film for the first time several months ago."

"Really? Did she say where he's from?"

"I only learned about this project an hour or so ago. I was at the front desk at the time, but I did check the registration book. He's from Atlanta. Susan said you used to live there also."

"Yes, I did. In fact, I only moved to Toronto about a year ago. It was a job move. Did you happen to get his name?"

"Um. I think Paul. No, maybe Phil. Phooey, I don't know for sure. Hey, look alive. I think I see him approaching from up the beach. On the count of five I'll be rolling. I'm turning on the CD now for the theme music. You'll hear it for background. Susan wants to give the two of you a little SIT ambience. Are you okay?"

"This is exciting," she said as she smoothed a wrinkle in her dress and made an effort to look down the beach with searching eyes. "Roll 'em," she said for effect.

Wysong had begun his hesitating walk, trying to recreate for himself the sense of Collier/Reeve having seen a woman on the beach at a distance, and that she would be the one of his fateful desire. Pete's moment had nearly arrived. As he drew closer, his image of Marlene's striking beauty was overlain by the real thing. His heart rate went up. Slowly walking towards her but still some fifty yards away, he was taken by her graceful carriage, at once joyful and poised. Now his heart took up lodging in his throat.

They moved closer, only twenty yards apart. Whimsically, he thought of a championship football game and that he was now in the 'red zone,' which is that proximity to a goal from where a team was expected to score. He was as up for this as he had ever been ready for anything in his entire life. As he neared that part of this unique beach with its patch of eerie, wind-twisted trees, Wysong was surprised to hear the film's theme music from Rachmaninoff, popularly known as *The Rhapsody*. Instinctively, he began humming along with the music.

As they closed to not more than ten yards from one another, he could tell that she was straining to make out his features. Wysong's thoughts turned to his newly found faith and the blessings he had since experienced through the Lord. He had finally come to recognize that Billy's time on this earth was much more of a blessing than his passing was a loss. But now he fancied that he was about to face what could lead to either hoped-for blessing or heartbreaking rejection.

Only about fifteen feet apart now, Marlene stopped. Ever so slowly—almost at a wedding pace—Pete continued to close the remaining gap until they were separated by a mere two feet. At that point they were definitely inside the private space of individuals. As he gazed upon her face—recalling every feature he remembered from across the restaurant's table–he wanted to reach out and caress her hair. Nevertheless, he kept his hands and arms loosely at his sides, as Collier/Reeve had done in the film.

Acutely aware of her acting purpose, Marlene's mind never-theless wanted to register a quizzical expression on her face, but she refused to give in to impulse. Preparing to deliver her line she slowly raised her fingers to just under her chin. At that instant her eyes brightened perceptibly, registering semi-recognition, but not knowing what to make of that. With the cameraman positioned at a quarterly angle to both of them, she looked into Wysong's eyes and said her line for the video camera: "Is it you?" It was spoken just as emotionally as had Elise/Jane Seymour, but more distinctly.

Wysong wasn't at all certain she knew who he was, but he wanted the moment to be dramatic. He said, "Yes, Marlene. It's Pete." Then, in sincere and carefully measured tones, he said, "I've waited two years and come a thousand miles for a second chance to make a first impression."

Marlene remembered Susan's comment that once she had said her line the filmed scene would be concluded and the cameraman would immediately dismiss himself, which by now he had done. She furrowed her brow in confusion and responded to his statement by saying as honestly as the moment allowed, "If it *is* you, Pete, why would you bother?" Her recollection of their single date was all too vivid with equal parts of attraction and disappointment.

"Because I'm a new creation," Wysong said with new-found confidence. "God has revealed Himself to me and I have embraced Jesus Christ as my Lord and Savior. I am not the jerk who tried to deceive you when we first met."

"Pardon me," she said, "but why should I believe you now when you lied once before?" She had no intention of sharing with him how he had hurt her with his earlier deception, even though that had been their first in-person meeting. She had been even more surprised after the aborted meeting at how long it had taken her to get over him. After all, they had only shared e-mails for two or three weeks prior to that fateful date.

Before he could respond to her opening salvo she found herself unable to resist lobbing a few more rounds in his direction. "Look, Mr. Peter-come-lately," she added, "I worked hard at scrubbing your image from my memory banks, and now you ambush me at my favorite event! If you have suddenly come to faith, where is your sense of grace?"

Wysong was stunned. It wasn't that he didn't deserve her discourse, but he suddenly realized that he had been seeing things merely from his perspective. "Marlene," he said, "I don't fault you for anything you have said and I deeply apologize if I have offended you in this approach. But I want you to know something. You are a big part of my having come to accept Jesus Christ as my Lord and Savior. I mean, before the Lord could ever draw close to me I had to want to draw close to Him. You are the reason I sought understanding of Him in the first place. Then, shortly after our date I met someone who began to teach me to want a relationship with the Lord. It was only then that God revealed Himself to me."

They were standing alone beneath the trees, a stone bench nearby. He glanced towards the bench and said, "Will you sit with me for a few minutes and allow me to tell you the whole story?"

She hesitated a moment before nodding. As they sat down Wysong softly called her name. "Marlene, listen. After we parted I shortly came to realize that something was terribly missing in my life. The bad news was that I had been chasing happiness everywhere, never realizing that nothing in this world could satisfy me. The good news is that I finally found glory."

"Glory?" she said. She was puzzled. That wasn't the kind of word the man she met a year ago would have used. "What do you mean by that?"

"The glory that comes from God," he said. "The satisfaction in life we find only in Him. Let me tell you how all of this happened. Not long after our short-lived meeting I met the man I just mentioned at a church outreach program. He's both a Stephen Minister and Bible teacher and he became my spiritual mentor, even though I didn't recognize that at first. He has been so helpful to me. His name is Will Shoemaker, but I call him the Cobbler. This is a man who is so satisfied and happy with his relationship with Christ that he could—and did—lose what others value most in life, and still he was content."

Wysong knew he was on fragile ground and that the potential for her to either bolt the scene or belt him was very real. *Get on with it* he told himself. "Marlene," he continued, wondering if he was overusing her name, "after a while I slowly began to realize that the world of the caring grows, while the world of the stingy shrinks. After the Cobbler's teaching and caring was well underway the message for me became this: If even good people—which I certainly wasn't—are challenged, what's in store for the bad?"

"Back up a second here," she said, not wanting to be steamrollered by anything this guy out of her deliberately forgotten past might be saying, "What was it your friend had lost?"

"His wife of 26 years."

"Through divorce, I assume," she said, still skeptical enough of Wysong's intentions to not grant him any passes.

"No. To cancer."

She put her hand to her mouth and said, "I'm sorry. I apologize."

"No need. Now get this. I was candid in telling him my whole sad story, including my deceitful role with you, yet he didn't bolt. And in the end he not only led me to Christ, he taught me what Biblical love, romance and marriage are really all about. All of that was managed through a combination of an exhaustive Bible study and one man's servanthood." Pete instantly knew he had left something out of what he had just said. He amended it by saying, "Well, that and God's grace."

Intuitively, Marlene felt as she had the first time they met–before the lie had been discovered—that she could be open with this man. Although she was still confused, she was also curious. "Whatever kind of man your Cobbler is," she said, "I can imagine he would also need a sense of humor in getting an unrepentant reprobate like you through a study of faith and marriage. Exactly what kind of a course did he put you through?"

Wysong was not offended by either how or what she said. He not only wanted to be transparent, it was important that she see that quality in him. "Hey," he said, "it was a ropes course with no safety net. That's a joke. Believe it or not he worked on me from a single book in the Old Testament: Song of Songs."

She couldn't have been more surprised with his answer to her question. "What?" she said. "I've never known anyone to study that book. It only has seven or eight short chapters. Are you telling me you went from Secular Man to Bible Pete in one easy lesson?"

With a look of mock indignation Wysong said, "Hardly. We went at it for months. And in the end it certainly wasn't anything either I or the Cobbler did. You know better than I that faith comes by revelation, not by sight. But what I *can* say on my behalf is that the Word now speaks to me."

Marlene was both surprised and impressed. And just as importantly, she was hopeful. "That, Mr. Wysong, is what I call change."

It did not escape him that she had just uttered her first tentative acceptance of both the circumstances and his story. He didn't want to betray his excitement prematurely, however, and settled for saying, "Thank you." Cautiously, he added, "And until God spoke to me through His Word, I couldn't change. It's interesting to me in reflection that I had to actually grow before I could even recognize and understand why my marriage had failed, much less repent of my ways."

Marlene blinked at that insight. She well remembered that his failure at marriage was something he had blamed mostly on his spouse. To that she said, "Praise the Lord."

Then, before she could say anything further, Wysong said, "Marlene, I'm asking for your forgiveness for my having lied to you. I deeply regret having done that."

She looked into his glistening eyes and wondered if he saw the same in hers. She said, "You might find this surprising, but I know you couldn't help your actions at that time. Spiritually speaking, what you did was in your nature because you were without Christ. I can forgive you because I, too, was once spiritually deficient. Because God has forgiven me so much, who am I not to forgive you who have repented of your actions?"

At that, Pete leaned forward and put his hands lightly on her shoulders in prelude to lightly brushing her lips with his.

Marlene responded warmly but didn't hold the kiss long. With a light tone to her voice she said, "Okay, Mr. Suddenly Charming, tell me, why did you come all the way up here and go to the trouble to personalize things in such a dramatic fashion? Why didn't you just call me?"

Wysong laughed and said, "Are you kidding? First of all, you not only vacated the phone book, but you checked out from the post office as well. Granted, I did Google you much later, but I was pretty certain you wouldn't have taken my phone call. Would you have?"

"No."

"How about a letter?"

"I'd have torn it up without reading it."

"How about if I had rung your door bell, unannounced?"

"A bucket of boiling oil poured onto your head."

"Okay, that brings us to why I'm standing here on a remote lake beach in a circa 1912 tuxedo, talking to you. I did what Jesus did."

Marlene gave him a puzzled look and waited for an explanation.

"Show and tell," he said with a knowing smile. Still, she betrayed no understanding. "Okay, look," he said. "You know very well that for our sake Christ became a part of humanity. That is, He showed up in person to live among us. Why? Because He knew it would be more effective than sending yet another prophet with words. Thus Jesus Himself *became* the ultimate Word. Now to my point. I came up here to insert myself into your world because I didn't know any other way of reaching you."

"Now *that* was very well put," she said. "I'm flattered beyond words. But the question is still why?"

"Marlene, I can see that I'm not explaining something very well. You see, even though we've only met twice, this is–for me, anyway— an issue of the heart. My spiritual pilgrimage actually started when I began to understand what it was that you would require of a suitor. You knew almost instantly that my behavior denied my relationship with God, yet you left me with something that had a profound impact on me."

"What was that?" she said, suddenly hoping that this man's obviously dedicated effort was not merely a clever stunt.

"I don't know if I can clearly describe it for you," he said, " but over our dinner you spoke of things I had never heard from another woman. The women I had been dating–and there were many–all had wide-ranging opinions on all sorts of subjects. But when it came to spiritual beliefs, their supporting positions were always shallow. I didn't realize that at the time because I was one of them."

Marlene was intrigued, both with Wysong's obvious transparency and with his apparent conviction. "So what did you take away from our meeting?" she said. "I mean, other than a kick in the pants?"

"Several things," he said. "If I had been capable of analyzing it at the time I would have known that what led me to a Christian dating service was the lack of any perspectives from the women I was dating offering me alternatives to my own life and spiritual struggles. And then there was the genuine disappointment you expressed concerning my dishonesty. At first, I didn't get that."

"That's deep, too," she said. "How did the Lord go about revealing Himself to you?"

Wysong smiled and said, "That's the second time you have asked that question of me."

"I know," she said as she returned his smile.

"It wasn't overnight," he said. "And it certainly wasn't all at once. Then, one day, after some months of the Cobbler's tutelage, he gave me a particular reading assignment. It was a sobering example in the book of Acts as to how God views dishonesty. The first time I read the bottom line verse in that example–*"You have not lied to men, but to God."*–I thought of you and of what you had said to me."

Wysong wasn't certain whether he was connecting with her or not. "What I'm trying to say is that there was something about you I couldn't get over. I tried to put you and the little that had happened between us aside. But after a while, I didn't *want* to get over it. Then, when I began seeking God for answers about myself I began to understand some other things as well."

"Such as?" she said. Her thoughts were racing. *What was he saying? Am I hearing correctly? Is he as genuine as he seems?*

Wysong knew he was going to have to put things more clearly, but he also knew he hadn't finished building his case. "I realized I wanted to find you," he said. "I got proactive and tracked you down through the SIT fan society. Then I confirmed through a new-found friend here at the hotel that you weren't married and would be attending this weekend event."

"Susan!" she exclaimed. "Wait until I see her again. I have to admit I suspected something, but of what I didn't know."

"She was a great help," Pete said, smiling. "Oh, yes. And there is one other thing. I bought a little something for you, something special with which you could boast of our Lord Jesus Christ." With that, he produced and opened a gift box containing a small gold cross on a necklace.

Marlene was completely taken by surprise. To her instant relief, however, the box didn't contain a ring. "How thoughtful, appropriate, and demonstrative," she said. "Thank you very much, Pete, but if it's okay with you I'm going to consider this on loan. Quite frankly, it's way too early to understand my feelings about things, or how they might develop." Then, in an obvious concession to the success of both the man and his story she added, "But I'm willing to find out."

Wysong wanted to embrace her, but he knew the timing was not right. Instead, he settled for an appropriate response, given the circumstances. "That's good enough for me," he said.

"Now," she said, "let me change the subject. How is your son doing?"

Wysong looked away and then back as he said in a halting voice, "He . . . Billy . . . is with the Lord."

"Oh, no!" she cried out softly. "Not your little boy!" Both of her hands flew to cover her face. Tears formed in her eyes. "I'm so sad for you. Please tell me what happened."

"Thank you," he said. "Automobile accident. It was terrible. His mother and her boy friend ran off the road. They were injured but Billy suffered internal bleeding from a punctured lung. I was at his side just before he went into surgery for the second time. That was over a year ago. I've been hurting ever since, but I'm making it now."

"How are you handling it?" she said. "I can't imagine the heartbreak over losing a child."

"Well, I have found a way to ease part of the pain, thanks in part to the chaplain who was at my side the night Billy passed away. Whenever I think of my loss I'm reminded that even God the Father lost His Son, the Son who was not only perfect but is the only one in history who never deserved to die. That, and the fact that I know I will see Billy again."

Marlene nodded and said, "I admire you for your attitude. Not everyone is able to lift up the Lord when tragedy strikes. But you are so right. How ironic that God knew—even before He created man—that we would need a Savior. I don't know what I can say to ease your loss, but thank you for sharing, Pete."

"You know," Wysong said in a suddenly upbeat tone, "you are the same wonderful person I remember from our conversation over dinner two years ago. The thing is, we didn't actually get to finish our meal. May I take you to dinner this evening?"

"Well," she cocked her head and took another moment before answering, "I suppose I could go for that, but first I have two questions. You said something interesting about your friend who lost his wife. Will, I think it was. Perhaps it was the way you said it. When you mentioned that he had since found contentment in Christ, were you also speaking of yourself."

Wysong had been looking down as he was listening. As Marlene finished he looked up and said, "That is very insightful. Yes, I was. Thank you for sensing that. What's your second question?"

"This may not be as easy for you, but I need to ask it. What is the single greatest thing you have learned since we met two years ago?"

"Wow! Is that all?" His countenance turned serious as he thought not only of the question but also of its implications. "I could tell you right now," he said, "but do you want to take the time for that as we sit here on this stone cold bench-by-the-beach?"

"Of course," she said with a bright smile. "It's a beautiful day and becoming more beautiful by the minute."

"Okay, girl. Here goes." With that, he turned to a better angle for taking her hand in his, which she allowed. "When my mentor first told me that God loves me, I didn't believe it. Maybe man, but not me, personally. But when I began to understand the love of God more clearly, I realized God's personal love for me. I learned that His love is not emotional and responsive like mine, but unconditional and unchangeable, constant and faithful. Paul tells us that in no uncertain terms when he wrote in Galatians 2:20 that Christ not only 'loved *me*'. . . but . . . 'gave Himself *for* me.'"

Marlene interrupted the beautiful words pouring out of the mouth and soul of this man who was rapidly fascinating her. "I have never thought of things in that way," she said. "You're saying that love is something God *does*, not just has."

"Yeah! That's it," he said. "And there is something else that flows into that same bowl. It is the love that God bestows on the few He calls *His people*. It was quite a revelation to me to learn that those who enter into a covenant–or right–relationship with God, despite the fact that we are unremarkable, unworthy and undeserving, that we nevertheless become God's children. Not just *loved* by Him, you understand, but are adopted as His children."

Marlene was quiet for several moments, contemplating things. "Twenty minutes ago," she said, "I could not have imagined what I am about to say. Quite simply, your words and your heartfelt sincerity have blown me away. Now before you get full of yourself I also have to say it isn't all you."

"What?" Pete said in mock dismay. "You mean my charm isn't working?"

"Well, maybe a little," she said with a poutish look. "But here's my greater point. How awesome is our God that He has revealed so much of Himself to you in so short a time?"

Pete nodded and said, "That's right. And when I contemplate what Paul tells us about the human mind not even being able to imagine the glory of what God has prepared for His people, I rest in awe of that promise."

"Well, Peter Wysong," she said as she put her other hand on top of his, "we have a lot to talk about." Then, with a twinkle in her eye she said, "But first, I want a word with that general manager."

-End-

EPILOGUE

Pete and Marlene spent the balance of the weekend getting to know one another, including his driving her all the way back to Detroit on Sunday. That left him time to visit her home for several hours in order to meet Marlene's eight-year old daughter, Amanda, before returning to the airport for his flight home. By the time they parted, they had committed to continue their relationship long distance until such a time as something else was in the offing. There was. Six months later they were married by a local church pastor at the Grand Hotel. Wally Barneveld was Pete's best man. Herb Holland flew up from Florida and Sam Sampson flew in from Texas. Both served as ushers and also worked closely with Wally in arranging for a surprise chivaree during the first honeymoon night at the Grand. And in an unusual note prior to the actual ceremony Will Shoemaker gave a brief talk to the assembled crowd on the Biblical aspect of marriage.

The couple decided that it would be better for Marlene to move back to the Atlanta area than for Pete to start over in his repping business in Detroit. Marlene was rehired by her former employer and Pete adopted Amanda. Within a year they had one child of their own, whom they nicknamed "Willy." They each continued their walk with the Lord and grew in their relationships with Him, worshiping through the Word and prayer, through service and gifts, and through joining with fellow believers in church, Sunday School, small groups, and mission trips.

Printed in the United States
132439LV00016B/95/P

9 781607 910411